About the auth

William R. Francis was born in Liverpool and educated at Alsager College (now part of the University of Manchester) where he gained an Honours Degree in History and English Literature.

After experiencing a variety of hospital jobs, he trained as an educator, working as head of department in schools in Kent and Herefordshire for a number of years. His students loved to hear him tell stories.

He has written four historical documentaries for BBC Radio and won hundreds of competition prizes by devising memorable tie-breakers.

His ambition is to write a screenplay for a major Hollywood movie.

THE WYVERN RING

William Francis

THE WYVERN RING

Vanguard Press

VANGUARD PAPERBACK

A CIP catalogue record for this title is
available from the British Library.

ISBN 978-1-80016-109-2

*Vanguard Press is an imprint of
Pegasus Elliot MacKenzie Publishers Ltd.*
www.pegasuspublishers.com

First Published in 2021

**Vanguard Press
Sheraton House Castle Park
Cambridge England**

Printed & Bound in Great Britain

Dedication

To my father, J. W. Francis, who many years ago, carried a little boy on his shoulders around the walls of Chester, thrilling the boy with astonishing stories about the Romans and inspiring a lifelong love of history. The torch you lit still illuminates my life.

"And so, the English groaned aloud
for their lost liberty and plotted ceaselessly
to find some way of shaking off a yoke
that was so intolerable and
unaccustomed."

Orderic Vitalis
Medieval English Monk

Prologue
October 1066

She wanted revenge. Bloody, brutal, revenge. But to achieve it, she must be free.

"Anglais! Tu dois mourir!"

Edith trembled, twisting in and out of trees, stooping under branches, running deeper and deeper into the wood. Mordiford Church was only a mile distant. But her pursuers were near.

She fell. But was up again instantly, her blue dress spattered in mud, her hands caked with dirt. The soldiers were close. She heard their angry Norman voices. Oaths filled the air, curses and threats promising retribution. Behind a clump of yew trees, English voices, hushed in anticipation, counselled patience.

She ran faster, splashing through a stream, her plaited blonde hair unkempt, her eyes permanently startled. Edith, wife of King Harold, was sentenced to death. If captured, she would be instantly killed.

The soldiers were closing in, matching her change of direction, shouting, avowing murder. A pitiless enemy, hatred in their eyes and murder in their hearts, scrambling past trees and smashing through the thicket. Her pursuers scented a kill. Preoccupied with Edith, they did not notice the swords and spears of the Silvatici hiding amongst the trees.

Edith stopped. Heart thumping, she knelt on a carpet of bluebells. This was Haugh Wood — impenetrable and dark. As a child, it was home but now it seemed to disown her. She could not continue. Her strength was gone.

Hands clasped, she closed her eyes, whispering a prayer, calling on God to punish those who murdered her husband. Before the first blow struck, she smiled, recalling happier times…

The ribbon around her wrist, the exchange of rings, the priest's blessing.

"You are now two people, sharing one life."

The birth of sons and daughters. The exultation of Harold's kingship. Memories tainted by the horror of his violent death.

"This is the king's body. I identify him by marks on his chest known only to me."

An English queen, a rallying point for resistance. Her death would prevent an uprising. She must die.

A hand grabbed Edith's arm. Fearing the worst, she opened her eyes, expecting to see soldiers with raised weapons.

A gust of wind blew across her face. Edith smiled, making the sign of the cross. God had listened.

Stigand, the peasant, helped Edith to her feet. An English fighter, willing to resist.

"Lady Edith. God preserve you. Bishop Wulfstan asked the Silvatici to help. Those who survived Hastings will continue the fight, using forests as their base. In time, we will drive the Normans off our soil and regain freedom. Your sanctuary, Mordiford Church is near. I will escort you, while my comrades deal with your pursuers. Killing Normans is not murder."

Stigand pointed his sword towards the path leading into Haugh Wood. It was late afternoon and growing dark. Behind them, muffled screams, Norman voices beseeching mercy. The bloodletting had started.

"Did you fight alongside your king at Hastings?" asked Edith. Stigand seemed trustworthy. But a generous reward might persuade even the most loyal Englishman to turn traitor.

"Yes," said Stigand, shaking his head resignedly. "A dozen men from Hereford joined the king's army. But only I survived. Murdered and defiled, my comrades lie in a mass grave. Many good men lost their lives. Their deaths must be avenged."

Edith nodded. Revenge dominated her thoughts, absorbing every moment and directing every action. If the people did not resist, they would be made slaves. As Harold's queen, she would be the focal point of English resistance. The sight of Harold's mutilated body confirmed her decision.

"There will be a reckoning," said Edith. "And when the Normans are defeated, Harold's battle flag will hang from the tower of every English church. The Wyvern Dragon will be triumphant. As queen, this is a covenant I make with my people."

Stigand grasped Edith's hand. They had arrived at the lychgate of Mordiford Church — the Church of the Holy Rood. Jesus looked down on them from a crucifix. The Son of God appeared astonished.

Inside the church, a single candle illuminated the altar. On the wall of the west gable, the Mordiford Dragon leant forward, eager to fight. Queen Edith had returned to the dragon's lair.

The Interim

With angry eyes, the wyvern dragon burst through the stonework of St Michael's church, beating its wings, baring its vicious teeth, contemptuous and defiant. A supernatural manifestation? Or an illusion caused by sunlight breaking from behind a cloud?

Osric did not see it. Coaxing bees out of a skep hive and keeping them calm required absolute concentration.

"Feel the warmth on your wings. Escape. Find a new home."

Gentle as a doting father, Osric tilted the skep, drumming his fingers against the wicker frame. The first bees emerged, the trickle becoming a flow, as the swarm headed for its new home—a skep in a recess of the garden wall. Osric admired bees for their industry. But he did not like being stung. St Dominic, the patron saint of bee keepers, advised talking to your bees. It ensured they remain your friends.

Wringing his hands, Osric eased himself down onto the wall. A hot sun. Bees humming. He was worrying about the journey. This day, 2nd October, marked a special anniversary—the feast day of Thomas Cantilupe, former bishop of Hereford, now acknowledged as Saint Thomas. Pilgrims praying at his tomb reported invalids cured, lepers healed and children raised from the dead. In light of what Osric knew, he craved the saint's blessing. Racked with guilt, Osric needed absolution.

Despite finishing his morning chores, Osric remained agitated. He was sure the bees were listening.

"Cuthbert and I will leave after noon. The journey to Hereford will take four hours. But we can't leave until Cuthbert collects the eggs from the dovecote. And he is obliged to prepare squabs for the refectory. The hospitallers get irate if their pigeon meat is not ready. Beans in vegetable juice may fill your belly but only God's provision will nourish the soul. God knows I need it."

Osric closed his eyes, feeling the sun's rays on his face. He listened intently, nodding his head, absorbed by every sound. Pigeons cooing. Sheep bleating. Wind rustling the leaves of the trees. Brother Kenway reciting Psalm ninety-one. The kitchener cursing as he scrubbed his pots. The rasping of the corn mill wheel. The buzzing of a single, discontented bee. A brief, happy interlude. Momentary respite from the scorpions in his mind.

The Order of St John at Garway had shaped every aspect of Osric's life. As a baby, Osric was admitted to the hospital with sweating sickness. Fearing plague, his parents abandoned him, disappearing into Wales. Osric's thirty years with the order saw him progress from novice to principal gardener, master of the dovecote, keeper of the bees, through to candlemaker and overseer of pensioners. Usually, his black mantle, with its eight-pointed cross, made him feel proud. But now he was thoroughly ashamed of himself and the dreadful secret Edmund shared with him.

A shadow fell across Osric's face. He opened his eyes. The soothing sounds diminished. Cuthbert was standing there, grinning broadly, arms folded under the sleeves of his robe. Half Osric's age, Cuthbert's great height and leathery skin made him seem much older. A year working in the dovecote, climbing ladders and snatching eggs from aggrieved birds, had given his skin a permanent deep brown tan. His black robe was streaked around the shoulders and down the back. Despite his repulsive appearance, Osric felt compelled to reassure Cuthbert whenever he could.

"Your clothes may smell. Your appearance maybe odious. But your soul is pure."

"This is not the time for slumber, Osric," Cuthbert said, shaking bird droppings from his hair. "There's a long walk ahead of us. I have apples, bread and a nugget of cheese in my bag. We can eat well during our journey."

Osric pointed to the wall, directing Cuthbert to sit down. The truth must be told. Osric felt compelled to share Edmund's poisonous confession with someone else or it would destroy him. He believed, with all his heart, there was no place in Heaven for those who denied truth. Evil would triumph if the righteous sat on their hands.

Osric's eyes were fixed on Cuthbert. His tone was soft, his words earnest.

"Edmund, the pensioner, died last night. I sat with him in the great hall, counting the hours, watching his life ebb away."

Cuthbert shrugged his shoulders. "His death was not a surprise. He was over eighty. I expect he is in Heaven now, enjoying God's benison. A deserved reward for a life free from sin."

Osric sighed. He and Cuthbert and all the other monks were deceived. Edmund was the antithesis of the wizened, grey bearded, biblical prophet his demeanour suggested. Edmund's life was not free from sin. It was, in fact, a life devoted to wickedness. A celebration of evil. His hands stained with the blood of hundreds of innocent victims. Cuthbert was wrong. Hell, not Heaven, would be Edmund's final unresting place.

"No," said Osric. "The everlasting bonfire is Edmund's destiny. I am loath to say it. But I have to tell you now. Edmund, our mild-mannered pensioner was, in reality, a cold-blooded murderer."

Cuthbert's mouth fell open, brown eyes wide as walnuts. He covered his mouth with his hands, whispering between his fingers.

"It's not possible. He was goodness personified. A gentleman who kept a quiet…"

Osric waved a dismissive hand. "All things are possible in a world blighted by original sin. Remember Adam's disobedience? Every man is inherently evil. It is our curse."

Cuthbert shook his head, bird droppings falling from his hair like winter snowflakes. Edmund was such an amiable old man. It beggared belief he could commit murder. Surely Osric was mistaken? "What do you know, which makes you certain Edmund is damned? Upon what evidence do you condemn him?"

Osric closed his eyes, mustering his thoughts into a coherent order. There was a terrible story to tell. "Last night, only a few hours ago, I was with Edmund in the great hall, sitting on a bench in front of the fire. No candles were lit. The glowing embers provided sufficient light to see his face. A dying man, seemingly ready to confess before God."

"Did he ask God's forgiveness?"

"No! Not once. I did not sense guilt or any attempt to reconcile with God. No remorse or contrition. He was obdurate, proud of what he had done. Listen to his dreadful narrative."

Edmund's raspy voice, confirmed his decline. His heart was failing. And he knew it.

"England is under occupation by a foreign power. In 1066, the Normans murdered our king and enslaved the English people. Harold was the last English king to rule this country. So far, all attempts to destroy the oppressors and free England have failed. Eadric and Hereward almost succeeded but they were betrayed and cruelly killed. Do not believe what the chronicles say about our English heroes. Remember, it is those in power who write the history.

"No crime was too awful for the Normans. Thousands of our people were hanged, tortured, mutilated and raped. Their lands and livelihoods were confiscated. Hundreds of villages obliterated. Around Hereford, many hamlets and villages were razed. Stane, Lincumbe and Cuple, once thriving communities, were pillaged and their inhabitants slaughtered. In the north, hundreds of thousands died when the Normans burned their crops, leaving them no food for the harsh winter months. An unremitting horror, no hope in sight for the English people… until the emergence of the Wyvern Ring. Wild men, or as the Normans called them, Silvatici, hiding out in forests and marshes, raiding Norman castles, slitting Norman throats. Men and women bound by a sacred oath to set England free. A solemn promise passed down to each successive generation. The assassination of prominent Normans was its speciality. Walter, Bishop of Hereford, stabbed to death by a female disciple. Walter de Lacy, thrown off the roof of Saint Guthlac's Priory. Wulfstan, Bishop of Worcester, poisoned by one of his staff—another loyal disciple of the Wyvern Ring… Just a selection of our more prominent victims.

"As for myself, I was proud to belong to the Wyvern Ring. I killed dozens of men and women. Normans and English collaborators. It was the honourable thing to do. I know my time is near. But I do not regret fighting for my people's freedom. I will die having led a life beyond reproach."

Osric used a sleeve to wipe away his tears. Cuthbert, bewildered, unsure what to say, chewed his bottom lip until he tasted blood in his mouth.

Osric took a breath. "A dark shadow hangs over this country, directly threatening our lives. The wyvern dragon is ready to strike."

A wyvern dragon. Osric jumped off the wall, running quickly, skirting around the perimeter of St Michael's church until he reached the west door of the nave. Chest heaving, breathing hard, he looked above the door to the niche which held the sculpted wyvern dragon... But the dragon had gone.

Chapter One

A hot summer's night in Hereford. Outside the tavern, two hungry dogs, searching for food, drag fish remains across the cobbles. Wild pigs, grunting in anticipation, stick their snouts into a dung heap. Tubs of water, positioned in case of fire, overflow with human waste. The smell of High Street during the Pestilence.

But inside the Saracen's Head — a different world. Laughter, raised voices, oaths, fists thumping on tables, the click of dice, the clinking of cups as deals are made or friendships confirmed. William the scrivener, unable to be heard, stabs the air with a finger, pointing to his cup. Alice, pushing through the tightly packed drinkers, replenishes it. William nods. Next to the hearth a group of merchants stand in a circle discussing business. Fine clothes and feathered hats mark them out as wealthy.

A touch on John's shoulder. An enquiry in a blunt male tone. John ignored the stranger's question. He was watching Alice charm the customers, men and women alike, smiling, laughing and exchanging ribald comments — giving as good as she got.

Geoffrey, the fiddle player, beguiled by Alice's brown eyes and confident of his potent appeal, grasped his fiddle, elevating it like a musical member.

Unimpressed, Alice sized up Geoffrey's fiddle, dismissively shaking her head.

"Your instrument is too small for my liking," she insisted, a smile playing across her lips.

"Besides, I prefer a trio to a duet. The beautiful music is so much more intense."

With Alice, John was assured of good food, fine wine and a safe summer's copulation. Alice had supported him since the death of his wife. John gulped down his wine.

The stranger did not give up, tapping John's shoulder and repeating the same question.

"By your leave, sir. Can you direct me to the bishop's tomb?"

The red wine had taken hold. John did not hesitate.

"God be with you, sir. But pray answer. Why would a person of sound mind wish to visit this God-forsaken city? Hereford lacks any discernible virtues. It is an ague-ridden, pernicious, pestilential bog. The lair of Satan. This cursed place is a nest of poison vipers. That is the opinion of our most Holy Father. In truth, your visit here seems perverse."

John's voice brought the tavern to silence. Customers bowed their heads or raised their cups to thirsty lips. John Dornell, schoolmaster, graduate in theology and esteemed citizen of Hereford — a man whose wisdom was universally respected — had spoken. However, this time, he was drunk.

The stranger pushed back the chair, slowly rising to his feet. There was menace in his deliberation. He was smiling.

Alice placed her hand over John's cup, forcing it down to the table.

"Leave it, John. Leave it be or by St Ethelburg, I'll break your head. This tavern is a refuge from the Pestilence. A respite for wayfarers, pilgrims and good Hereford folk. Leave your anger outside. Inside, we make merry."

The stranger removed his red felt hat offering his hand. John shook it. Disappointed, no blood had been spilled, the locals returned to their parochial chatter.

"My name is Thomas Gascoigne," the stranger said. "The best butcher in Norwich. I've travelled to Hereford to worship at the tomb of St Thomas. My wife and son are suffering with the sweating sickness. I must confess I have enjoyed the delights of my prosperity but neglected the demands of my faith. I want to put that right."

"Well, you're only a fart's distance from the cathedral," said Alice. "If you wish, you can rest here. Sleep by the hearth. Tomorrow, you can visit the bishop's tomb and pray your heart out."

"Like a good butcher boy," John whispered.

The Rhenish wine jug was empty but the excess had not dulled John's brain. He noticed there was only a spatter of mud on Gascoigne's clothes. Odd, for a pilgrim who claimed to have journeyed from Norwich, two hundred miles away. And his upright bearing. It reminded

John more of a soldier than a butcher.

Gascoigne bowed. "Madam, you are an angel in human form. May St Augustine keep you safe."

"And may St Christopher watch over you," said Alice. "The roads of England are crawling with robbers and outlaws. Nothing is what it seems. Now, put away your cares. I will find our music men. There's time to enjoy true merriment before curfew… and still time to purchase more of my special Rhenish wine."

Smiling, Alice turned heel, forcing her way through the tightly packed drinkers. Geoffrey and Robin, the musicians, were somewhere in the throng.

John turned to Gascoigne. "Surely, St Sebastian would be more deserving of your prayers?"

Gascoigne pursed his lips. "I believe St Sebastian is the patron saint of warriors. I am a butcher. St Jude is looking out for me. My needs would keep him occupied, I assure you. But which saint guards your soul?"

"St Gregory is a great comfort to me. As is St Dubricius," said John.

"St Dubricius?" Gascoigne was puzzled.

"St Dubricius hails from my village, Madley. A few miles from here. He is the patron saint of wine drinkers. Therefore, I have a double respect for him."

Gascoigne laughed, banging the table with delight.

"And Alice?" asked Gascoigne.

"St Vitalis of Gaza," said John. "But don't mention it to her. Or you'll leave this tavern minus a vital part of your anatomy!"

"Gentlemen and gentlewomen," Alice's stentorian voice hushed the customers. Heads turned. Conversations stopped.

"Before the entertainment begins. Remove the tables please."

A well-practised routine. Cups were drained and placed on the hearth. Tables, chairs and benches, stacked against the walls. A space to dance. Alice hitched up her skirt until the tops of her boots showed. Time to perform.

"The Saracen's Head now presents a tremendous, even tumescent, trilogy of terpsichorean turpitude."

"She's amazing," whispered Gascoigne.

21

"And she's mine," John replied.

Alice was in full flow. "Everyone, link arms. And form a tight circle. You will skip to the left or right around me while I sing… You must join in the chorus. Musicians, are you ready?"

Geoffrey, fiddle under his chin, raised his bow. Robin, whistle in mouth and drum in hand, nodded. Alice began to sing.

"My dame is sick and gone to bed
And I'll go mould my cockle bread."

A multitude of discordant but exuberant voices replied.

"She'll do it with her arse,
She'll do it with her arse,
She'll do it with her arse,
She'll do it with her arse."

Bumping, dodging, skipping and twisting side to side, the tavern revellers repeated the chorus. A respite from the Pestilence beyond the tavern door.

Alice raised her voice even higher.

"A feather of St Michael's wing,
A toenail drawn from Adam,
A diamond from our bishop's ring,
A pustule from a madam."

With increasing gusto, the customers repeated their refrain.

"She'll do it with her arse,
She'll do it with her arse,
She'll do it with her arse,
She'll do it with her arse."

John caught his breath and stopped dancing. He was hot and far gone in wine. It was nights like this which helped bury the memory of Matilda — his wife. She died in agony. Not recognisable as the beautiful woman he married. A fleeting thought. His mood darkened.

John fixed his eyes on Alice. Alice was a Hereford girl. She and John had an understanding. She was passionate and mysterious. Alice had become a second mother to William, John's son. John could not conceive of a life without Alice.

The faint sound of the curfew bell, broke John's reverie. An excuse to leave. A quick wave to Alice. She waved back, clearly disappointed.

Tonight, her bed would be cold. But she understood why John wanted to return home. Besides, a man of his reputation could not risk being arrested during curfew. Gascoigne watched John leave. The revellers continued dancing. Good fortune or ill fortune. Whether you lived or died. It was all in God's hands anyway.

John closed the door of the Saracen's Head and stepped straight down into the yellow mud of High Street. That was a good session. The world was a better place after an evening of alcoholic excess. John felt no guilt. Even Jesus enjoyed wine.

Narrowing his eyes, John looked left towards Eign Gate and right towards High Cross. It was dark as Hell. There was no one about. The bells of All Saints Church had sounded curfew. John knew he must get home before a watchman caught him. He did not want to spend a night in the city gaol. Beggars and cutpurses were dangerous companions. Still, that red wine from Gascony was excellent. Alice knew what her customers liked. God bless her. She ran a reputable drinking house with clean mats on the tables, fresh straw underfoot and a privy in the backyard. King Edward III himself would be proud to drink at the Saracen's Head.

Arms outstretched to steady himself, John picked his way through the clinging mud of High Street. The pungent smell cleared his head. It focused his eyes and his mind. A herd of cows had passed through on the way to market. The stench was all-pervasive.

John knew these streets. Down Cabbage Lane, into Broad Street and home. The passageways were silent. Shops were boarded up and those houses still occupied, had their shutters firmly closed. The Pestilence had overwhelmed Hereford. Shaking his head in bewilderment, John stepped over a putrid drain, spilling over with human waste and rotting food.

Then pain. Sickening pain, smashing straight into the back of his head, knocking him over, spinning him into the mud. Fingers searching the pockets of his cloak. His purse, ripped away in an instant. His boots dragged off. A red felt hat. A dazzling pain-filled darkness.

John lay stretched across the cobbles. Hours passed. A hungry dog nosed over, tentatively licking the dry blood from John's lifeless face. A pig, contemptuous of the offering, gave a token sniff and trotted up the street in search of better pickings.

Another victim of the Pestilence dead on the streets of Hereford. Another corpse to commit to God. The tired watchmen picked up the corpse and flung it on the cart with the others. By order of the bishop, all victims of the Pestilence must be buried within two hours of being found. Only John's flickering eyelids revealed his terrifying dream.

***

A third-floor room in Butchers' Row. A silver candlestick on a trestle table. The candle's flame pierces the darkness like a burning dagger. The window shutters are fastened. The heavy oak door is locked from within. The chosen seven, Elders of the Wyvern Ring, sit on benches either side of the table. Silent. Solemn. Respectful. Weighty matters demand contemplation. The candle burns slowly. Time is measured in drops of wax. Until, at last, Edwin's voice punctures the silence.

"When God wills, may the end be good. Rise up and drench our land with Norman blood."

Lifting a purse from his belt, Edwin threw it down. Coins spilled across the table. Silver pennies. Each one bearing the portrait of a king. Harold Godwinson. King Harold, king of the English.

Morcar pulled back his cowl. Snow-white hair and beard. Piercing blue eyes. His words slow and measured.

"Bishop Trilleck deserves to die. He must be killed. He is a demon, masquerading as a man of God. We have endured twelve years of his pious hypocrisy and his Norman iniquity. By his actions, he has signed his own death warrant. Signed it with his own corrupted blood."

For a few seconds, no one spoke. Grim faces illuminated by a flickering candle. The gravity of Morcar's words needed consideration. The murder of a Bishop would provoke a terrible vengeance.

Magnus spoke first. "He could be kidnapped and tortured. We could nail him to his own cathedral door. Our actions would show that English resistance is not broken." Morcar shook his head.

"Or blackmailed," suggested Magnus.

"We could torch the Bishop's Palace," said Leofgar. "That would be a statement. Normans are not wanted here."

Morcar shook his head. With chilling logic, he explained what had to be done.

"This country is under occupation. God's chosen people made slaves. We are ruled by foreigners who consider the English an underclass of servile peasants. Trilleck works night and day to maintain this subjugation. As the Wyvern Ring, guardians of the English people, it is our responsibility, our sacred duty, to destroy all vestige of Norman influence in this country. The issue is not the death of one loathsome bishop. What's at stake is the freedom of the English people. This noble cause requires Trilleck be eliminated. Is there one amongst you, who does not want England to be free?"

Morcar lifted the candlestick above his head. No ordinary candlestick. A holy object from Waltham Abbey, the resting place of the last true English king.

The whole room was illumined. No shadows or dark corners. Morcar examined each face. Edwin, Leofgar and Magnus sat to his left. Young, fanatical, full of anger. The cause was safe in their hands. To his right Wulfstan, the Black Monk. Not so animated but perpetually wise and utterly reliable. Hengist, the old campaigner, leaned forward. A soldier with King Edward at Caen, his loyalty was beyond question.

Alitha sat slightly apart from the others. Brown, beguiling eyes fixed rigidly on the candle flame. Morcar smiled. He recognised the white-hot anger of real resistance.

"When God wills, may the end be good. Rise up and drench our land with Norman blood."

A solemn oath. An unbreakable promise to God.

"Let me have the honour," said Alitha. "By tomorrow morning Trilleck will be dead. Our French oppressors will realise the English are not beaten, simply waiting for the moment to destroy their enemies."

Alitha scooped up the pennies from the table. Long, fingers counted the coins into the purse. Each silver penny, a tribute to a fallen king, a reminder of an ignoble death. Alitha threw back the hood of her cloak. A cascade of red hair. Pouting lips. The unmistakable eyes of a woman. A deadly threat to the life of a deeply troubled bishop.

***

The Pope stretched out his right hand, suspending his long fingers above the lighted taper. Engrossed in thought, he did not feel the heat or smell his own flesh burning.

"Hereford has become a nest of vipers. A city odious to our senses. Like a serpent stalking its prey, atheism imperils our religion. Hereford has become a bastion of defiance. Bishop Trilleck has failed his faith… and his God."

The Vicar of Christ was resolute.

"If I were to light every candle in Christendom, it would not illumine the darkness within Trilleck's soul."

A clenched fist. The candle flame extinguished. The tranquillity of the papal library, the largest book collection in Europe, shattered by an explosion of anger.

Chest heaving, hands gripping the arms of the papal throne, Pope Innocent VI held court at Avignon. He was angry. So angry, his skull cap lifted, struggling to contain the rage inside. So angry, he pulled off his boots and flung them at Cardinal Beyssac sitting ten paces away. Stoic and used to casual violence, Cardinal Beyssac fell off his chair. It was not wise to complain.

"Why do kings and queens kneel at my feet?"

Beyssac jumped up, straightening his cap.

"Your Holiness. You are God's link with His created world. Your dominion extends…"

"Everywhere!" the Pope snarled. "My supreme authority is accepted in all Christian countries, except in one little island. That heretical, stew of perdition — England!"

Arms outstretched, eyes firmly shut, Innocent continued to rage.

"Have I not brokered peace between England and France?" Beyssac nodded.

"Have I not delivered our own King John to them, left rotting in the Tower of London, like a beggar?" Beyssac nodded more vigorously.

"Are the English not three million gold crowns richer? A king's ransom!" Beyssac nodded furiously, wringing his hands and stamping his feet like a man on hot coals.

The Pope's face turned from scarlet to grey. A sign that worse was to follow.

"Eternal damnation on them!" Innocent screamed. "Why do they defy me? Do they want to burn in Hell? Bishop Trilleck must be dismissed. He's useless. A spent candle. The citizens of Hereford are savages. Never have I known men so lax in their morals, so wild in their rites, so impious in their faith, so barbarous in their laws, so stubborn in their indiscipline and so unclean in their lives. Yes, Christians in name. But in truth, they are pagans... And those mumbling monks refusing their taxes. They must be whipped into line... Don't mention the Knights Templar. Rich as Midas. Yet they will not pay taxes... And now... ...I've got cold feet!"

He motioned to Beyssac. With a respectful flourish, the cardinal handed over the pope's boots. Innocent struggled to put them on.

"In the bowels of Christ. What is happening?"

The library shook. The bookshelves cringed. A heavy book thumped on to the carpet. Thucydides, a description of the Pestilence. A banner, depicting a wyvern dragon, tore away from the wall, clattering to the floor. A pane of stained glass cracked. The impenitent thief lost his head.

Innocent lowered his voice. Gradually he regained control. His ominous words, more frightening than his rage.

"The trouble is, my predecessors did not know how to be Pope. Beyssac, I grant you a most singular privilege. As my ambassador, you will go to England. You will subdue all opponents of our Holy Church. You will bring Hereford back under my control. You have my authority to use all means necessary to silence those who defy me." Innocent smiled benignly.

Beyssac stopped nodding his head, wringing his hands and stamping his feet. For a few seconds he stood motionless, a confused look on his face. Then, twisting like an Archimedean screw... he fainted.

***

Bishop Trilleck threw down the parchment. He understood its message. He had pored over it for hours. Sleep was a luxury he could not afford. His eyes ached. As did his heart. He stretched his fingers up to the light.

Sunlight. Dawn breaking. Twisting his ring finger, he marvelled at the amethyst stone. Violet sparks of fire. A symbol of the Spirit of God.

An inspiration to the heart. Protection against tempests, evil spirits, moral pollution and perhaps… the Plague.

He coughed. A fit of coughing broke his reverie. Some blood, not much. "God's tokens." A persistent headache. A burning thirst. Strange thoughts undermining his faith. Submission to God was best. Men sin. God is angry. Men suffer.

"You must eliminate the causes of the Plague — the outrageous sins; the blasphemies against God; the schools of atheism; the pernicious usury."

The letter from Archbishop Zouch offered an explanation. Hope to cling to in the face of the Plague. Words urging obedience to the will of God. Crumbs of comfort.

"The Plague is a broom in the hands of the Almighty. He sweeps evil from the world."

Another painful bout of coughing. Difficulty breathing. A bloated tongue. More blood. Constant worry.

"Take action, take action and you will defeat the Plague."

Bishop Trilleck sighed. The parchment rolled under his desk. What more could he do? Every day for three months, he had held services at the cathedral — that most holy, glorious house of God. He had invoked the protection of the mother of God, Mary herself, beseeching mercy. How many candles had been lit? How many hymns sung and prayers earnestly whispered? But still the Plague continued to devastate Hereford. Disobedience and sin anger God. The Plague is evidence of God's wrath. Divine retribution. Three hundred people a week were dying in Hereford. A dark, unending horror.

Orders had been given and precautions taken but to no avail. Noxious odours must be removed. Offal must be collected, tanners and leatherworkers banned from trading. Fouling of streets and byways, a criminal offence.

But the greatest cause of God's anger was moral pollution. Harlots, rogues and atheists, must be arrested. Heaven is reserved for those who serve God. Hell is the place for those who defy Him. In Hell, an evil man shall weep more than all the water in the Earth. He is damned forever.

Bishop Trilleck felt the stubble on his chin. No time to shave. Yet, there was still hope. The people should throw themselves on God's mercy. The bishop would lead them barefoot, with heads bowed, to the tomb of St Thomas. This manifestation of obedience might save them.

Standing up, he pressed his face against the window overlooking the herb garden. The Kyrie eleision began. "Lord have mercy" drifting on the breeze, delicate as angel wings. Shafts of brilliant sunlight revealed rows of blue flowers. Hyssop, its distinctive minty aroma, a tonic for those in distress. "Thou shalt purge me with hyssop and I shall be clean." A chance of atonement.

Enraptured by the liturgy and distracted by the heady scent, Bishop Trilleck did not hear the door open or the footsteps. A delicate kiss on his cheek. He turned. A woman. The sharp blade of an axe. Blows chopping into flesh. No time to cry for help.
Death came quickly. In the distance, the monks raised their voices. The Kyrie episcopes grew louder. Inspired by their love of God, the Benedictines were joyous.   Kneeling down, the woman placed a silver coin on each of Bishop Trilleck's lifeless eyes. Like a gruesome gargoyle, he appeared to smile.

***

A candle flame illumined the altar. Dragon's eyes, vivid and terrible. Jagged red jewels, threatening and deadly. An elongated, twisted, glittering head. A mouth dripping blood. A lascivious, forked tongue hinting at unspoken corruptions. Uplifted wings adorned with green and gold scales. The Mordiford dragon, imperious and pagan, yearning to attack. An appropriate place for the Wyvern Ring to gather.

"Here in this ancient church of Mordiford. In this house of God. We must pledge ourselves to renew the struggle. Our glorious, sacred, struggle."

Nods of agreement. Clenched fists. Grim resolve etched into angry faces. Morcar spoke quietly. A tone of cold conviction. A fanatic devoted to a single cause.

"The Normans are a deadly yoke. A burden on the English people. England has become the home of outsiders, a wretched colony, dominated by foreigners. Today, no Englishman is an earl, bishop or abbot. Strangers gnaw away at the very innards of our nation. There seems no hope for an end to our misery. What is to be done?"

Leofgar did not hesitate. "We must intensify our policy of assassination. The Normans must understand Hastings was the beginning, not the end of our resistance. Cleansing the world of evil is a moral act. It is not wickedness. It is our sacred duty."

Wulfstan, the Benedictine monk raised his hand. His eyes were stern and cheerless.

"Killing still goes hard with me. I've been a brother at St Guthlac's priory these twenty years. I've seen many bad things. The evil men do. Brutal, merciless, sadistic deeds which erode my faith. I've asked God a thousand times how can the English reach salvation? The answer is always the same. The Normans must be destroyed."

Words and voices of approval, acceptance, enthusiastic agreement. Edwin, Morcar, Leofgar, Hengist and Alitha. Not one dissenting utterance. Even the Mordiford dragon, painted on the chancel wall, appeared to smile.

Confident in the righteousness of their cause, the Wyvern Ring were exultant. The shackles were loosened. A mandate for unlimited murder.

Hengist rubbed the knuckles of his left hand under his beard. A sign he wished to speak. A reverential tone.

"We have forgotten our manners. A great deed was accomplished yesterday. An implacable enemy was eliminated. Bishop Trilleck was hurried to Hell. We must thank Alitha. She is a blazing torch amidst the Norman darkness."

Alitha slipped a silver ring from her finger, holding it near the candle. An amethyst ring. Purple and violet in relief against the shimmering flame. Passion in her voice.

"I have fulfilled my obligation to my people. I did not steal this ring. I liberated it from a Norman lackey. I retrieved the rightful property of the English people. I did not murder Bishop Trilleck. I carried out the sentence against him."

"Boudicca is reborn!" whispered Magnus"

"An English St Olga," said Hengist.

"Or simply, Alitha. A true English patriot."

Morcar's words were definitive. All present turned to listen.

"Our struggle has entered a new phase. The Pestilence has made

Hereford ungovernable. This is our moment. We will make Hereford a fortress of resistance to Norman rule. We can regain our birth right. We can once again, rejoice to see an English king proudly seated on an English throne. We have an obligation to Harold and Hereward. Men who gave their lives fighting the Norman devils. This is our destiny! When God wills, may the end be good. Rise up and drench our land with Norman blood! I vow the River Wye will be clotted with the blood of our enemies."

Euphoric with the prospect of victory, the Wyvern Ring disappeared into the night. To all appearances, ordinary, law-abiding Hereford folk, heading home before the curfew and the gates are closed.

The Mordiford dragon thrashed its wings. Streaks of moonlight pierced the stained glass. Myriad colours danced across the stone floor. Vivid green melted into subtle yellow, dissolving into splotches of royal blue. Then red... scarlet... vermillion... copper. Back to red. Red as a dripping wound.

Chapter Two

Powerful images filled John's head. Each jolt of the cart unleashed a cascade of memories. A bell-mouthed cannon blasted shrapnel into screaming enemy soldiers. A red dragon scampered over bleeding bodies. Thousands of coins rained down from the sky. The face of Matilda, his dead wife, engraved on each penny. Black coffins stacked in rows, reached higher than the tower of Hereford Cathedral. John raced up the steps. He looked down. The streets were deserted. The Pestilence had triumphed. Hereford was a dead city.

But the wound to the back of his head, the dried blood and the smell of corpses, confirmed he was alive. Sore, bewildered and miserable, laying under prostrate bodies destined for the cathedral graveyard, John knew he must act fast.

Peter and Thomas, the watchmen, dragged their cart around the corner of High Street, into the narrow confines of Cabbage Lane. This was a street of grocers' shops, fishmongers and spice merchants. The stink of corpses combined with salted fish and pungent spices to create a nauseating plague perfume.

Peter flopped down on the cobbles, puffing out his cheeks. Thomas leant against the cart, wiping the sweat from his brow with a sleeve. This cargo of corpses was heavier than they anticipated.

The weight of corpses, pinned John to the bottom of the cart. He could not move. His breathing was shallow. A bearded old man, eyes protruding like a fish, nuzzled John's cheek in mock affection. If John could not escape, he would be thrown into a plague pit along with the dead. The prospect of being buried alive horrified him. A choking darkness beckoned.

Summoning up his strength, John squeezed into a gap, pushing hard against the corpses. He shoved aside the be-whiskered old man's flopping head, pushing his hand clear of the disobliging bodies and into the air. Blue sky. Warm sunshine.

"By the bones of St Ethelbert. I am alive!"

Nonplussed, Thomas the watchman stood up, rigid as a statue. His eyes were distended. His chin, hanging like a bag of grain.

Older and more accustomed to death, Peter leaned over and grabbed John's flailing arm. John's head emerged. He blinked his eyes sensitive to the sunlight. One powerful tug and John was clear of the corpses.

"I expect you be Lazarus," said Peter smiling. "I've never seen a man raised from the dead before. And I've been a Christian these sixty-four years."

"Not dead," said John, twisting and stretching his neck. His confinement had left his limbs stiff.

"Somebody smashed my head and robbed my purse. I think I know the culprit."

"Aye. There's a lump on the back of your head and your hair is thick with blood. You took a mighty wallop and that's no mistake…" said Peter. "For God's sake, Thomas, get up!"

Thomas, eyes tightly shut, was on his knees, facing the cathedral, invoking the Trinity. He had witnessed a miracle. A plague victim had come back to life in Cabbage Lane, Hereford. News would spread. Pilgrims would descend on the city from all corners of Christendom to worship at this sacred spot. It could rival Canterbury. This wonderful occurrence could wipe away his sins, guaranteeing him a place in Heaven. The benison of God was infinite. There was money to be made.

"I was not, definitely not, dead," said John, deliberately stressing his words. "Unconscious for a while but not expired. There has not been a miracle! The only miracle is how I've managed to survive, pinned down under a heap of corpses."

A crowd of onlookers assembled. The cart's grisly cargo ensured they kept their distance. Heads, legs and arms entangled in a human haystack. Every night the grim harvest was gathered. The Pestilence remained indiscriminate and ultimately fatal. Peter and Thomas were directing their cart towards an abyss.

But John had other concerns. He smacked the dust off his tunic and smoothed down his hair. He must return home. His son, William, would be frantic. And, besides, the cathedral boys needed instruction. Without a master, they might sneak into town and be seduced by lascivious pleasures.

John shook Peter's hand.

"You have done God's work today. You have saved me from a premature burial. I hope to enjoy many summers before God calls me."

"Our business is with the dead. Not the living," said Peter.

Still dubious about John's mortality, Thomas pulled a quizzical face. "You be no resurrected man?"

"No."

"You be no wraith or unquiet spirit?"

"No. Just John Dornell, cathedral school master."

"And you haven't been to the other side?"

"Well, I have been to Worcester. Just once. And it did seem a damned place. Much wailing and gnashing of teeth. Without doubt, an abode of miserable sinners. But no. I have not died and returned to life."

Thomas pulled a knife from under his tunic. John jerked back. Thomas did seem a strange man. But not an assassin. Thomas pointed with the knife. Dried blood darkened the blade.

"I be needing a lock of your hair. That would be God's own proof of this wondrous occasion. I have seen a dead man come to life. Christians would pay much silver to see such a glorious relic. Can we agree terms?"

Peter shook his head, an amused smile dancing around his lips. Thomas was a money-grabbing codger but you couldn't dislike him. Putting his arm around Thomas' shoulder, Peter motioned John to leave.

"Put the knife away, you reprobate. You've given me an idea that could make us a barrel load of money."

Peter guided Thomas down Cabbage Lane, holding his attention by explaining an ingenious scheme to make them rich. After a minute, the two watchmen, deep in conversation, disappeared from view. John discretely slipped into an alleyway, glad to be alive and relieved not to have fulfilled Thomas' suggestion. John needed to see his son.

Meanwhile, beguiled by Peter's scheme, Thomas floated down the lane in a state of financial euphoria.

"Richer than Augustus Caesar. You will bathe in liquid gold. Trembling knaves will serve you sumptuous meals on diamond-encrusted plates. You will drink only the finest wines. Voluptuous maidens, renowned for their beauty and acquiescence, will pander to your desires. How do we achieve this life-changing wealth? I will explain..."

Peter glanced over his shoulder. He was pleased to see that John had gone...

John stood at the door of his house, looking up to the second floor. He composed himself, scraping spots of blood from his face and patting the hair down around his wound. He would pass muster. He could hear the cathedral boys arguing, shouting and blaspheming. William must have let them in.

A few tiles were missing from the roof and one of the wooden shutters hung crazily. Not the Bishop's Palace. But it was home. Two rooms downstairs. One for cooking and one for sleeping. The top floor was the schoolroom. The cacophony came from there.

John used echoing, exaggerated footsteps to climb the stairs. They should be aware of his approach. The sound of voices ebbed away. John's attitude to teaching was simple. Unruly students do not learn. Only discipline and unremitting hard work would yield results. Quiet, heads bowed, the boys waited for their master.

There were eight boys in the class. John earned a stipend by charging each one a fee. The cathedral authorities appointed him, impressed by his degree in Canon Law. They provided him with a home and placed him in charge of the singing boys. His son William, golden haired and golden tongued, sat on the front bench, eyes as big as florins. Silent, expectant, slightly in awe, the boys waited.

"The Pestilence is entirely amongst us. Church bells are worn thin due to the number of funerals. The Dance of Death seems unstoppable. Close your eyes, while I call upon St Sebastian."

As John spoke, the bells of All Saints Church could be heard across the city, tolling a morning knell. Shops were out of candles. The graveyards overflowed.

"St Sebastian, guard and defend us, morning and evening, every minute of every hour. Diminish the power of that vile illness which threatens us. Protect and keep us and all our friends from this scourge. We put our trust in God and Mary and in you, our Holy Martyr. Amen."

While the boys repeated the prayer, unanswered questions filled

John's head. Who had stolen his purse? Was Thomas Gascoigne involved? Would the Pestilence kill everyone in Hereford? It seemed the inevitable conclusion. The triumph of Death. A grinning skull, leering at the afflicted.

In unison the boys completed their 'Amen'. John ceased brooding.

"We must now consider this week's Bill of Mortality and contemplate God's purpose. The bailiff has supplied every school in Hereford with this melancholy document. Any questions, complaints or declarations before I start?"

Thomas Scudamore instantly raised a hand. "My father says God's purpose is unfathomable. Mere mortals should never seek an explanation. We must accept God's will. My father says it's the Devil's work to question God. My father says…"

John gritted his teeth. "I'm a supercilious, smug, insolent bag of wind, with the face of a constipated baboon," John whispered to himself. The blow to the back of his head was still raw. He was hungry and needed a shave. He had no time for fatuous remarks made by conceited schoolboys.

John raised his voice. "…That we must respect authority and obey our elders. Or be ready to accept a rightful punishment."

John pointed towards a thin hazel rod standing in the corner. Thomas Scudamore lowered his head. He was not stupid. Just obnoxious.

Holding up the parchment, John began reading aloud. He walked between the tables, carefully watching, until he was certain he had their complete attention. His sonorous voice, distinct as a funeral bell.

"This morbid epistle is a register of causes of death in Hereford, as reported to me, Bailiff Bartholomew this last week of May 1361. God has called these souls to final judgement. May the Lord have mercy upon them. Amen."

The boys repeated the 'Amen' with respectful gravity. After pausing, John continued his monologue.

"Aborted and still born, 8.

Aged, 23

Atheism and disorder of the brain, 12

Bloody Flux, 10

Buggery, 7

Colic and the wind, 9

Enchantments and spells, 10

Griping in the guts, 8

Hanged and made way with themselves, 3

Improper relations with beasts, 18

Pestilence, 268

Sheep Pox, 16

Teeth and worms, 30

Unnatural practices, 18

Wild shites, 27."

Slowly and with flamboyant deliberation, John put down the parchment. He stared out of the window, looking across the city. Buildings, roofs, the grandeur of the cathedral. This inventory of death evoked thoughts he had tried to suppress. God's reckoning. Each life, a lighted candle, struggling to defy a tempest. Human beings, each one a miracle of creation, reduced to inky statistics on calfskin. Was God aloof from this suffering?

The miserable moment passed. John faced the boys.

"Put your hands up if you can tell me the number of victims claimed by the Pestilence last week?"

All hands were raised. Robert Westhope looked particularly eager.

"Two hundred and sixty-eight, Sir."

"Correct. But can you explain why so many died?"

"Disobedience and sinfulness invite the Pestilence. God is demonstrating His anger and His awesome power."

"So, the victims brought death upon themselves? You are saying they deserved to die?"

"God decides who lives or dies. Who goes to Heaven or who goes to Hell. I can't speak for God. But the lessons of history suggest, that impious people who fall away from God are always punished. Hereford is a dangerous, evil city. God's retribution must inevitably follow."

Robert's profound pessimism held sway. For a few moments the room was silent. Hope and joy in life melted away. Robert's words had destroyed any prospect of salvation. Hereford and all its inhabitants, were doomed. Then, unexpectedly, a shrill voice piped up from the back of the room. Walter Kivernoll would not be quiet.

"It's all the fault of those Lollards. They're always mumbling and grumbling or chanting and ranting. They're poisoning our wells."

John nodded, his face a mask of agreement. But inside he was reeling. Walter had touched a raw nerve.

"Yes, a dangerous and violent gang of heretics. Now, Walter, explain the logic underlying your conclusion."

The boys turned to listen. Tall and thin, a pale, almost bloodless face. His hair, shiny and black as a raven's wing.

"They want to kill our Holy Father. They want the Church to surrender its wealth to the poor. They demand the Bible be printed in English. They kidnap Christian children, drain their blood and eat them. They spread pestilence to undermine our faith and question God. They must be exposed and ripped out of the world."

"Are you telling me these scoundrels have reached Hereford and are actually living amongst us?"

"Yes, sir. We are being slowly poisoned. Every day is a step nearer the grave."

"So, what can we do to save ourselves and our Holy Church from these devilish apostates?"

Walter lowered his voice. His words rational, numbingly cold.

"The Lollards are a cancer. When a patient has cancer, the cancer must be removed to save the whole body. Quite simply, all Lollards must be discovered and executed. It would be righteous to destroy them."

A simmering noise. Murmurings of approval from the other boys. Voices in agreement. Hushed threats. Oaths uttered between clenched teeth. A ground swell of burgeoning malice and hostility. Palpable hatred.

Until... a single defiant voice. One prepared to defy the majority. William could not be restrained.

"Walter, you are talking out of your fundament. I've never heard such gratuitous nonsense. God should strike you dead for advocating such horror. Yours are not the words of a Christian. Yours are the words of..."

"Serious problems, demand serious solutions," Walter interrupted.

"But how is killing people doing God's work? Where in the Scriptures does Jesus order us to kill our enemies?" William's eyes sparkled with determination.

"You're missing the point," Walter snarled. "If we do not defend ourselves and our religion against these heathens, there will be no Catholic Church. It will be smashed to pieces. We will be living in a tormented, Godless universe, waiting to die and go to Hell. Stop cavilling. Your very soul is at stake here."

John scratched his chin. He was proud of the boys. Opinionated, articulate and argumentative. But it was time to step in, to quell the schism.

"I am pleased with your enthusiasm. I admire your willingness to express your views. It is a privilege to serve as your master. However, time is short. We will continue this sophistry tomorrow. Now is the time for hard learning."

John pointed to each boy in turn.

"Pick up your wax tablet. Have your stylus in your right hand. I'm not accepting any sinister behaviour. I will read Thucydides' account of the Pestilence. You will write down my words neatly. Write in English. No need to translate into Latin. I won't go too fast."

Heads down, attentive to the task, the boys began to etch the redolent words.

"The bodies of dying men lay one upon another. Half-dead creatures reeled about the streets and gathered round the foundations in their desire for water. The sacred places were filled with corpses. Men, not knowing what was to become of them, became careless, whether sacred or profane. It was an age of evil extravagance…"

John stopped mid-sentence. Loud footsteps could be heard. Scudding up the stairs. Nearer and nearer. Someone was panting, struggling towards the door. A thud. The door opened. George Winnal. A jackass with a grotesque smile. Gasping for breath, George struggled to speak. He waited until his chest stopped heaving.

John was offended. Arriving late for class, interrupting the master's oration and diverting attention away from Thucydides, the greatest historian of them all. Such behaviour was unforgivable.

"Well, George Winnal. You have stopped any learning taking place and undermined my pedagogy. No doubt, some trivial calamity prevented you arriving on time. What have you got to say before I thrash you?"

Like a cornered fox resigned to its fate, George spoke in a matter of fact, emotionless tone.

"On my way to school, I stopped at St Ethelbert's Well. I was hungry. A man there sells eel pies to pilgrims. Really good pies. He told me and he got it from the night watchman."

John was losing patience. "Told you what? This story is lasting longer than the Peloponnesian War!"

George closed his eyes. "Bishop Trilleck is dead. Murdered. His head cut off. His eyes gouged out. A most bloody, horrible crime has taken place."

"God preserve us," John whispered, striving to digest the news.

"God preserve us," the boys repeated.

Chapter Three

Seething with anger, Morcar rose from his chair, pushing the visitor to one side. He unbolted the window of the wool loft, looking over the rooftops towards the bowling green. It was an unrivalled view across the city. Pestilential, Hereford.

'Senlac' house was the most prestigious building in Widemarsh Street. Four storeys high, built entirely of stone, it boasted glazed and shuttered windows. An immaculate rose garden surrounded the house, confirming it as the residence of a very important man. But a man, apoplectic with rage.

"Why is John Dornell alive? Your mission was straightforward. Dispatch him. Make it appear he was the victim of a robbery. But he still lives! You have failed our cause!"

Tom Gascoigne closed his eyes. He placed a hand over his mouth, biting his tongue in frustration. He could not believe John Dornell survived the attack. A cudgel, smashed against a man's head was unerringly fatal. As a skilled assassin, he had never before failed to eliminate an intended victim. What must he do to regain the respect of the Wyvern Ring?

Morcar turned away from the window. His furious blue eyes fixed on Tom.

"John Dornell is an enemy of our movement. He has corrupted my daughter. He poisons the minds of his pupils by instructing them to collaborate with our oppressors. He encourages and celebrates licentious appetites. He is a wanton wine drinker. My life… will be improved… by his death."

An opportunity for redemption. Tom did not hesitate.

"I vow by all that our disciples hold sacred, John Dornell will be dead by nightfall. Separating his head from his body,will guarantee his demise."

Clearly eager to complete his mission, Tom stretched out his arms, twisting the palms of his hands upwards in a gesture of almost religious supplication.

Deep in thought, Morcar leaned back in his chair. He hated John Dornell — the shameless drunkard who he blamed for corrupting his youngest daughter. Morcar believed it was his duty to kill John Dornell. A father must defend his children.

—Twisting the dragon ring around his finger, Morcar spoke in a low, restrained tone. Tom trembled, expecting another rebuke.

"No," said Morcar. "I shall execute him. He will suffer before he dies. Leave him to me. We have identified four other targets which require your attention."

Tom smiled. Morcar still trusted him. He would move Heaven and Earth to confirm Morcar's faith.

"It is a glorious honour to be chosen for such a mission. To be selected as the instrument of retribution fills my English heart with pride."

Morcar nodded, joining his hands together as though in prayer. In essence, Tom's mission was a holy one. A sacred crusade to subdue Norman tyranny. The day of the Great Rising was near. Scruples were the property of cowards.

Morcar spat out the names with palpable disgust.

"These parasites must die. Richard de la Bere, our esteemed high sheriff. Bartholomew le Clerk, our bailiff, a particularly loathsome man. And Henry de Catchpole, the member of Parliament for Hereford. He is an immoral, manipulative crook and a rival to my business. A man who has exploited the citizens of Hereford for too long. The killing of these men will signal the rebirth of the English nation and end three hundred years of slavery. The day is near, when once again, we will have an English king, upon an English throne and a king who speaks English! Do you accept this mission?"

Tom tucked his thumbs into his belt puffing out his barrel chest. He was elated but also puzzled.

"I accept. But you mentioned four targets?"

Morcar leaned back in his chair. His ice blue eyes seemed focused on an issue far beyond their conversation. For him, the liberation of the English people was not the most important aspect of the Great Struggle.

As long as he could remember, he had yearned for a state of affairs more profound and nationally significant — the emancipation of the English soul. Pope Innocent and his myrmidons were the antithesis of Morcar's hopes. The Bishop of Rome was the real enemy.

"Yes, there is a fourth. Our disciple in Avignon reports that Cardinal Beyssac is embarked on a pilgrimage to Hereford, supposedly to pay his respects at the tomb of St Thomas. In reality, he is concerned to investigate the collapse of the Catholic faith in this diocese. I believe he has reached Canterbury. The destruction of a cardinal would be trumpeted throughout Christendom. You must kill him, at the most expedient opportunity. Your other targets can be dealt with in due course."

Tom chuckled inwardly, a beaming smile unfurled across his face.

"Canterbury. A most propitious place to execute a celebrated cleric. The success of this enterprise is guaranteed. I will leave this afternoon."

Morcar leaned over, placing a coin-filled purse in Tom's pocket. Tom nodded. No words were necessary. The purse foretokened violent death. A resolute handshake. A red cap placed upon a head. Heavy footsteps descended the loft stairs. Tom Gascoigne was impatient to get to work.

***

Eight o'clock. The bells of All Saints Church were precise and resonant. A warm, summer's day in Hereford. Morcar was delighted. His meeting with Mr. Gascoigne had been productive. Both parties were satisfied. A profitable deal had been struck. A good bargain, ahead of breakfast.

Morcar was a ruthless businessman. His determination and will to win were extraordinary. His rivals, in awe of his business skills, maintained he could convince a saint to purchase shares in the fires of Hell.

His wealth came from trading English wool. He sold hundreds of sacks a week to the textile factories of Flanders — Hereford wool being considered the finest in the world. A profit of sixteen shillings per sack, confirmed Morcar as the richest merchant in the city. A solid citizen, untouched by impropriety.

Alitha tiptoed up the stairs, carrying the tray with her father's breakfast. White bread and honeyed cheese. Chicken breast in gravy. A flagon of Gascon wine. A substantial meal to start the day. The bells of All Saints Church indicated it was time to eat.

She hesitated outside the door, listening. Not a sound. The visitor had gone. A gentle knock before entering. A room filled with wool sacks from ceiling to floor. Morcar stood in front of the open window, a dove perched on his wrist. It fluttered its wings. But soon settled, remaining placid as he stroked its feathers, comforting and soothing an anxious heart. Relaxed, eyes closed, perfectly innocent. Like a trusting child, certain of its parents' love.

Quietly and carefully, Alitha put down the tray. Startled, the dove took flight, darting out of the window, heading for the safety of the cathedral tower. Alitha felt ashamed. Only Morcar understood the significance of the moment. Reflecting on it, he sat down to eat.

"A magnificent meal, provided by a dutiful daughter. I am blessed that you remain loyal."

Indignant, Alitha tucked her red hair behind her ears.

"You do have two other daughters."

Morcar drained his cup.

"Elizabeth married well. Mr. Barton is the richest man in Witney. He will provide all the necessities for a comfortable life. Her duty is to provide him with children."

"I fear it is a loveless union. An arrangement and not a marriage. Don't you want Elizabeth to be happy?"

Morcar sighed. "She will grow into her marriage. In time, a partnership can become a successful union. When the absurd dreams of youth give way to the comforts of old age, Elizabeth will be fulfilled."

"Fulfilled! More likely enslaved! Trapped in frigid, passionless, confinement!"

Morcar's spoon clattered to the floor. Alitha was like her mother — volatile, opinionated, argumentative. But strong. And possessed of a fearsome temper. Emma, Alitha's mother, had died twenty years before, a victim of the sweating sickness. Morcar had raised his daughters, without the attenuating influence of a sensible wife.

Alitha lowered her voice. "And Beatrice? She is never mentioned. It seems your first child, my eldest sister, has ceased to exist."

"I do not wish to speak of her. She betrayed our cause. She absconded and thrust her family out of mind. I consider her deceased."

A dismissive tone. In her secret heart, Alitha yearned to embrace Beatrice, to share experiences and reaffirm the intimacy of sisterhood. Alitha despised Morcar's mood but a daughter's respect for her father, persuaded her not to react. Over time, Morcar's indifference towards Beatrice, had awakened in Alitha, a bitter, festering resentment and a private, unspoken grief.

Alitha sat in a chair opposite her father, waiting for him to finish eating. A fragile silence descended. Snow-white hair. azure blue eyes. The deep lines etched on his face, a poignant reminder of the hundreds of killings he had sanctioned. A man of integrity and cruel determination. It seemed immaterial to him, whether a man lived or died. But despite his vindictive nature and his obdurate pride, Morcar, chief disciple of the Wyvern Ring, remained her adoring father.

At last, Morcar pushed away his plate.

"The Scriptures are right," he said emphatically. "There is no greater joy for a father, than to hear his children, walking in the truth. You have proved your devotion to me and our cause. The severed head of Bishop Trilleck confirmed it. But your decency is besieged by base temptation and easy immorality. Your liaison with John Dornell is not acceptable to me."

In her mind's eye, Alitha collapsed into a black void. Desolation, shame and rage, all combined, ready to explode. Morcar braced himself for the expected onslaught. Venting her anger would certainly dissipate it. But Alitha did not raise her voice. Her indignation expertly kept in check.

"He is a good man but prone to excess. His drinking is rooted in the death of his wife. The Saracen's Head provides a respite for him."

In embracing the role of Alice, the convivial proprietor of the Saracen's Head, Alitha confirmed she was a brilliant performer. She transformed into the quintessential lady tavern keeper, incorrigible, flirtatious and unwilling to tolerate rowdy behaviour. Even John Dornell had not seen through her act. Used to deception, her true feelings were easily concealed. Alitha judged it expedient, not to contradict her father.

She needed time to think.

Morcar frowned. "Hereford has many watering holes where he can find strong drink. I'll make it known he is forbidden to enter the Saracen's Head. That will keep him away from you."

Alitha, in the guise of Alice managed the tavern. But Morcar was the owner. Only a few members of the Wyvern Ring were privy to this. A busy tavern in the centre of Hereford, was an ideal place to gather information and monitor potential enemies. Profits raised were used to buy weapons and provide funds for the disciples of the Wyvern Ring. Morcar often said that ownership of the Saracen's Head allowed him to make a killing.

Alitha scooped up her father's breakfast dishes, placing them on the tray with cold deliberation. A jagged shaft of sunlight entered through the open window. Alitha shielded her eyes, hiding her angry tears. In an instant they were gone, her composure regained. She carried the tray as far as the door. She stopped to speak but did not turn around.

"You are asking me to choose between John Dornell and our sacred cause?"

"Yes," said Morcar solemnly.

Alitha opened the door. With head bowed, she hurried down the stairs.

Chapter Four

Cardinal Beyssac closed his eyes. It was warm inside the awning of the coach but the bumpy road and constant jolting made sleep impossible. Only twenty miles to Hereford.

The rumbling monotony of the heavy wheels focused his thoughts. He despised the English and their roads with an equal passion. Plague-ridden, uncultured, quarrelsome, violent, consistently perverse. Their king, Edward III, a warmonger and a whoremonger. A monarch who found God's approval in all he did. A lustful king, cavorting with a thirteen-year-old mistress. Edward's erotic feasting guaranteed his damnation.

Beyssac recalled how the first miles of the journey from Avignon had been straightforward. His retinue consisted of six trustworthy companions: four experienced soldiers, Raymond, Pascal, Gaston and Tristan; Antoine, the cardinal's personal chef and Jerome, the papal equerry. All God-fearing, reliable men.

They set out on their journey filled with pride and optimism. A large flag, emblazoned with the Pope's emblem — a golden lion — fluttering proudly on top of the coach. It demanded the respect of French villagers, creating excitement wherever they stopped. Every true believer was obliged to support the papal emissary and help him accomplish God's purpose. A most holy enterprise. A sure way to reserve a seat in Heaven. But the English were not good Christians. In Heaven, there was no place reserved for them.

The descent into Hell began with crossing the Channel. Cardinal Beyssac, now incognito, became Monsieur Beyssac, journeying with friends to worship at the shrine of St Thomas in Hereford. The Pope's flag folded away and hidden. Military men changed into pilgrims. Bishop Trilleck should not have any knowledge of his impending dismissal. The people of Hereford must continue to wallow in Stygian filth, until Beyssac, inspired by the light of God, could save their souls.

London, consumed by the Pestilence, must be avoided. Ankou, the Grim Reaper, was abroad. Each night, he selected victims, scything them down, piling their corrupted bodies on his wagon. A creaking axle heralding his arrival ahead of the next gruesome harvest. Even Henry Grosmont, the Duke of Lancaster and hero of Auberoche had died. London, wallowing in venality, needed to be punished for its wickedness. Canterbury, protected by the spirit of Thomas Becket and free of Pestilence, would be a safe place to start their journey.

But the road from Dover to Canterbury only confirmed the Plague's insidious progress. Abandoned villages indicated an evil visitation. Plague pits and heaps of charred, cremated corpses, the remains of a demonic feast, indicated the presence of the Pestilence. Worst of all, were the stupefied peasants, arms outstretched, begging for help, staggering along the potholed road. Their swollen necks, black tongues and livid crimson spots, sure signs of imminent death. Victims, their faces twisted in puzzled agony, were everywhere. A black shroud had descended over England.

"Behold, with a great plague the Lord will smite thy people and thy children and thy wives and all thy goods." This was evidence of a wrathful God, punishing an ungodly people. Beyssac hid in the coach as it trundled along the dismal road to Canterbury. He feared the sight of such misery could erode his faith.

Thankfully, Canterbury proved a balm to the spirit. Pilgrims from every diocese in Christendom thronged the noisy streets. Honest hawkers and plausible peddlers shouted and jostled, all vying with each other to make a sale. Votive offerings, candles, statues and bottles filled with the blood of St Thomas were on offer at bargain prices. A feather of St Michael's wing. One of Adam's toenails. A gobbet of spit from Moses. All genuine relics, available to devout Christians — if a deal could be struck.

After prolonged haggling, Jerome, the equerry, was delighted with his purchase. For just two gold angel coins, he acquired the actual sponge lifted to Christ's lips as he suffered on the Cross. An incredible, authentic relic.

Antoine, the chef, did even better. For three gold coins, he purchased what appeared to be an ordinary leather bucket. But inside, lay its miraculous contents — soil from Calvary, saturated with the blood of Jesus Christ. Antoine had guaranteed himself a place in Heaven. A soul destined for eternal joy. Suffused by the immediate presence of God, Antoine knelt down next to the coach. Gulping down a cup of wine and offering up a fervent prayer, he did notice the guards, sneaking into the Jackdaw Tavern.

Meanwhile, Beyssac, waving away the relic sellers, joined the multitude of pilgrims toiling up the steep road to Canterbury Cathedral. There were no raised voices. The pilgrims were reverential, speaking in whispers. Beyssac was shocked to hear three archbishops had fallen victim to the Pestilence. Now, Simon Islip, the present archbishop was ill and not expected to live. How could an archbishop incur God's wrath? This definitely was the Year of Annihilation.

Beyssac entered the Trinity Chapel, taking his place among the pilgrims. As Cardinal Beyssac he would be feted and given preferential treatment. The English monks would bow to him. But now he was incognito and determined to remain unrecognised.

The Benedictines pulled on ropes to lift the wooden cover from Becket's tomb. Beyssac felt exalted. The coffin was silver and gold, adorned with precious stones. It dazzled his senses.

"I am the light of the world. He who follows me, shall not walk in darkness but have the light of life."

In that transcendent moment, Beyssac embraced Becket's sacrifice and martyrdom. Now he understood his unique place in the world. A calm enveloped him. Becket's murder was not a defeat but a triumph over death, a victory for Christ's promise to humankind. Putting his hands together, Beyssac knelt, praying to God in earnest silence.

Meanwhile at the Jackdaw Tavern, the guards were also enjoying a life-changing experience. An epiphany inspired by Hippocras — a spiced wine. A piquant potion, beyond all understanding.

Every cupful sharpened their thoughts and deepened their wisdom. Every flagon increased their perception and strengthened their resolve.

"Let us toast Cardinal Beyssac," said Raymond. "May his mission be a triumph."

"No," Pascal insisted, his restraint weakened by the wine. "Let us toast Cardinal Sin. A much more seductive master."

"That's naughty," Gaston purred, eyes closed, enjoying his fantasy. "But I must admit, the only mission that inspires me… is the missionary position."

Tristan nodded. "English girls," he mumbled, draining his cup in one, slurping mouthful. "English girls are beautiful. And hotter than a blacksmith's forge."

To Hell with Beyssac and his sacred task. They would stay in Canterbury, drink wine and each find an English wife. Three hours of consistent drinking had brought them to their senses. It was their duty to foster good relations with the English. They would achieve this by supporting the wine trade and by each marrying a local girl. Besides, the Pestilence made it too dangerous to travel any further. Confident their collective insight had reached a profound truth, the guards settled down to sleep. Wine begets wisdom. If Canterbury proved a turning point for Beyssac, it had become a point of no return for his guards.

***

That night, Jerome drove the coach the short distance to St Martin's Church. He positioned the coach next to the bell tower. They would be safe there. This was the church St Augustine had used as a base for his mission to convert England to Christianity. A tranquil sanctuary away from the temptations of Canterbury. A pious place in which to gather their thoughts and enjoy a meal.

A black marble tombstone served as their table. The inscription revealed a man and wife lay beneath — victims of the Pestilence. More food for the worms. Beyssac, Antoine and Jerome were hungry. Their makeshift meal would be respectful, not sacrilegious.

Antoine scooped a portion of beef stew into each bowl. Simple fare but delicious. Beyssac took a mouthful, chewing it with scrupulous propriety. The bell tower loomed over them like a stone sword. Beyssac gestured with his spoon.

"The dissolute are easy prey for the Archfiend. I am not surprised our guards succumbed to sensual temptations. Their adherence to God was clearly facile."

Jerome rubbed his bald head. He spoke in a whisper, attempting to gauge Beyssac's mood.

"They were good men, only somewhat distracted."

"Distracted!" Beyssac threw down his bowl. "We are privileged emissaries of Pope Innocent, engaged in a sacred mission to investigate the demise of the Christian Church in Hereford. Those guards deserted us in order to satisfy their depraved appetites. No more. No less. They are destined for damnation!"

Antoine shook his head. The face of St Bertha, immortalised in stained-glass, was looking straight at him.

"Only God decides who is damned and who is saved. We are filled with God's light but we are not divine."

Beyssac gritted his teeth, incensed that a mere chef would dare to question his theology. Beyssac unleashed his rebuke.

"The Pope is God's man on Earth. Did not our Lord say to Peter 'I will give you the keys of the kingdom and whatever you bind on Earth shall be bound in Heaven and whatever you loose on Earth shall be loosed in Heaven'. The Pope's judgement, inspired and directed by God is infallible. Therefore, those contemptible guards are wicked, godless sinners. Please assure me you are not challenging God. People have been burned at the stake for less."

Antoine retreated into his thoughts. Beyssac was wrong. Every man is liable to sin. No one is perfect. But Beyssac's threat was real. It would be prudent to concede defeat. Contrition would be a sensible attitude.

"I am deeply sorry. My brain was fuddled. I would never criticise the authority of the Holy Father. In truth, I am more confident holding a ladle than holding an argument. I can prepare a ragout but I should not speak about religion. Please accept my apology."

Jerome stroked his head. A sure sign he was nervous.

"And when I said 'distracted', I meant distracted by evil. Pure evil. I hope you don't think I condone their scandalous conduct? No. Not at all."

Beyssac scowled. He had made his point. False thoughts had been corrected. Antoine and Jerome could still achieve salvation but they must be vigilant in matters of faith. Religion is a fortress against Satan. Any breach in that fortress would be a catastrophe for the world.

"You must pray to St Jude. You are witless and need guidance. You are one footstep away from stumbling into a quagmire of sin. Pray hard, pray deeply and pray passionately. Above all, pray for God's forgiveness."

Beyssac stood up, making the sign of the cross.

"Now it is time to rest. Tomorrow we continue our pilgrimage to Hereford. A perilous road lies ahead."

The discussion was over. Beyssac climbed into the coach for private prayer and welcome sleep. Jerome unhitched the horses, watching them graze amongst the tombstones. Antoine washed the bowls and packed his cooking utensils away. Life seemed to be one long travail with little to enjoy and much to endure. Yet as St Bertha silently looked down on him from her stained-glass heaven, she seemed to flutter her eyelashes…

As they journeyed north, Antoine concluded that St Bertha's delightful smile would be his last uplifting experience. England presented a scene of faith-damaging desolation. The Pestilence ruled. Life or death depended on mere chance. It was a danse macabre impossible to escape.

Abandoned villages presented a pitiful sight. Open doors, broken hinges, smashed shutters, ruined farmsteads and looted cottages provided depressing evidence of the Pestilence. Fields remained uncultivated. Animals were unfed. Dead cattle lay in ditches, chunks of flesh hacked away by starving peasants. Wolves could be seen, sniffing blood in the air, determined to find prey. There were stories of cannibalism and of corpses disinterred by hungry villagers desperate for food.

Whole communities moved away, in search of respite from the horror. The roads were choked with coughing, sneezing and vomiting fugitives, dragging their pain-filled bodies in the direction of any town or village which they thought free of the deadly scourge. Black tongues offered earnest prayers to God, pleading for His mercy. It seemed as if the whole world was on the move.

Chapter Five

The procession halted at the Wye Bridge gate. Without hesitation, the brotherhood knelt down in submission, acknowledging the authority of the master. Flanked by two subordinates, holding a banner depicting the Crucifixion, he extended his arms in a messianic pose, shouting at the top of his voice.

"For on this day, you cross the River Wye. You will know for certain that you will die. Your blood is on your own head."

Too frightened to deny them entry, Peter and Thomas, the watchmen, quickly opened the gate. A short walk across the bridge and three hundred men, their faces hidden under black cowls, would enter the city. Men of God — their white tunics decorated back and front with a blood-red cross. The flagellants — fanatics who believed punishing their bodies would appease God's wrath. Their penance would satisfy God. He would stop the Pestilence.

Insistent feet, marching in unison, stamped across the wooden bridge. An ominous, rhythmic, portent. Below them, the River Wye continued its search for the sea. Eyes open, staring up at the clouds, the corpse of a young girl floated slowly down the river, rising and sinking at the current's behest. A victim of God's anger?

Stamping their feet whilst chanting the Stabat Mater, the brotherhood marched along Wyebridge Street, heading for St Nicholas' Church. Strident voices declaring their desire for pain. Agony, the foundation of their ecstasy.

"Holy Mother, pierce me through

In my heart each wound renew

Let me share with thee His pain

Who for all my sins was slain."

People lined the street. Bewildered shoppers, anxious traders, worried mothers clutching children, mystified monks and nervous nuns, pilgrims, beggars and errant servants absent from work, all bemused by the bizarre spectacle. Hundreds of fierce-looking, belligerent men, chanting, shouting and raising dust, pounding their feet into the ground.

St Nicholas' Church. They stopped. The grand master raised his right hand, stretching up high, holding a silver crucifix directly up towards the sun. A signal. The torment must begin.

Each man, resolute and intoxicated by religion, stripped off his tunic, leaving only a linen cloth wrapped around his groin. No misgivings or fearful faces. An army of saints, made pure by self-sacrifice. Zealots determined to defeat the Pestilence. All carried a scourge — three leather thongs, tipped with blacksmith's nails.

Concealed by the hood of his cowl, the master remained aloof, directing activities and issuing orders. His rich, resonant voice, commanded respect. His distinctive blue eyes scrutinising every onlooker, alert for any threat.

"Ply well, the scourge for Jesus' sake

And God, through Christ, your sins shall take."

The scourging began. Grim fanatics, eagerly thrashing their chests and shoulders with nail-tipped whips. Red pearls of warm blood flew through the air, splashing the faces of onlookers, standing too close.

An elderly woman screamed as a gibbering monk fell to his knees, smearing blood across his eyelids, certain the Apocalypse had begun.

Wyebridge Street staged a pain-filled pageant. Twisted, agonised faces, groans, sobs and plaintive, piercing cries, shrieks and gasps of men suffering bloody self-inflicted torment. Blood everywhere. Flowing wounds, oozing gore, lacerated shoulders and heaving chests crossed by scarlet stripes. The relentless fury of men obsessed by one brutal belief. Appease God and the Pestilence would end.

Awed bystanders tore pieces from their garments, dipping strips of cloth into the spilt blood. Sacred relics to earn God's mercy and deter the Angel of Death.

Some onlookers, overwhelmed by the spectacle and convinced of the flagellants' virtue, knelt down, sipping mouthfuls of blood from still warm puddles.

The bystanders inevitably succumbed to the prevailing mood. The actions of the flagellants combined with the hostility of the onlookers, to create a violent, hysterical mob, hell-bent on destruction. The moment the master planned for, had arrived. St Nicholas' Church, Hereford's oldest religious building, lay only a stone's throw away.

Before his death, King Harold regarded St Nicholas' Church as the most sublime place of worship in his kingdom. A blissful Christian temple, glorious in the sight of God, a stunning celebration of Christianity — awe-inspiring, life changing and utterly indestructible. The Master disagreed.

The screams of men in distress were negated, lost amidst the noisy tumult of the mob. The master narrowed his eyes. Issuing instructions at this juncture would be futile.

Thinking quickly, he mounted the box seat of a wagon. Once again, he raised his crucifix. But now he pointed directly at St Nicholas' Church, aggressively jabbing his finger like a murderer plunging a knife into a body.

Demented minds need little encouragement. Shouting curses and blasphemies, threatening gruesome death to anyone who defied them, flagellants and citizens, surged along Wyebridge Street, knocking aside terrified adults and trampling over quaking children. It was a madcap, frantic rush to reach the focal point of their hatred, St Nicholas' Church.

Racked by the pain of his wounds, a flagellant brother was first to the church. Yelling profanities, naked except for a loincloth, he seemed a biblical savage, "having no love for what is good." Wild-eyed, unshaven, covered in bloody gashes, he barged at the priests' door, forcing it open. The anger of a dispirited community towards an institution indifferent to its fate, was about to be unleashed. Hundreds of shrieking rioters, men and women, impossible to control, a turbulent, seething mob, stormed into the chancel.

Two Norman monks, wary of danger, remained in the chantry, cowering behind a curtain. They listened, aghast at the wanton destruction of St Nicholas.

The marble altar table was toppled over and shattered. A gold cross, candlesticks, valuable vestments, furnishings and even a flagon of sacrament wine, were looted. The stained glass, a vibrant masterpiece depicting the kings of Mercia was smashed. The font became a pissoir for adults and children. Standing in the church doorway, watching the destruction, the master shook his head. He was still not content.

Driven by an all-consuming hatred, the master lifted the silver crucifix high above his head haranguing the bawling mob. In deference to his eminent position, sated for the moment, the rioters fell into a begrudging silence.

"You are saints, acting out God's will. You must now purge this place of Norman contamination. For too long our English Church has been befouled by foreign oppression. Two priests are hiding in the chantry. Find them and hang them. Do not spare collaborators! God has promised all men will be made equal and the idle rich will be punished… You must execute His will…!"

That night, the flames which engulfed St Nicholas' Church dazzled all those watching. Burning and blistering, red and blue. Timbers cracked. Tiles slipped, crashing down into the blackened skeleton. Noxious smoke irritated noses and gaping mouths. Smouldering embers blew ash into curious upturned faces. At the end of the street, two corpses, nooses around their throats, hung from the Wye Bridge. The city of Hereford glowed red.

Smiling, the master twisted the ring around his finger until the dragon appeared. Today had been a good day.

Chapter Six

The last mile of the road into Uxbridge almost cost Beyssac and his companions their lives. They had agreed not to stop the coach and to remain deaf to any cries for help from plague-infected travellers. It was too dangerous. This was a promise they kept until the feast day of John the Baptist. For on that day, slightly obscured by the morning haze, a gang of beggars, waving their arms and shaking their heads, came gradually into view.

They straggled the road, their torn and filthy clothes, hanging down in strips, their hopeless, apathetic faces, suggesting Death was near. Too much for even the hardest heart. It must be possible to help these people. Compassion is a Christian duty.

Jerome pulled back the reins, easing the horses to a gentle trot. The coach slowed. But narrowing his eyes to focus on the beggars more intently, Jerome realised he had made a terrible mistake.

For blocking the road, directly in front of the coach, stood a dozen, fierce-looking naked men. It was not their torn clothes hanging down in ribbons but wasted flesh, covered in pus-filled buboes. Every dirty hand brandished a knife or a cudgel. Desperate for food, resigned to inevitable death, they were prepared to kill.

Meanwhile, inside the coach, unaware of danger, Beyssac lay under a blanket. A night of fervent prayer, a full stomach and the unceasing motion of the coach wheels, encouraged a deep, untroubled sleep. As for Antoine, he remained engrossed in reading the religious manuscript, Beyssac had put down. Antoine considered the manuscript deeply. He pondered all its possibilities and analysed all its aspects. He evaluated every viewpoint and perused every potential problem. It was a truth beyond dispute. Rich men attract beautiful women.

As for Jerome, he took a more pragmatic approach to life. Repeatedly screaming as loudly and deafeningly as he could.

A shaggy-haired, blaspheming beggar, leapt up to the box seat, snatching the reins from Jerome's trembling hands. Jerome felt a knife against his throat. Stinking, bearded, naked, bestial creatures. Ogres, wild men of the woods. Homme savage, the antithesis of civilisation.

"Silence! You puling priest. Stop whining or I'll cut your bowels out and chew them in front of your face!"

The coach came to a stop.

Jerome noticed flecks of blood in the beggar's beard and red smears around his mouth. His flatulent breath made Jerome feel sick.

Slowly, menacingly, the beggars encircled the coach. Expectant mouths hung open. Glittering knife blades caught the sunlight. The beggars were hungry — fresh meat was now readily available. An unholy Communion was about to take place.

"I warn you, hell hounds. Your lives are in peril. I have a sponge!" Jerome was resolute. His faith steadfast.

An instant reaction. Horrified by Jerome's warning, the beggars burst into laughter. Some, unable to stand, knelt down, stomachs heaving, guffawing into the dust. Others, delirious with disbelief, thumped their chests, struggling for breath. One man rolled around, wailing like a wolf. What drollery? Was this priest insane? He has a sponge! What else was in his weapon store? The Pope's penis?

Under the awning, inside the coach, Beyssac remained asleep. His eyes flickered. In his dream, Sarah, wife of Abraham, met with three angels. Despite her great age, one hundred years old, God promised, she would give birth to a son and name him Isaac. Sarah laughed out loud. She continued laughing and did not stop.

But Antoine was alert. Those beasts outside were cannibals. Very soon, he and his companions would be murdered and eaten. Were all English men so brutish?

Antoine considered what to do. Thoughts flashed through his mind. Some ingenious but all impractical. He recalled his childhood in Rennes. Everyone, young and old, feared the Ankou, the henchman of Death. He drove a black coach pulled by four black horses. He wore a black robe and a black hat. His skeleton face was plague-pit black. It was believed those who met his gaze would be taken straight to Hell. Damned souls, destined to eternal torment — condemned to pain beyond human understanding.

Quick as a harlot's wink, Antoine emptied the contents of the sacred leather bucket over his head. Soil, worms and nuggets of blood streamed down his face. Bubbles of gore dripped from his lips. His features twisted into a savage, feral mask. It seemed Hell had unleashed a demon, ready to kill.

Antoine threw on his cloak. God's power must prevail. Howling like a rabid dog, he tore the awning. A bellowing, yelping, anguished cry, emerged from the depths of his lungs. When the gruesome apparition appeared, the laughter suddenly stopped.

Waving his fists, Antoine seemed possessed.

"I am Ankou!" he boomed. "Harvester of the damned. This is my chariot. You are my mortal crop. Your time has come. Join me in my Dance of Death. Remember you are dust and unto dust you shall return."

Astonished jaws dropped. Blood-stained tongues dangled from foul-smelling mouths. Silent as statues, the beggars stood aghast. Were they only seconds away from Hell?

Heads full of images of punishment. Contorted faces reflecting tormented souls. Ankou must obey his master. Hell was waiting.

Antoine's voice reached a crescendo. He was in full flow and enjoying it. He unleashed a spell to summon Lucifer.

"Life is short and shortly yours will end;

Death comes quickly without respect,

Death destroys. It shows no pity.

You are near to Death. No one can help you."

Only one thing for the beggars to do. Run. Run fast. Keep on running. Don't look back.

Screaming, shouting, cursing, wailing, falling over, flailing their arms, crashing into each other, banging heads, the naked, desperate beggars scattered in all directions. Bubonic beasts. Human ripples dispersing across a pond. Antoine sighed with relief. Jerome fainted, twisting like a falling leaf. Beyssac remained asleep.

That evening, they pitched camp in the garden of St Margaret's Chapel of Ease. It was a warm night. Aromas of lemon balm, rosemary and apple mint, lulled their senses. Beyssac sat on a wine barrel, listening to Antoine's vivid account of the day. Jerome nervously rubbed his pate. God had saved them. But Beyssac's face was solemn.

"How appropriate we should rest at St Margaret's Church — the patron saint of the dying. Today nearly ended in disaster but the Lord kept us safe. The forces of Antichrist were defeated. But Antoine should be penitent. He destroyed a holy relic. I hope he is consumed with guilt."

Antoine dug his spoon into the cooking pot. Lifting out a portion of veal, he stared fixedly at Beyssac.

"Consumed? Those beggars were cannibals. If it wasn't for me, we'd all have been consumed today. And I doubt if they would have said grace either!"

Beyssac crossed himself. He accepted the rebuke without reply. In his secret heart, he was just glad to be alive.

Chapter Seven

The warmth of the sun and the weight of the coffin on his back, made Nicholas breathless. He needed frequent stops. But he was determined to reach the cathedral. He halted and put the coffin down, resting for a moment. He unbuttoned his jerkin and tightened the knot in his trouser belt. It was early and the streets were quiet. Fear of the Pestilence discouraged all but the most courageous. Or the most foolish.

Convinced he would be arrested, or at least attacked, Nicholas took a deep breath as he rolled up his sleeves. He wanted to cause trouble. He hoped his sermon would outrage the citizens of Hereford and provoke a response. Real anger was more authentic than passive acceptance.

Moreover, his promise to stand on a coffin outside the door of the cathedral — the focal point of Christian faith in Hereford — and condemn the Church for its wickedness, was bound to stir up a hornet's nest.

Looking around, Nicholas spotted two Carmelite nuns, clothed in white gowns and dark scapular, hurrying across the Cathedral Close towards the infirmary. Clearing his throat, Nicholas stepped onto the coffin lid, shouting directly at them.

"Good ladies. Harken to the truth. Behind me, corrupt and shameless, stands a mansion of immorality, a place offensive to God. The Pestilence has confirmed God's determination to punish this church and its money-mad followers. You are innocent. God knows you are decent, righteous people. But the Pestilence is the price you are paying for the idolatry and duplicity of the Catholic Church."

The nuns stopped, angelic smiles adorning their innocent faces. An older woman, clearly senior, arm in arm with a young novice, a girl obviously under instruction. They walked over, hands tucked under their cloaks. Exalted seraphim in direct communication with God.

Uplifted, Nicholas considered himself to be on the threshold of a major spiritual experience. Eyes sparkling like votive candles, the older nun spoke in a calm, reassuring tone. The accumulated wisdom of fifty years quietly unleashed.

"You yelping, shit-faced abortion! You are full of conceit! You dare to claim knowledge of God's purposes? Remember the warning of Proverbs. Every man, arrogant in heart, is an abomination to the Lord and deserves to be punished… And remember my words, the words of Sister Kathryn. Take your demonic doctrine and stick it up your crack!"

Radiating dignity and warm humanity, the Carmelites hastened on to the hospital. Delighted by this reaction, Nicholas knelt on the coffin lid, offering up a prayer. The song of Moses, warned of the fate awaiting evildoers.

"I will heap calamities upon them and spend my arrows against them. I will send wasting famine against them, consuming pestilence and deadly plague."

In Hereford, at least twenty people a day were dying from the disease. The law courts had been adjourned, the weekly market shut down and schools and brothels closed. Dozens of shops had ceased trading and were boarded up. Each dawn revealed unclaimed corpses lying in the streets. In despair, many townspeople had taken flight to the countryside. To Nicholas, the high death rate proved that God had identified Hereford as an evil city, deserving to be punished.

Nicholas jumped to his feet. A man turned the corner of Milk Lane and was walking briskly across the close. His black cassock suggested a cleric although his head was not shaved. He seemed angry. Nicholas anticipated a furious debate. He waited until the man was within earshot.

"Good sir. Do you believe all churchmen should abandon their wealth and focus on their faith?"

John Dornell stopped. He did not want to engage in a discussion with an obvious fanatic. His son's illness, the love affair with Alice and the cathedral school closed, leaving him jobless, were worries he could do without. A curt response would quash the young man's zeal.

"Yes. I believe they should focus on their faith."

Nicholas blinked in astonishment. He had expected an ill-tempered argument not gentle acquiescence. Perhaps this man had a grievance with a priest which influenced his thinking. It would quickly be mended. Soon, he would be eager to defend the Church. Still, the second question was bound to provoke a dispute.

"Do you agree that every Christian has the right to study the Scriptures and come to a personal belief?"

John stroked his lips, apparently absorbed in thought.

"Yes. Every Christian should have access to the Scriptures and develop a personal relationship with God... But I have important business. I must go."

Nicholas stood on his coffin, open mouthed. Was this man mocking him? Providing derisive answers until the watchman arrived? Then, labelled a heretic, he would be thrown in prison? One more question.

"Sir. Before you attend to your important business... Do you agree the Pestilence is God's vengeance against black-hearted sinners?"

John felt anger spuming in his stomach. A boiling, seething mix of bitterness, resentment and exasperation. His son, William, was ill. John could not admit to himself what it might be. But he did know William was not a black-hearted sinner and did not deserve to suffer. The Pestilence was not God's vengeance against the world. No, it was clear, the horror was directed at corruption, idolatry and false worship. Ordinary people were blameless. The inexorable truth was the Catholic Church, the most powerful institution in the World, had set in motion its own doom.

"No!" John shouted. His strident voice piercing the silence of the close like a soul falling into Hell.

"That is an outrageous assertion. The Pestilence does not discriminate. King or pauper, citizen or rustic, saint or sinner. Death can strike anyone, anywhere, any time. How can this torment be God's vengeance against the wicked? Thousands of devout Christians, monks, nuns and priests, people who give their lives to God, are dying every day. Only a dullard would suggest such dedicated people are actually agents of Lucifer. No, I find your assertion sordid and offensive. A kicking would be a good remedy for your addled brain."

Shrugging his shoulders Nicholas stepped down from the coffin.

"A soft answer calms wrath. But a harsh word stirs up anger. The instant I saw you walking this way, I knew you were vexed. You were incensed about something even before I spoke. Vehement words cannot disguise your distress."

John's fury began to recede. How could this zealot, a complete stranger, instantly recognise he was a worried man, under severe strain? William's illness, particularly his repeated vomiting and inability to swallow food, were pitiful symptoms of a malady John did not understand. Mr Spicer, the apothecary, had recommended laxatives and opening a vein. In his opinion, William had an excess of blood which needed to be drained and investigated. John dreaded the prospect of William spilling his lifeblood into a copper bowl.

Stepping forward, the young man placed a hand on John's arm. His sympathetic face showing genuine concern.

"The Lord can be a fortress against evil," he whispered, his kind words, a balm for John's distress. John relaxed. He sat down. Considering the world was on the verge of Armageddon, taking a seat on a coffin seemed appropriate.

"I am John Dornell, schoolmaster at the cathedral."

"And I am Nicholas of Credenhill, herbalist and freethinker… perpetually in awe of God's wrath."

They shook hands, sitting next to each other on the coffin.

"You have impressive knowledge of the Scriptures," said John. "Nahum is a minor prophet. Only the most learned scholars quote him."

"I cherish wisdom," said Nicholas. "It would be a foolish man who ignored a prophet's advice."

"Or perhaps a deceitful man, intent on evil."

Nicholas nodded, pointing at the cathedral. "Yes, the Devil has countless disguises. That palace of putrefaction being one of them!"

John frowned.

"It is a palace but a very powerful one. Your criticism is unfair and too severe. The Church provides great solace to those in distress."

"The Church is the cause of their distress," said Nicholas.

At that moment, John grasped the reason for Nicholas' anger. Resolutely hostile and intolerant of support for the Church, Nicholas adhered to a scandalous faith. He was a Lollard, a man who believed the Pope to be Antichrist. A heretic who wanted to destroy the Catholic Church.

John shifted a little on the coffin. He could be arrested for talking to Nicholas. Time to relieve the tension.

Clenching his fist, John knocked on the coffin lid — three, slow, heavy blows — like a phantom banging on a church door in the dark hours.

"Why such a melancholy companion?" asked John.

Lost in thought, Nicholas stroked the coffin, his fingers following the grain of the wood. Larch wood — a defence against evil spirits and enchantments — protection against the Evil Eye. A Christian needs every resource they can find to combat Satan. His musing finished, Nicholas jumped up.

"This coffin is a perpetual reminder of my mortality. All of us are only a heartbeat away from death... and the Lord's judgement."

"From dust you are born," John hissed.

"And to dust you shall return," Nicholas interrupted.

John's anger had dissolved into despair. His downcast face betrayed a heavy heart. Nicholas did not hesitate.

"Your eyes reveal a man in low spirits. You are clearly burdened by a great concern. Can I help?"

John shook his head dismissively.

"My son, William, is laid up sick. He vomits continually and refuses food. He has a fever and pain in his limbs. I will be straight with you. I fear... I fear, he has the Pestilence."

Nicholas scratched his head, pondering what John had told him. Undoubtedly William was ill but John's suspicions of the Pestilence were premature. As a herbalist, Nicholas had examined and prescribed treatment to dozens of victims of disease. Common sense suggested the Pestilence could not be to blame for every illness.

"How old is William?"

"Twelve."

"Is his skin blotchy or black?"

"No. Not at all. But he does have a rash on his face and tiny butterfly-shaped spots on the bridge of his nose."

"That is significant. But it's a good sign. Does William have any swellings in his neck, armpits or groin?"

"No."

"Thank God. Have you seen livid, scarlet marks anywhere on his body?"

"No."

"Does he complain of headaches?"

"Yes."

"Does he prefer to rest in the shade, away from strong light?"

"Yes! How could you know that?"

Nicholas exhaled, a pensive look on his face.

"William may be very ill," he said grimly. "But I do not think the Pestilence is responsible. I must examine him before I confirm my judgement."

Overwrought but exhilarated by Nicholas' diagnosis, John sprang up, hurdling the coffin in one bound. William might be very ill but certainly not at death's door. John raced towards his house in Broad Street, pushing through a group of choirboys on their way to the cathedral and almost colliding with a dung cart heading for the river.

"Come on," he shouted, catching his breath at the corner of the street. "But remember — leave your coffin outside the door!"

Eyes closed, his face covered in beads of sweat, naked, except for a blanket, William lay motionless on the bed. The room was dark, lit only by a flickering wall sconce, dripping wax on to the floor. The dim light confirmed a blood-red rash covered his face and chest. An indistinct scent perfumed the air, its fragrant aroma nestling in every corner. As William slept, a respectful silence dominated. Time seemed to have stopped.

Gently, with a father's loving care, John wiped the sweat from William's forehead.

"He's still asleep," said John. "All that vomiting must have exhausted him."

Nicholas felt the pulse in William's neck. It was faint. With his nails, he pinched the boy's face. William did not stir. Lifting his eyelids, revealed dilated pupils, staring fixedly at the ceiling. William was not asleep. He was unconscious. Nicholas needed more information.

"When did William first tell you he felt ill?"

"Yesterday afternoon on his return from the cathedral."

"And from that moment he has complained of headaches and fever? Does he vomit frequently?"

"Yes."

66

"This room has a peculiar smell. It reminds me of something nasty I have encountered before. Can you smell it?"

John sniffed the air, breathing in deeply to catch the scent.

"I can smell sick. That's all."

Nicholas shook his head.

"Do you have flowers in this house?"

John bowed his head, struggling to contain his anger.

"I invited you here to identify William's illness and suggest how he could be cured. I don't understand the need for all these questions!"

Nicholas closed his eyes. John loved his son. He was worried and angry. He did not understand.

"And you will know the truth and the truth will set you free," said Nicholas under his breath. "One last question. Did William pick flowers yesterday?"

"No," said John emphatically. "But he said he did help an old man, a pilgrim visiting the tomb of St Thomas. The man claimed he was infirm and too weak to climb the cathedral steps. He promised William a silver penny, if he agreed to place a garland of flowers on the tomb. As a sign of respect, William was asked to kiss the flowers before he set them down."

"What colour were those flowers?"

"Blue," said John. "Definitely blue."

Nicholas gasped, his mind racing with conflicting emotions.

"I have to tell you now. Your son has been poisoned. I do not think he will survive the night!"

Chapter Eight

Richard Corner held the rosary beads between the fingers of his two hands. Eyes closed, he whispered the Lord's Prayer. He felt the amber beads caress his thumbs. A brief moment of serenity.

St Giles Hospital, Wycombe, was full of sick and dying patients. Miserable, hopeless souls. As Master of St Giles, Richard was responsible for the physical and spiritual needs of nearly one hundred invalids. He doubted he could cope. His compassion was being overwhelmed by the sheer number of those needing help. He was fighting a losing battle.

And the Pestilence raged unabated. Every day, increasing numbers of victims begged to be admitted to St Giles. Medical supplies were low. Rye bread with vegetable soup was the only meal available. Patients slept two in a bed or found a coveted space on the floor near a window. A master, four chaplains and three women, struggling to care for so many incurable patients. How could such suffering be part of God's plan? St Giles himself, patron saint of cripples, would falter under the burden of this misery. A Maison Dieu — built to accommodate the needs of pilgrims— now transformed into a Maison Morte, concerned to meet the needs of the dying.

The majority of the sick, occupied beds in the Great Hall. A few, due to lack of room, lay on pews in the chapel. Men, women and children were not separated. Vomiting or incontinent patients, groaned out their woes. The smell was dreadful. Richard looked pensive. On average, he performed the last rites five times a day.

Most patients were beyond help. If it be God's will, some might survive. But most would die. Take Michael Makejoy, erstwhile fiddle player, juggler and favourite buffoon of Alice Perrer, the king's mistress. He would probably die before supper.

A skeletal hand stretched out. A bony finger poked Richard's belly. Michael Makejoy, cursed by God and shunned by society. His affliction, a divine judgement for a sinful life. Deformed and repulsive, an affront to Christ and his kingdom on Earth. Michael was a leper.

Richard felt nauseated. Sick to his stomach. Not by Michael's physical state but by Michael's suffering. Red, ulcerated sores covered his whole body. A gaping wound, replaced his nose. His hair had fallen out. His bulging eyeballs reminded Richard of a stone-carved gargoyle. Thank God the other patients were too busy dwelling on their own misfortunes to realise a leper was amongst them. As an outcast, Michael was condemned to a living death. Michael's condition was a test of Richard's courage and the certainty of his faith.

Slowly and carefully, Richard raised a jug of water to Michael's mouth.

"Cyprus wine," said Richard. "A most appropriate beverage for such an esteemed performer."

Eyes closed, lost in a memory, Michael gulped it down.

"Cyprus wine," he whispered. His voice faltering when he spoke. "The wine of kings and the king of wines. Much loved by Richard Lionheart. This is pure nectar. You, sir, are a man of refined taste."

"No, just a man of God," said Richard.

Despite his awful predicament, Michael sparkled. Beneath his rotting flesh, lay an indomitable spirit. His dancing days were over. He was not strong enough to hold a lute or juggle heavy swords. But he responded to wit. After all, life itself was just one big cruel joke. That jug could contain whatever Michael wanted it to contain.

Stretching down, Richard retrieved a dark crust from the wooden platter under the bed. Black rye loaf. He gave it to Michael.

"All sorrows are lessened by good bread," said Michael. He chewed slowly, squeezing the crust into his mouth, relishing and enjoying every crumb. Richard recited the Messiah's words. They seemed appropriate.

"I am the living bread that came down from Heaven. Whoever eats my bread will live forever."

"No," said Michael firmly. "Not forever. But maybe until the next empty belly. This is Wycombe, not Nazareth."

"Cling to your faith," Richard retorted. "At all times. When things seem hopeless. You must cling to your faith."

Michael raised himself. "What faith? Your gentle, loving,

compassionate God has made me a monster. A repulsive human animal. I disgust everyone. My life is a trial. Every day is an ordeal. A struggle from dawn to dusk. Each morning is a wound that bleeds afresh."

A challenge to his faith. Richard raised his voice.

"This life, your life, however hard, however difficult it seems, is simply a preparation for eternal life. Submit to God's will. Then you will secure a place in Paradise."

Michael shook his head dismissively. He spoke quietly, his words full of indignation.

"Did not the leper say to Jesus? 'Lord, if you are willing, you can make me clean'."

"Yes, Jesus was asked that question."

"I have prayed to Jesus a thousand times to heal me and make me clean. Yet, he has ignored me. He is deaf to my suffering. I am excluded from his mercy."

"No one is excluded from God's mercy. I say again. You must cling to your faith. Our time on Earth is but the blink of an eye. You must be ready to meet God. Do not give up the struggle."

"When Jesus believes in me, I will believe in him."

Michael turned his back on Richard and lay facing the wall. A woman cried uncontrollably. Her baby son, lifeless in her arms. A man spat, cursed and struggled, as two chaplains tried to spoon medicine into his mouth. Someone knocked loudly on the heavy entrance door. Richard ran the rosary beads between his fingers. Michael was dying and would be dead by morning. Another wasted life. A further erosion of Richard's faith. In all his life, he had never felt so alone.

Chapter Nine

'Diabolical' was Antoine's description of the road between Uxbridge and Wycombe. Jerome considered 'hellish' a more appropriate adjective. Beyssac judged the road 'a damnable, wretched, accursed, purgatorial, quagmire'.

Deeply rutted by cartwheels, intermittently blocked by fallen trees and ankle-deep in clinging mud, progress was slow. The horses struggled in the mire, slipping and losing grip, sweating hard, snorting with fear, desperate to stay upright and avoid sinking into the ooze.

While Jerome walked alongside the coach controlling the horses, Antoine enjoyed the privilege of carrying Beyssac on his back. A papal envoy must maintain decorum. It was not seemly for Beyssac, the Pope's emissary, to trudge through smelly, English mud. Beyssac was not heavy but he was prone to flatulence.

Antoine was worried.

Hour after hour, mile after mile, mud sticking to their clothes, they slogged on towards Wycombe. The plan was to spend a comfortable night at the Red Lion Inn, a hostelry used by pilgrims. Beyssac was of the opinion, that although the road to Wycombe was pure purgatory, Wycombe itself would be pure heaven.

The sun was beginning to set when Jerome turned the coach into St Margaret's Lane. With care, he steered the exhausted horses towards the welcoming courtyard of the Red Lion Inn. A hot meal and a soft bed were only minutes away.

Antoine bent his back, allowing Beyssac to step down on to the road. Muttering a prayer, Beyssac stretched his arms. All three were tired and hungry but in good spirits. Jerome's unerring sense of direction and fluent English had brought them to their destination.

A Carmelite friar they met at the crossroads, confirmed the details. The best hospitality in Wycombe — the friar had emphasised the word 'hospitality' — was provided by Richard at his blessed establishment in

St Margaret's Lane. Richard followed the maxim of St Benedict. "Let all guests that come, be received like Christ. For He will say, I was a stranger and you took me in." Thus, filled with anticipation and keen to meet their host, Antoine, Jerome and Beyssac, knocked on the oak door of St Giles Hospital.

Geoffrey, the chaplain opened the door. He saw three plague victims, desperate for help. The Pestilence did not discriminate. Merciless, unforgiving and relentless. It seemed unstoppable. The punishment of a God, beyond human understanding. Still, these men were suffering and needed his support.

Pushing Geoffrey aside, Beyssac marched in. The hostelry seemed popular. There were beds along every wall. There was even a chapel. This was a sign of the proprietor's Christian credentials.

Beyssac removed his cloak, draping it over Geoffrey's arm.

"Have your groom tend to our horses and stable them. Instruct your servants to take our bags to your superior rooms. We have clothes which need washing. Start work immediately. We are hungry and expect a lavish meal. But first, we need refreshment. Spiced wine is my preference but care, not too much cinnamon. It engenders lustful thoughts. Inform Richard we are here. I must question him."

Geoffrey's jaw dropped. He thought quickly. He knew the Pestilence could cause disorder of the brain. These men may be rogues or more likely simply deranged. Their faculties poisoned. Victims of a cruel, cosmic joke. Best to accommodate them. They might turn nasty. He listened to their conversation. Three very odd individuals. Geoffrey nodded, bowing respectfully.

"Gentlemen, give me your cloaks. Take a seat while I fetch Richard." Geoffrey pointed to a bench. "Richard will be delighted to welcome you to our hostelry. I can honestly say, you will never forget your visit."

With a deferential flourish, Geoffrey strode across the hall, disappearing into a side room. The air was filled with a pungent smell. It adhered to their clothes, permeating every corner of the hall. It reminded Antoine of boiled pork.

Geoffrey described to Richard his three new patients. They were dangerous. The leader, Beyssac, was clearly a megalomaniac. He seemed intoxicated by his own importance. The impostor calling himself Antoine, claimed to be a chef. But he had mistaken vegetable stew for boiled pork. And as for Jerome. He was not a squire. Rather a horse-obsessed idiot. They were probably armed and hell-bent on robbery, mutilation and murder. Time to alert the watchmen. Intuitive, discerning, proud of his penetrating insight, Geoffrey urged Richard to put his trust in God… and keep a dagger close to hand.

Assuming a benign face, Richard whispered a psalm and swept out of the room. The sound of his footsteps echoed across the hospital stone floor. Deep in conversation, the three guests broke off their discussion. Their faces bore the unmistakable look of unhinged criminals. Intimidated but armed with his faith, Richard offered a hand in greeting.

Beyssac ignored Richard's hand. As a cardinal, he expected deference not familiarity.

"We have travelled a long way. We are very hungry. Lombard tart would be a good first course. I prefer quails' eggs to those of chicken. Our next course should be venison or partridge. Whatever is more convenient for you. I have a weakness for sparrows in fruit pottage. Plum, cherries, grapes or strawberries would suffice. Baked apple is also acceptable. A cheese platter to finish would be good. As for drinks — spiced red wine would definitely complement the food. How soon can this snack be ready?"

Taken aback, Richard struggled to maintain an amiable face. Geoffrey was right. These men were lunatics or despicable rogues. Twisting the rosary beads between his fingers, Richard knew he must be honest.

"In this house we specialise in spiritual and emotional nourishment. A satisfied soul is more pleasing to God than a full belly. I can offer you vegetable stew, with a cob of black rye bread."

Jerome and Antoine looked offended. But Beyssac smiled. He immediately saw through Richard's stratagem. The offer of such poor victuals was a test of their Christian credentials. Richard was calculating their devotion to God. Once they had passed the test, Richard would entertain them in the style they expected.

With a few whispers, Beyssac explained Richard's ploy to Antoine and Jerome. The way forward was to agree with everything Richard said.

"Vegetable stew is my absolute favourite," Antoine enthused.

"The fewer vegetables, the more I like it," Jerome declared.

Not to be outdone, Beyssac raised his voice.

"Rye bread is an outrageous luxury. Far too splendid for me. A small crust of horse bread would satisfy my hunger."

This humility left Richard confused. He judged them to be arrogant scoundrels. Now, they appeared humble and even submissive. Still, best to remain vigilant. They might be planning mischief.

Richard sat on a stool, opposite his guests, examining their faces. Jerome, the groom, seemed bewildered. His rolling eyeballs suggested fear. Antoine, the chef, exuded calm. His broad shoulders and trim waist hinted at a man more used to fighting than cooking. But Beyssac was clearly the leader. He had an air of gravitas which demanded respect. He reminded Richard of a magistrate or conceited papal official.

Richard exhaled gently. They must be told.

"I cannot provide you with individual rooms. All our beds are taken. You must share or sleep on the floor. You may discover your bedfellow has the Pestilence. Or, God forbid, leprosy."

Beyssac admired Richard's skill at inventing stories. To devise such an elaborate charade, in order to test the depth of their Christian faith, was a master stroke.

"It would be a privilege to share a bed with a sick stranger, covered in weeping sores. That would be a good test of my faith."

Beyssac chuckled, proud of his self-abasement. Not to be outdone, Antoine was eager to demonstrate his compassion. Even St Sebastian would struggle to match Antoine's humanity.

"Bring forth all those with dysentery, syphilis, Pestilence or the king's evil. Lepers, you are welcome into my bed. The more lesions, the better. I will sleep with the afflicted, to demonstrate my faith in Jesus."

Unconvinced by Antoine's display of brotherly love and fearful of Beyssac's anger, Jerome stood up.

"And, I'll sleep with… the horses," he whispered. In a second, he was out of the door and running across the courtyard. Jerome would choose horses over humans, every time.

"Your kindness is clear evidence of your faith," said Richard, warmly.

"But what brings you to Wycombe? Why did you choose this place to relieve your distress? You can see we are full to the brim with unfortunate souls."

Beyssac slipped effortlessly into his cover story.

"We are pilgrims. Our destination is the tomb of St Thomas in Hereford. I have always admired his undaunted faith. To visit the Lady Chapel and light a candle for Thomas would be a life changing experience. A Carmelite friar we encountered on the road, confirmed your legendary hospitality. Thus, we sit before you, tired, hungry and much vexed."

Beyssac smiled, his face radiating absolute sincerity. At that moment, an ominous, groaning sound filled the hospital. It rolled around the walls, bouncing off the ceiling, rumbling in each corner and piercing every eardrum. Michael Makejoy was struggling, breathing his last but determined to be noticed.

"Maybe, he didn't like the vegetable stew," said Antoine, nodding in Michael's direction.

"No," said Richard. "Not in this case. Most of our guests are only short stay. They leave us for a new life, far away from here. A place where there is no sin. The Celestial City."

"You mean Gloucester," declared Antoine.

Eyes closed, hands clasped, oblivious to Antoine's comment, Richard whispered a prayer for Michael's soul.

"O Lord. Grant eternal rest upon him and let your perpetual light shine within him. May he rest in peace. Amen."

So be it. Michael Makejoy was dead. A man whose cheerful nature had disintegrated into a cheerless existence. Now, God was the only one laughing at his jokes.

Richard unclasped his hands. His knuckles remained white.

"You say you are much vexed? What is your own complaint?"

Beyssac did not hesitate.

"The food in England is horrible. The population is composed of lawless, illiterate peasants. It rains perpetually. Every highway is a river of viscous mud. But my biggest concern is I may have contracted a parasitical infection. The streets of Canterbury were crowded with foul-smelling pilgrims. The Cathedral itself was standing room only. I took my place amidst the unclean multitude. Look at my itchy skin and these sores. There are creeping eruptions right up my arms."

Beyssac thought he had worms. No evacuation or laxative had helped. Perhaps Richard knew a possible cure.

Richard doubted Beyssac's diagnosis but agreed to examine him. As the cardinal undressed, Richard was shocked by Beyssac's spindly arms and rickety legs. His skin was very red. Small blisters ran the length of his forearms. Bloody scratches crisscrossed the back of his calves. Scarlet swellings reached from his knees up to his groin. Richard recognised the signs. Beyssac might give his complaint a fancy name. But those marks were simply pressure sores. Beyssac had spent too many hours sitting down. Indolence was his real affliction.

"I have a brew which I am confident will heal your sores," said Richard. "Flax seed oil, fired in goat's fat. A preparation devised by St Hildergard. I value any guidance from the esteemed Sibyl of the Rhine."

Beyssac nodded. Visionary and polymath, Hildegard had inspired Beyssac all his life. He wished he could again experience the exhilaration of exploring her ideas and sharing her perceptions.

As Beyssac contemplated the vagaries of his faith, a feverish calm descended. Shouts turned to whispers. Screams faded into sighs. The sick and the dying occupied every bed and every corner of the hospital. The quiet of dusk was broken only by the murmurings of a few fretful patients. Fear of the Pestilence, subdued even the boldest spirit.

While Antoine's mood was downcast, his stomach saw fit to complain. Gurgling, grumbling and growling, Antoine's empty belly rumbled like a wagon, jolting along a cobbled street. Beyssac's reverie was broken. Antoine was famished.

"Geoffrey will be here with your food very soon," said Richard.

"This night may be a last supper for many of our clients. Geoffrey considers it his holy duty to give them a respectful send-off."

"Such devoted service!" Beyssac enthused.

"We are all sincere Christians here. We are obliged to follow the example of Jesus. We have a duty to ensure the comfort and security of all who pass through our doors. Love your neighbour as yourself. No other commandment is greater than this. Only a fool, or one concerned to perform the Devil's work, would contradict Jesus."

Racked by hunger, Antoine stood up. Richard's pious banter was not putting food in his belly.

"I'll help in the kitchen," said Antoine. Desperate to eat, Antoine would hurry things along and ensure the preparation of a meal fit for a cardinal. Guided by his nose, Antoine entered the dining hall and made for the kitchen at the far end. A familiar smell of boiled pork intrigued his nostrils.

In the stable, Jerome was attending to the horses. The comforting smell of hay, leather and animal sweat, calmed his nerves. It was a privilege to work with these beautiful animals. They were hackneys, not proud war horses, but tough and strong, easily adept at coach work.

Hippocrates was his favourite. Thirteen hands and blessed with a striking champagne coat, she could pull a load of five hundred pounds yet show no fatigue. She was an animal with more intelligence and determination than most people.

Jerome cleared his throat. Stroking Hippocrates' leg and squeezing her tendon, he began to sing. A lullaby. A gentle lullaby from his childhood. A comforting song to reassure the horses.

Hippocrates relaxed, completely under his spell. For Jerome, human relationships had always been perilous. Whereas horses were uncomplicated, trustworthy and loyal. There was no doubt about it. Jerome had more respect for horses than humans.

Heads down and exhausted, the other horses slept. A soft, pale light from the tallow candle flickered intermittently, throwing shadows up against the stable wall. Jerome used the hoof pick rigorously but gently — Hippocrates was happy, whimpering like a baby. Her nose thrust forward. Her eyes, tolerant and trusting. She watched Jerome expertly remove stones and debris from inside a hoof. An unspoken, emotional bond. Leaning down, Hippocrates stuck out her tongue and licked Jerome's bald head. Mewling in a subdued tone, Hippocrates showed her appreciation.

Jerome stopped. He put down his tools. Listening hard, he heard the distant sound of a baby crying. The blubbering of an infant in distress. Jerome raised the candle above his head. The feeble light reached into a corner of the stable. Twitching horses fast asleep, oblivious to the world. The sobbing grew louder. Jerome stepped forward. He pushed aside a bale of hay. There he saw the body of a woman half-buried in the hay, her arms outstretched, beseeching help. A naked baby lay just beyond her reach. She was dead. Another victim of the Great Dying.

Jerome picked up the baby boy, cradling him in his arms. The words of Saint Peter resounded through his head. "I have called you out of this darkness and into His marvellous light."

A baby born in a stable. An event central to the faith of millions. This night Jerome had expected a decent meal, a warm bed and a sound sleep. Instead, he faced only deep frustration. He had never stayed in a hostelry like this one. What was he to do with a corpse and a newborn baby? He pondered, his predicament, polishing his head with the flat of his free hand. Surely, Antoine would know what to do. He was wise to the world. Yes, consulting Antoine would be the most prudent course of action.

Encouraged by his musing, Jerome tucked the baby under his arm and slipped out of the stable. The kitchen was just across the courtyard. As long as the horses were happy, fed and rested. That was the most important thing.

Antoine nodded. He considered the dining hall a magnificent building. An oak wainscot enclosed the entire room. Above this, painted in vibrant colours, were scenes from the life of Jesus: the Annunciation; the Nativity; the Temptation and the Crucifixion. The central panel featured Jesus sitting on a rainbow, his feet resting on the Earth. The Sun, Moon and Stars, glorious but deferential. A powerful spiritual message, reinforced in dazzling red, ochre and azurite blue.

But the agony within the dining hall resembled a scene straight from Hell, as those without hope, the dead and the dying, sought relief from the Pestilence — God's merciless punishment.

Dozens of men, women and children, all plague victims, occupied makeshift beds or lay sprawled on the floor. Above them, the benign face of Saint Sebastian stared down from a marble statue — apparently unmoved by the anguished prayers of those kneeling at his feet.

A bedridden teenage girl, racked by violent convulsions, sobbed as a stream of dark blood, spurted from her mouth, soaking her blanket. Preoccupied with their own survival, the other patients turned their backs. Gradually her breathing became intermittent and ceased. The plague pit was choked with corpses. The girl's body would be burned.

Antoine realised his mistake. It was not the sweet smell of boiled pork filling the air. But the distinctive smell of death. This dining hall was a charnel house. He watched as husbands and wives embraced, finding redemption in each other's arms. He listened to whispered prayers, begging for God's mercy. A little boy, hands together, wept over his mother's corpse, his tears splashing on her bodice. Antoine had arrived in Wycombe looking for hospitality. But he had discovered a hospital ravaged by Death.

In contrast, Beyssac's laughter echoed around the entrance hall. He relished debating with Richard. In England, it was rare to find a man of piety and useful learning. Antoine and Jerome were good fellows but intellectually bereft. If Richard had concocted a charade to test their faith, so be it. Clever argument was preferable to drunken disputation.

"Yes," said Beyssac jovially. "I know I am 'afflicted'. I have been 'afflicted' these forty years." Having worms was distasteful but something Beyssac accepted.

Richard looked down at the floor, shaking his head. Beyssac was deranged. Laughter, indicating a disorder of the brain, was a well-known symptom of indolence. Richard's face was serene. His concern, genuine.

"Have you attempted any medication or treatment?"

Beyssac nodded. "Hard prayer. I regularly ask Saint Jude for mercy. Bleeding has no effect. The bad moods keep returning. Purgatives? I once gained some temporary relief from an enema of rabbit bile. But I found thrusting a metal tube up my fundament too painful. I have made pilgrimage to Santiago de Compostela and Rome itself. But my affliction remains. Like Cain, I am cursed to live without hope, scavenging but never reaping."

Richard's soothing smile concealed his fear. Beyssac had exhausted all possible cures. But with the eternal optimism founded in potent faith, Richard wanted to offer Beyssac hope.

"Have you tried rubbing your afflicted parts with fried onions? I believe some patients have found relief using this method."

"I have tried," Beyssac confirmed. "Once. But never again. I found it engenders lustful thoughts."

Richard blushed. He could not understand the link between sexual arousal and fried onions. He speculated it was a practice, peculiar to the French.

Taking a moment to think straight, Richard stretched the rosary beads between his fingers. His next question required some delicacy.

"Your companions, Jerome and Antoine. Are they also afflicted?"

Beyssac erupted. "Yes, they are both seriously afflicted and their faith is in peril! Antoine carries a malignant disease which corrupts his soul. Once identified, it must be eradicated. Antoine has a penchant for atheism!"

Richard crossed himself. His faith consumed him. It was all he had. He must speak out.

"The fool has said in his heart. There is no God. They are corrupt. They have done abominable works."

"Amen," said Beyssac earnestly. "And as for Jerome. He is an excellent groom. His understanding of horses is unsurpassed. But he is vexed by melancholy. An excess of black bile has depressed his spirit. He has been known to question his faith."

Richard understood Jerome's dilemma. In a world full of evil, how can we stay good? Richard found comfort in the letters of Saint Paul. Christians would be saved. But as for atheists.

"They are dark in their understanding and separate from God."

"Amen," said Beyssac nodding in agreement. A growling sound emerged from his empty belly. Hunger gnawed his insides. Now he must have had passed Richard's examination of his faith. It was time to be pampered.

Beyssac stood up. "Richard, you are clearly a man of God. I welcome your rigorous scrutiny of my Christian faith. I commend your careful and considerate actions. I approve your wish to restrict hospitality to those who deserve it. But..."

A commotion. Raised voices. The sound of running feet as Antoine raced down the corridor, followed by Jerome carrying a bundle under his arm.

"Monsieur! Monsieur! We must leave immediately!" Antoine was panting, struggling to breathe.

"No!" said Beyssac, angrily. "I have waited long enough."

"We are duped," Jerome said timidly. "We have made a terrible mistake. I have found…"

"Silence," said Beyssac, placing a finger to his lips. He turned to Richard. "I look forward to: a delicious meal prepared by your chef, a ventilated room with a private toilet and — an undisturbed night's sleep. As esteemed proprietor of the Red Lion Inn, I expect you to meet my needs. Why do you look bewildered? Am I being unreasonable?"

Richard closed his eyes. Beyssac was unhinged.

"This is Saint Giles Plague House. Our 'guests' are victims of the Pestilence. When you arrived, I assumed you and your companions were afflicted. You expected to enjoy lavish hospitality, in an overcrowded, pestilence-ridden infirmary. Your arrogant attitude defies belief."

Beyssac's eyes rolled in his head. He felt giddy and overheated, struggling to accept his mistake. It was a plague hospital, filled with infected and dying people. It was not the Red Lion Inn. Best to leave now, while they could, rather than be carried out later in coffins.

Within ten minutes, their coach was rumbling along the waterlogged road to Tetsworth. In Saint Giles Hospital Richard lit three wax candles. The bright light illumined a small wooden statue of Saint Roch. As a Christian, Richard bore no grudges.

Chapter Ten

A baby! Beyssac poured scorn on Jerome's rescue act. It was not their responsibility to look after a child. A baby was a burden, a puling hindrance. Their orders were to visit Hereford and investigate Bishop Trilleck. It was not a recruiting drive for a children's crusade.

The heavy rain forced Antoine and Beyssac to shelter under the canopy, while Jerome, shaking his head and uttering profanities, steered the toiling horses along the saturated road. This was a dangerous area, notorious for cut-throats. In France, it was thought English civilisation began at Oxford. The rest of England was a barbarous wasteland.

Antoine carefully wrapped a blanket around the baby's body. Such a handsome little boy. A leather water bottle filled with cow's milk had done the job. The regular motion of the coach and a full belly meant an untroubled sleep.

Beyssac rested on a leather-bound Bible. A pottage of peas, herbs and bacon had satisfied his hunger. Emotionally drained, he quickly fell asleep. Their destination, Thame Abbey, home of the White Monks, lay twenty miles to the north. Beyssac was sure they would receive a respectful welcome. The monks were virtuous, hardworking and especially helpful to pilgrims. In addition, as Antoine pointed out, they brewed the most sublime beer in England.

A deep rut jolted the coach. Jerome cursed. The baby muttered, raised a hand, yawned and twisting into a more comfortable position, returned to sleep. A scrap of humanity at the beginning of life. No worries. No doubts. No fear of hell or burden of guilt. Rather the warm certainty of safety in Antoine's arms — like Antoine's own twin girls — before the Pestilence carried them off. Antoine pulled the baby closer, gently stroking his head.

Beyssac woke. He sat up, struggling to focus his eyes. A pietà? The soft candlelight revealed the Virgin Mary cradling the body of Jesus. An English miracle? Beyssac rubbed his eyes with his thumbs. Filled with spiritual excitement, bursting with religious exultation, heart pounding, ready to prostrate himself before this blissful vision, Beyssac opened his eyes.

"This baby has evacuated his bowels!" declared Antoine.

Beyssac's spiritual euphoria was shattered. Mary and Jesus were not present. Only a delusion born of fatigue. One would have to be moonstruck to confuse Antoine with Mary, Mother of God. Beyssac sighed.

"I hope for salvation. You offer me defecation. I yearn for sacrament. You present me excrement. That child must go. We have been instructed by His Holiness to investigate the Church in Hereford. That is our sacred task. The child is a burden and a hindrance. Besides, you are a cook not a wet nurse."

Antoine nodded. "But this is no ordinary child. Born in a stable in adverse circumstances. Doesn't that remind you of anyone?"

"You cannot equate the birth of Jesus Christ in Bethlehem with the birth of a baby in Wycombe. Your comparison is fanciful and arguably blasphemous."

Beyssac scowled. This upstart cook needed to be put in his place.

Antoine licked his fingers, smoothing down the baby's hair. He spoke slowly.

"This child has survived Pestilence, a terrible danger which has threatened to destroy us all. This is no ordinary baby. It is part of God's plan we found him. We should rejoice in this baby, not banish him. You said yourself. All that lives is Holy."

As the coach rattled along the road, Jerome cursed the horses pushing them hard. He admired their beauty, their strength and their natural power. But Thame Abbey was still far off. Any dawdling along the road might attract robbers. The horses dripped sweat. Confounded beasts! Could they not gallop faster?

Beyssac's speed of thought was swifter than any horse. He considered Antoine was right. This child's presence was not a coincidence. There must be a sacred purpose. As God created the world and all things, it follows that everything must possess a divine spark. All that lives is Holy. This is a special child. He will be named Sebastian, in honour of Saint Sebastian and stay with us until we get to Hereford. That is God's decree.

"Well?" said Antoine tentatively. Beyssac was officious, a man on a mission. All his decisions were based on reason, not emotion. Antoine was not optimistic.

Beyssac smiled, making the sign of the cross as he spoke.

"I have given the child a name. Sebastian is a good name and appropriate to our predicament. I agree he can stay until we reach Hereford and find a suitable mother. My decision has taken much deliberation but I know I am right."

Antoine jumped up, holding Sebastian above his head like a piece of the True Cross. A miracle had taken place.

"Stop this coach. Stop this coach now! An event not explicable by natural or scientific laws has occurred. I see a cardinal who is spiritually happy and a baby who desperately needs a clean nappy. We are truly blessed."

Jerome slowed the horses, guiding them to a slithering stop in the mud. What was all the shouting about?

Chapter Eleven

Brilliant rays of morning sunlight pierced the mist. Jerome slowed the horses shielding his eyes from the glare. To his right, up on a hill, a line of oxen struggled to pull a plough through the soil. The driver shouted, brandishing his whip. But to no avail. The ploughman shook both his fists and collapsed into a heap. A parliament of rooks descended looking for food. The perpetual struggle for survival.

Gradually, through the fading haze, Thame Abbey came into view. A magnificent, awe-inspiring, House of God. The most respected Cistercian foundation in England. The abbott, John Esingdon, revered in every part of Christendom for his devotion. A good shepherd, watchful of his flock.

Jerome stopped the horses outside the abbey hospital. It was quiet. There seemed to be nobody around. The Cistercian brothers were famous for their piety. That would explain the tranquil atmosphere. Everyone, the lay brothers and the choir monks, preoccupied doing God's work. The Bible says 'Through laziness, the rafters sag; because of idle hands, the house leaks'. The brothers were diligent workers not hedonists. Jerome noticed a freshly dug mound of earth, opposite the fish pond. Discarded spades and pickaxes lay to one side.

Beyssac and Antoine climbed out of the coach. Sebastian, wrapped in Beyssac's red silk cape, slept. Beyssac smoothed down his cassock, tilting his green hat slightly forward. He wanted to make an impression.

Beyssac pointed. "This magnificent building is a tribute to God's inspiration. Expert craftsmen, imbued with the spirit of their Creator, have constructed a homage to the Lord and a celebration of our faith. In addition, Abbott Esington is a living saint."

Jerome rubbed his head. "It will be a privilege to meet him. I hope he is in residence."

Beyssac nodded. "As the presbytery is the most holy part of the abbey, what better place to find the holiest man in England. Let's try there first."

"Is that near the brew house?" asked Antoine. "The most sublime beer in England is brewed here. Only a brute would spurn an opportunity to taste it."

Beyssac frowned. "Everything has its time. There is a time for strong beer. And there is a time for strong faith. Now is the time for strong faith. Devotion is more potent than drink. We need to find the presbytery."

For a bustling community which attracted countless pilgrims, Thame Abbey seemed uncannily quiet. An insidious silence prevailed. Jerome, Antoine and Beyssac strained to hear a human voice or an animal cry. There was nothing. Not even the chirp of a sparrow or the chatter of a magpie. The only sound was their footsteps crunching on the gravel path leading to the chapter house.

Antoine placed an ear against the studded chapter house door. He shook his head. Turning the handle Jerome pushed it open. They did not see a meeting of brothers debating Christian beliefs nor witness the abbot holding chapter. The hall was deserted. A high-ceilinged, octagonal room, with sculptured angels looking down. These were complemented by brilliant stained-glass windows, celebrating God the Creator, surrounded by the starry heavens and His unique achievement — the Earth. A room filled with the spirit of God. But empty of human beings. Beyssac remained philosophical.

"The situation is perfectly clear. I should have grasped it before now. Today is the feast day of St Raymond, the patron saint of silence. I have many times placed padlocks on his altar to stop gossip and hurtful lies. I am sure we will find the abbot and his flock engaged in silent prayer in the presbytery. I am not worried by the silence. I am exultant. It confirms we are in the presence of ardent devotion."

Antoine looked up at the stained glass. He was not convinced by Beyssac's explanation. In one section, an image depicted the Fall of Mankind. It showed a serpent deceiving Eve. In the next frame, a smiling Adam accepted the forbidden fruit. To Antoine's mind, circumstances were usually more complicated than they seemed.

Antoine's cynicism, always just below the surface, could not be restrained.

"You speculate Abbot Esingdon and the monks of Thame Abbey are in a state of blessed quietude, observing the feast day of St Raymond. But where are the farm workers and the servants? Where is the noise of their conversation? Where are the animals? The pigs, the sheep and the chickens? I've never heard of animals taking a vow of silence! And the birds of the air. Where are they? Is this place a Christian house or a charnel house?"

Jerome nodded. "It's not right." He sensed through his empathy with animals, something extraordinary had happened. He discerned an evil atmosphere. His instinct was to hurry away.

Beyssac closed his eyes. He was angry. But he acknowledged Jerome's fear and Antoine's logic. He was convinced their worries would vanish, once they saw the brothers at prayer in the presbytery. Seeing would be believing. He smiled, gesturing to them with both hands.

"Follow me. And I will show you wondrous things."

Meticulous as ever, Beyssac adjusted his hat and straightened his cassock. With a spring in his step, he marched off, following the path through the physic garden, leading towards the south transept. Antoine and Jerome trailed behind.

The physic garden reflected the ordered lives of the monks. Hedged and precise, divided into quarters, super abundant with medicinal plants.

Antoine recognised rhubarb. A cure for constipation. There was liquorice. Strong smelling and easy to cultivate, a tonic for the blood. Next, white iris, good for teeth but a sad reminder of home. The fleur-de-lis the symbol of the Capet kings.

But was it an illusion? There was clearly a problem. Antoine knelt down to investigate. Wrinkled leaves fell apart between his fingers. Plant stems snapped at the slightest touch. Every plant was withered or dying. The soil was hard and dry as a bone. The plants had not been watered for many days or even weeks. Indolence was out of the question. Relentless hard work was the defining feature of Cistercian life. This beautiful abbey was hiding a grotesque secret. Hitching up their cassocks, Antoine and Jerome raced to catch Beyssac.

Above the door of the south transept, seven carved heads guarded the entrance. Only virtuous souls had the right to enter this building. Finding the door wide open, Antoine rushed in without a blink of conscience. As a young man, he had worked his way through all the deadly sins. Jerome hesitated, dithering outside the door, until Antoine grabbed him, dragging him inside. Two massive rose windows dominated the transept. As the sunlight flooded in, they were submerged in a tempestuous yellow and red sea. Beyssac sat on a chair, delving into a wooden chest, turning over the contents — books, vestments and ceremonial dishes. It was eerily quiet.

They found themselves next to the presbytery, the holiest part of the abbey, the building in which the most sacred mysteries took place. Beyssac was certain this hallowed location would confirm the immaculate faith of the Cistercian brothers and bear witness to their respect for St Raymond. With a beaming smile, Beyssac turned the handle of the presbytery door.

Straight away, they were engulfed by a cloud of buzzing, swooping, inquisitive flies. An incredible noise. A profane sound in a sacred place. But after much waving and flailing of arms, during which Jerome had to extricate flies from his nose and mouth, the noxious cloud twisted and veered away down the transept, out of the door and into the garden. The profound silence returned.

The smell was awful. The pungent, sweet fragrance of death. A vile perfume. But the scene which met their disbelieving eyes came straight from the bowels of Hell.

Making the sign of the cross, they knelt down. Beyssac mumbled a desperate prayer. In front of them, stretching up to the crucifix on the rood screen, stood a macabre monument — a pyramid, entirely composed of the corpses of hundreds of Cistercian monks — their white robes smeared with blood and suppuration. Gaunt faces, weeping boils and black, blotchy skin, confirmed the Pestilence had attacked Thame Abbey. Christian lives devoted to work, prayer and denial, callously extinguished.

A pyramid of the deceased. Purple-faced old men, spreadeagled, crushed, entangled, pressed down on the faces of novices, whose innocent bulging eyes yearned to question God. At the top, was Abbot

Esingdon, desperate for salvation, his right hand clutching the feet of Jesus hanging on a shimmering cross.

Eyes shut, Beyssac prayed hard. Antoine and Jerome, heads shaking in disbelief, circled around the heap of rigid bodies. Jerome pinched his nose to filter the smell. Antoine could not hold back.

"I refuse to believe this horror is part of God's plan. They were good people. They did not deserve to die!"

Jerome instinctively rubbed his head. "The Pestilence is God's punishment upon a wicked world. Evil must be punished."

"Yes!" said Antoine emphatically. "That is the point. These were not evil men. Innocent, God-fearing Christians are suffering as much as the wicked. It makes no sense."

Antoine pointed to the body of a novice, laying face up on the tiled floor. A shaft of sunlight pierced the Catherine window, accentuating his twisted face. Just a boy. His protruding tongue was black. Splashes of blood smeared his white cassock. Purple boils covered his neck, face and even his hands. A halo of sunlight shimmered around his head, bathing him in a golden glow. He seemed a demonic angel, expelled from Heaven.

Antoine erupted, struggling to contain his rage. "How has the world profited by this boy's death? What advantage is it that he should suffer? Has there been an increase in virtue and a reduction in vice? No. I see pointless, unending misery. Another wasted life. Another nameless corpse for the plague pit. Has God forgotten us?"

"No!" shouted Beyssac. "The opposite is true. We have forgotten God!"

Lifting the hem of his cassock, Beyssac scurried around the pyramid of corpses, stopping directly in front of Antoine's face. A meeting of opposites. Beyssac narrowed his eyes. He was vexed Antoine had the impudence to question God. Beyssac did not need a pulpit to deliver a sermon.

"This pestilence is a consequence of human sin. God created a perfect world which Man by his wicked behaviour, has corrupted. Do not blame God for your failings."

Antoine scowled, unconvinced. "Baby Sebastian is asleep in our coach. He is innocent yet the Pestilence could kill him in an instant. A baby does not deserve to die."

Beyssac exhaled. He found it insulting he must explain things to an untutored mind.

"Yes, there is evil in the world. But there is more virtue. Remember that. This pestilence is a punishment from God. It is not the end of the world. It is not the Apocalypse."

"But why do innocent people suffer?"

"Through suffering we grow spiritually. God does not want us to remain as children, inhabiting a trivial, undemanding, world. That would lead to childish imbecility, not reverent maturity."

Antoine frowned. He considered Beyssac's words an apology for God's actions, not an explanation of them.

"It would be preposterous tell a man whose family had been killed by the Pestilence, don't worry, you will soon find joyful consolation in your spiritual growth. That is a cruel deception."

Unflinching, Beyssac looked straight into Antoine's eyes. Logic could be a double-edged sword.

"Do you consider anyone in this world, king or pauper, exempt from the wrath of God?"

"That's not possible. No one can claim to be exempt from God's wrath."

"Then you have quashed your own doubts. God created this world. We are obliged to accept the pleasure along with the pain. Triumphs or tragedies, they are part of His world. It is not proper or rational to question God. Greater scholars than us have concluded: God is inscrutable."

Beyssac raised his hat, affirming his theosophical victory. The debate was over. Antoine retreated into the bolt-hole of his common sense. Jerome, overtly righteous but inwardly fearful, rubbed his head. He needed to talk.

"This is the most dreadful thing I've ever seen. It's an absolute affront to God in His own house. What happened to these poor souls?"

"The Pestilence," said Antoine resignedly. "That mound of earth near the fish pond is a burial pit. I should have realised."

Beyssac nodded. He had worked out the sequence of events which engulfed the monks.

"An act of unparalleled self-sacrifice took place in this presbytery. Overwhelmed by pestilence but determined not to spread it beyond the abbey walls, the monks decided to remain here and confront the affliction."

Jerome contemplated the tangle of bodies. Squashed human beings, sprawled out, stacked like carcasses in a magnificent abattoir. He did not understand.

"Why are these brave men piled up in such a bizarre way?"

Beyssac explained. "The bodies of the dead monks became stepping stones for the living. Each dying man, desperate to embrace the crucifix, climbed over the bodies of their brothers, trampling them. Until they themselves died and became part of this hellish construction. How appropriate Abbot Esingdon should be at the top. I regard his determination to reach the pinnacle of this hideous pyramid, as a triumph over Death. One day, he will be made a saint."

Beyssac pulled up a stool and sat down. Emotionally drained, he needed time to assess their situation. Absorbed in thought, he did not notice Antoine and Jerome leave by a side door.

The abbey, once a consummate model of Christian life, was now an imposing monument to a squalid death. To stay in this cursed place, amidst a multitude of diseased corpses, would be tantamount to suicide. They must leave immediately. Thame Abbey was a colossal coffin.

Brow furrowed, Antoine considered the matter deeply. He pondered all the possibilities and analysed all the different aspects. He evaluated every viewpoint and perused every potential problem. It was a truth beyond dispute. Dead men don't drink beer.

Motivated by thirst, Antoine's epicurean intuition, complemented by the sweet aroma of toasted malt, led him straight to the brewhouse.

Antoine and Jerome stopped outside. Closing his eyes, Antoine bowed his head. Hands together, he whispered a prayer. What alcoholic delights awaited them? Perhaps they might discover a beverage beyond belief or a brew straight from Heaven. Cistercian beer was celebrated throughout Christendom.

Antoine's throat was parchment dry. Taking a dignified breath, he raised his voice.

"Among men, it is called ale. But amongst gods, it is called beer."

Pushing open the brewhouse door, he grabbed Jerome, hauling him inside. They stared in wonderment. Floor to ceiling, barrels, rundlets, firkins and hogsheads. Each one, brim-full with sweet-smelling malt beer.

Jerome scooped the frothy brew with a ladle. He sniffed its creamy aroma. He sipped a mouthful, swirling it around his tongue, trickling it down his throat, delighting his shrivelled taste buds.

"I swear by St Arnulf and St Gambrinus, this beer is a liquid miracle. It was created not by Cistercians but by Seraphim."

Proud of this insight, Jerome scooped up more beer, gulping it straight down. He was pleased. So, while Jerome enjoyed his second mouthful, Antoine finished his second pail. It was a wonderful testament to the expertise of the monks.

Raising his pail, Antoine sniffed the contents. He took a mouthful, running it round his mouth for a few moments before spitting it out. Antoine would never mock the afflicted. But he would mock the affected.

"My palate informs me… This is a full-bodied, idiosyncratic beer, dominated by a ginger nose yet subdued by subtle notes of cinnamon and Banda Island nutmeg… In other words — It's bloody amazing!"

Antoine sank to his knees. His chuckle turned into a howl, which rapidly became a roar. Soon, both Antoine and Jerome were rolling on the floor, sniggering uncontrollably. Experience confirmed in them an unspoken belief. Good beer is a certain remedy for bad trouble. A wise conclusion to which only a select few adhere. But not Beyssac.

"I knew I would find you in the brewhouse!"

Beyssac stood in the doorway, indignantly shaking his head. Did these miscreants have no respect for the dead brothers?

Antoine got up. The monks surrendered their lives for a virtuous cause. Jerome and I salute their bravery. We recognise their sacrifice. In tribute to them, we agreed to run this beer across our palates. Would you care to participate in this homage to the dead monks and their brewing skills?"

"No thank you," said Beyssac dismissively. "I don't drink beer. It engenders lust."

Jerome pulled himself up, taking a deep breath to clear his head. Distracted by the brewhouse, they had forgotten baby Sebastian. Jerome was worried Sebastian's life could be extinguished by the Pestilence at any moment. The monks were healthy adults yet they succumbed. Sebastian was not baptised. If he died, he would go to Limbo, twixt Heaven and Hell, an abode of unbaptised, howling infants. A destiny too awful to contemplate.

"We should leave this place," said Jerome. "Thame Abbey is the most woeful site on Earth. But we cannot leave until Sebastian has been brought to God. He must be baptized to secure his soul. It would be sinful not to do it."

Beyssac nodded. "I agree. Besides, I resent travelling in the company of a heathen baby. Fetch the child and bring him to the baptistery. I will perform the sacrament. It will be an honour for Sebastian to be baptised by a cardinal."

"I'll go with Jerome," said Antoine. "We need a hogshead of beer. I hear the road to Oxford is particularly dusty. We'll meet you at the font."

Scenes from the life of John the Baptist decorated the walls of the baptistery. Vivid images of John preaching, John baptising Jesus and John's decapitation. Beyssac was pleased. Baptism was the sacrament especially close to his heart.

As a baby he had been baptised at Saint Jean in Poitiers — the oldest Christian building in France. But the Thame Abbey font, decorated with two large hands clutching a pregnant belly, was bone dry. Without holy water, there could be no baptism. Sebastian would remain burdened by Adam's original sin. Only a Christian baptism could set him free. A supply of holy water, blessed by a member of the clergy, was essential for spiritual cleansing and protection against evil.

While Sebastian lay asleep in the font, Antoine took furtive sips of beer from a stoup under its belly. Jerome rubbed his head, racking his brains, to find a way out of their dilemma. Beyssac, eyes closed and resting on his knees, prayed for divine guidance.

"There can be no baptism unless we have water blessed by God," said Beyssac. "We are not pagans."

The situation appeared hopeless. Sebastian remained cut off from Christ, unable to be received within the bosom of the Church. He would sit forever on the edge of Hell, never able to enter Heaven.

Antoine was thinking hard. Inspired by his admiration for Thame Abbey beer, he conceived an ingenious stratagem. First, he must convince Beyssac.

"My lord. Our situation puts me in mind of the wedding in Cana. The first miracle of Jesus was to turn water into wine."

Beyssac stood up. Religious debate stimulated him. It was his lifeblood.

"Yes, it confirms Jesus as Creator. Only He has power to transform and create."

"Therefore, alcohol is not inherently sinful?"

"No. But drunkenness is!" said Beyssac emphatically.

"So, beer is actually a gift from God?"

"Yes. God has provided all things in Heaven and Earth. Even beer is part of his divine plan."

Antoine put his hands together. His face was solemn. This was a momentous occasion — perhaps an epiphany. He emanated wonder.

"Therefore, it follows, a most excellent beer, lovingly created at Thame Abbey by devoted servants of the Lord, must by definition, be morally and spiritually, sublime. We have discovered the ultimate libation — hallowed, sacred, divinely inspired. Without doubt, this is Holy Beer."

Joyous, Jerome punched the air.

"You are right! By the bones of St Arnulf. You are right. This is a heavenly brew. We can proceed with the baptism!"

"No!" said Beyssac dismissively. "We cannot proceed. Your proposition is blasphemous. Besides, we need salt blessed by a cleric for the baptism to be acceptable to God."

"There are blocks of salt in the brewhouse," said Antoine. "The brothers used salt to flavour the beer. This beer does meet the required criteria. It is marvellous in God's eyes."

Beyssac smiled. Gently, almost father-like, he cradled Sebastian. Antoine held up a stoup of frothy beer. Beyssac dipped a finger, tracing a cross on Sebastian's forehead.

"I baptise you, Sebastian, in the name of the Father. And of the Son. And of the Holy Spirit."

Sebastian gurgled, blowing a bubble of saliva into the air. No tears. No tantrums. Only innocent acceptance.

"This baby is now free of original sin. An errant lamb has joined God's righteous flock."

"Time to wet the baby's head," Antoine declared.

Chapter Twelve

As Jerome steered the horses through the East Gate and down the high street, the smell of death prevailed. The Pestilence, God's punishment for the evils of mankind, had taken control.

Merton, Exeter, Oriel and Queen's colleges were closed. The students had fled. The high street, normally bustling with scholars searching for academic materials, was deserted. Most businesses were boarded up. The high street was dead.

Even the shops at the Carfax crossroads appeared moribund: pallid shanks of lamb hung under the butcher's canopy; threadbare cloth lay in piles on a draper's stall; the vintner, a white-bearded Methuselah, sat on a wine barrel, attempting a smile; stinking trout, salmon, roach and eels, heaped up on the fishmonger's cart, stared stupidly at passers-by; a pot-bellied spice merchant doffed his cap whilst loudly extolling the delights of his fare. Any fool could see his mustard was mouldy, the fennel was fetid, his pepper putrid and the saffron clearly spoiled.

Corn merchants, cordwainers, mercers and alchemist shops competed to attract the few brave customers who dared to venture on to the streets. It was clear, Oxford was a desolate and ultimately doomed city.

Without warning, a boisterous gang of men spilled out of the Bag O' Nails tavern. Their loud voices and discordant laughter, indicating an afternoon of heavy drinking. Four young men — students, judging by their white vestments — undaunted by the Pestilence, refusing to relinquish their pleasure despite the horror poisoning the city. Jerome smiled begrudgingly. They were either lionhearts or idiots.

Hippocrates, the lead horse, began to slow, treading cautiously through the mud. He curled his upper lip, his ears twitched back and forth, straining to hear. He swished his tail. His anxiety felt by the other horses. Despite Jerome's encouragement, the horses dragged their hooves, reluctant to push on. Hippocrates was in control and Jerome had to accept it.

A black shape. A lurching, nimble figure. Bellowing profanities, one of the students jumped in front of the horses, blocking their progress. The coach stopped dead. Jerome grasped the initiative.

"Good friends. We are pilgrims on a mission to Hereford. We delight in keeping company with law-abiding Englishmen. But our time is precious. We adhere to Paul's advice to the Ephesians. 'Use time well, for the days are evil'."

The tallest student stepped forward, stroking each horse until he drew level with the box seat. Beer stained the front of his white shirt. His blue eyes examined Jerome's face.

"I respect your knowledge of the Scriptures. But I do not understand your desire to visit Hereford."

Jerome detected hostility. He must be discreet.

"We are cheerful at the prospect of praying at St Thomas' tomb. He was a great friend to the poor."

The student's face twisted into a scowl.

"It's a hard fact, my name is Tom Latimer. And it's a hard truth St Thomas was a friend of the Pope and the Catholic Church... But not the poor. The Catholic Church is a cabal of parasites."

Jerome grimaced. They were Lollards, extremists opposed to the Catholic Church. He knew of their excesses. They assaulted monks. They smashed stained-glass windows. They demanded the Church be dissolved and its riches given to the poor. They believed in an invisible Church of the elect, rather than the visible Catholic Church. Arrogant scoundrels. A thoroughly bad lot.

"Your opinion is pernicious and quite wrong," Jerome countered, letting the reins slip through his fingers. "You hold an opinion, which true Christians consider heretical."

The students moved closer, forming a semi-circle around Jerome's box seat. Angry, vindictive faces. Young men, intoxicated by beer and beguiling beliefs. Tom Latimer, Jack Bradby, William Clanvowe and John Ball. In tranquil times, four scholars eager for academic success. In troubled times, four dangerous fanatics.

Jack extended both index fingers, pointing upwards, looking to Heaven. His cherubic face suggested a choirboy, not a religious diehard. He gushed solemnity.

"Only God can decide who is a true Christian. The Pope is Antichrist. He insists the faithful are not saved unless he gives permission. That is against God."

Beyssac seethed. He had heard enough.

"No, young man. You are totally wrong!" Beyssac's voice resonated along the high street. Emerging from the canopy, his face red as a cardinal's hat. Such heresy must be confronted. It must be excised from corrupt minds.

"Pope Innocent is the Vicar of Christ — God's representative on Earth. He is the Holy Father caring for his children. We should…"

"Stop blaspheming!" Tom shouted. "There is no justification for the papacy in the Holy Scriptures. You are rejecting the supremacy of Christ and denying the Holy Spirit."

Tom's great height and copper-coloured hair, reminded Jerome of a candle snuffer. But he was a fanatic, determined to extinguish the light of God in those who opposed him.

"Such apostasy!" shouted Beyssac. The core of his faith was under attack. He must strike back.

"You are heretics. You betray the true Church. No wonder God has sent a pestiferous wind to punish the English! You are a base nation. A multitude of brutes!"

William clambered up a wheel, placing his fist under Beyssac's chin.

Bull necked and ruddy faced. His faith was straightforward. Theological debate was for priests. The truth was the rich exploited the poor. An evil state of affairs. William enunciated each word, his rage barely in check.

"The Pestilence is a judgement on the Catholic Church, not on the people of England. When you agree, I will remove my fist."

Beyssac looked directly into William's eyes. He sensed William could be subdued.

"Why do you seek strange gods?" asked Beyssac.

A singular moment. William was left dumbfounded. Beyssac's question pierced his confidence, undermining his faith.

Confused, unsure how to react, he lowered his fist. Doubt overwhelmed him. Had he placed his trust in an empty delusion? A fascinated moth, fluttering around a lamp? If Beyssac was right, his life was based on a specious belief. A life corrupted by false ideas. A futile existence. Beyssac's question, left him devastated.

William clasped his hands together. A prayer, pleading God's forgiveness seemed appropriate. William knelt down in the mud. Beyssac eased into a smile.

Indignant and averse to servility, John grabbed William's arm, twisting it, forcing him to stand up. John Ball was angry, permanent anger being his natural state. He abhorred the Catholic Church; he hated the idle rich exploiting the common people; he loathed the French who subjugated his country; he detested all the judges, lawyers and legal swindlers who used sharp practice to deceive the ignorant.

But he was most disgusted — by himself. For despite all his actions and menacing bluster, his anger had not changed a single thing. Apoplectic with disbelief, John narrowed his eyes.

"Spineless coward! Get to your feet! No English man should grovel before a French priest!"

Offended by such disrespect, Beyssac shook his fists.

"You don't realise who I am. I am not some simple village preacher. I am Cardinal Beyssac, right hand man of Pope Innocent. I deserve your approbation, not your contempt."

"A cardinal? The fact you exist is a crime — a cardinal sin. You should be hanged," said Tom.

"Or have your head separated from your body," said Jack.

"Or better still, you should be burned alive as a beacon of hope for all those you have oppressed!" shouted John.

A crowd of onlookers, attracted by the raised voices, gathered. Shoppers, passers-by, stallholders, itinerant peddlers and opportunist thieves, all watching the preposterous pageant unfold.

Beyssac, the arrogant outsider, with his retinue of subservient lackeys versus loyal John and his band of steadfast, honest English companions. The conflict promised better entertainment than a mystery play.

Jerome trembled. His throat was dry. His legs felt heavy as milk churns. He rubbed his head vigorously, turning his pate strawberry red. It did not help. Their situation was dire. They were stuck in a city tormented by plague. The road was blocked and they were surrounded by a mob — scoundrels growing increasingly hostile. Their dilemma had turned into a spectacle for the citizens of Oxford. A drama borne out of their predicament. All that was missing was a vendor selling cakes and a troupe of musicians.

"Sweetmeats, sweetmeats, come and buy my sweetmeats." The hawker's trumpeting voice echoed along the high street.

"Liquorice, raisins, treacle cakes, figs, juicy oranges."

Jerome dropped his head in his hands. And missed.

Inside the coach, hidden from the rabble outside, Antoine was worried. This was Sebastian's sanctuary. The baby had been fed — breadcrumbs soaked in goat's milk and spiced with mead, washed — scrubbed from head to toe with lye soap and changed — a one-piece cassock cut from a horse blanket. Now, after a discordant lullaby, he was asleep. The atmosphere inside the coach was calm. But outside, the situation was growing worse. Some onlookers were baying for blood. While across the street, tumblers, jugglers, musicians and a woman dancing on stilts, entertained the crowd.

Having regained his composure William wanted revenge. Jack, wounded by Beyssac's disparaging remarks, was eager to lash out. And Tom, certain of his knowledge of the Scriptures, would not tolerate opposition. As for John, after applying logic and verifying the facts, he decided it would be in the best interest of all good Christians, if the strangers were burned to death. Morcar would be pleased.

Beyssac rose to his feet, standing as tall as possible, seeking to reaffirm his authority. With exaggerated dignity, he adjusted his papal hat. This confirmed his dominion over these English peasants. The box seat would be the pulpit from which he could castigate the sinful citizens of Oxford. God knows, they deserved it.

But as he opened his mouth, a mind-numbing drumbeat erupted across the street. The woman on stilts began to kick her legs increasingly higher, seemingly possessed by a malevolent spirit. Despite the cacophony, Beyssac remained defiant.

"Depraved people of Oxford. There is still time to embrace virtue and renounce vice. My superior position as cardinal from Avignon..."

The noise increased. Beyssac struggled against the din. The uproar, a hellish tapestry of wicked threats, monstrous music, barking dogs, loathsome profanities and aggressive hawkers calling attention to their wares. Beyssac would not give up. He shouted.

"I repeat. My superior position as cardinal, gives me the authority to absolve sins and guarantee you a place in Heaven. My eminent standing..." Beyssac broke off. A plaintive question.

"When Adam delved and Eve span
Who was then a gentleman?"

John Ball's carefully chosen words. Beyssac's speech foundered.

This was the moment John had waited for. Encouraged by Beyssac's silence, he leapt across the box seat, shoving Beyssac backwards through the canopy. Whimpering, Jerome put his fingers in his ears. While John, burning with righteous zeal, started to harangue the rabble. Despite Beyssac's best efforts, his repeated attempts to emerge from the canopy, only brought more punches to his face.

"This arrogant Frenchman! He savages our faith, like a wolf tearing at carrion. How can he judge our morality when he works for the most corrupt institution in the world! I am sure he has poisoned our wells and rivers. He delights in our misery. He relishes the agony he has unleashed upon us. He is watching our children suffer and die. He is a spy for the French and an emissary of the Antichrist. His annihilation in the purifying flames of a bonfire, is the only way to protect ourselves. What is to be done?"

Hatred unleashed. Insidious venom, increasing fury, escalating hysteria — a rapid decay of common sense.

"Cremate the prelate!" Tom shouted.

"Torch him!" yelled Will.

An outpouring of vitriol and spiteful abuse. Dejected men and women seeking a scapegoat for the Pestilence.

"Flames will feast on the corrupt French priest!"

"Burn the coach. Burn all the foreigners to a cinder!"

The bedlam reached its crescendo. A screaming, baying, impulsive, vindictive rabble. Crippled with fear, Beyssac collapsed into gloomy reflection. Jerome closed his eyes, whispering the Lord's Prayer, over and over again. Startled by the noise, Sebastian started to cry.

Already fuming and spoiling for a fight, Antoine considered waking the baby as the last straw. It was rude, unacceptable behaviour which could not be endured. Gritting his teeth, Antoine exploded, bursting through the canopy, kicking John up the backside and off the box seat, face down into the mud.

"You English idiots. Where is your respect? You have threatened the life of a cardinal. A sacrilegious act in itself. And now you have woken the baby! You are the ones who will burn... in the tormenting fires of Hell!"

The uproar began to diminish, dwindling in a minute to a peevish murmur of discontent. The musicians put down their instruments. The hawkers ceased shouting. The barking dogs were mute. Even the woman dancing on stilts stopped, uncertain what to do next.

But Antoine knew exactly how to proceed. Pushing Jerome aside, he jumped on Hippocrates' back, digging him in the ribs. Hippocrates shied and bolted. The other horses followed, galloping out of pure fright. In an instant, the coach was hurtling along the high street, heading for the North Gate. Clinging to Hippocrates' neck, Antoine felt ill.

Further along the high street, hands on hips, well breakfasted and content, John Studley, Lord Mayor of Oxford was standing outside his apothecary shop. He admired his diamond rings, sparkling in the morning sunshine. He had recently acquired more land and his business was thriving. A fur coat and long-toed shoes confirmed his wealth.

Oxford seemed quiet today. Although listening intently, he could hear a commotion at the top of High Street. Probably a reprobate being hanged — a cutpurse or murderer. Normally, Oxford was a settled, studious, law-abiding town. One could walk the streets in safety. The pace of life was unhurried, almost serene...

John Studley, Lord Mayor of Oxford, did not see the horses, until it was too late.

A confusion of noises: pounding hooves, warning shouts and deafening screams. A panorama of fitful sights: bulging eyes, spinning buildings, fetid, mud-lined streets. Twisting and whirling, John flew through the air like a sycamore leaf tossed in the breeze. He hit the ground hard. He was alive. But his fur coat was ripped to shreds.

He looked down. The toes of his shoes were missing, sliced off by the coach wheels. His back was sore. But he was alive. Racking his brains, he recalled a Latin phrase. It seemed appropriate. Medice, cura, te ipsum. Physician heal thyself. Despite his predicament, John broke into a defiant smile. Racing down High Street, dashing through the North Gate, speeding along St Giles Street, the horses only began to ease off, two miles out of Oxford on the Eynsham road.

Grasping the reins, Jerome gained control, bringing the horses to an uneven stop. Antoine slumped on to the road. Beyssac leant against a wheel, recovering his breath. Emotionally and physically drained, too tired to speak, they sat in silence, listening to Sebastian burbling and gurgling in his cot.

Beyssac spoke first. "Eynsham Abbey is quite near. It is a Benedictine house. I'm sure they will afford us food and shelter."

Antoine stood up. His natural exuberance returned.

"Do they brew beer?"

"I expect so," said Beyssac. "It is a skill for which the Black Monks are celebrated."

Looking pensive, Jerome felt it was the right time to speak out. "I'm never going to Oxford again," Jerome declared. "It's a madhouse!"

Chapter Thirteen

The journey to Eynsham Abbey meant travelling via the heavily potholed Witney Road. In good times it was a thoroughfare used by wagons and horse-drawn vehicles of every sort. But in bad times, such as when pestilence threated the extinction of whole villages, it became a melancholy highway, a road to ruin, best avoided by decent people. Antoine considered it the most dismal journey of his life.

Each side of the road provided evidence of the misery brought by the plague. Fields remained uncultivated, mature crops, the lifeblood of every village, withered and rotted. Emaciated cattle, bones protruding, wandered uncontrolled, searching feverishly for food. The herdsman had gone. Was he dead? Or had he run away when the plague arrived?

Ordinary people, unwilling actors in a bleak, unscripted drama. Depressed by what he had seen, Jerome stopped the coach outside the door of the Seven Stars tavern.

A large green canvas, depicting seven golden planets, hung from a pole outside the door. The canvas trembled in the breeze. The wooden shutters were latched back, welcoming the sun's rays, flooding the interior with brilliant, dazzling light. Insects murmured. It was warm. A mood of benign drowsiness prevailed. England, at its most beguiling.

Parched throats demanded refreshment. Beyssac preferred white wine. He refused to try beer, convinced English beer encouraged lustful thoughts. More easy-going, Antoine would drink anything put in front of him. Always consistent, Jerome looked forward to a cup of frothy, oak beer. While Sebastian, encouraged by Antoine, had developed a taste for white mead.

Beyssac entered the tavern first. A pungent smell met his nostrils. He identified it. The distressing miasma of death. Antoine and Jerome knew it too.

Corpses, ravaged by pestilence, lay somewhere in the tavern. They looked in the front room. It was sparsely furnished: a trestle table on which stood two cracked ale jugs; upturned benches; a stout wooden chest, its lid thrown open; a cold hearth surrounded by ash and four ale casks, their lids smashed and contents gone. Undoubtedly, thieves had ransacked the tavern. But where was the owner?

Antoine raised his shoulders, sighing deeply.

"In there," he whispered. He pointed at the back room.

"Welcome to Hell."

Antoine had seen death before. He witnessed the murder of his father and was present at the death of his children. Ordinarily, he was immune to desolation. But this was an atrocity. A savage abomination beyond understanding. An indifferent God had ignored this cruelty. Where was the Almighty with his much-vaunted compassion?

In the back room, four entangled corpses lay on a blood-soaked mattress. Four adults. A man and three women. Their hands tied behind them. Puncture wounds to their chests. Repeatedly stabbed. Perhaps tortured. The final degradation — each one without a head.

Nauseated by the horror, Jerome bolted out of the tavern, kneeling down in the garden, praying as hard as he could. Beyssac withdrew to the front room and slumped down on a bench. Closing his eyes, he pleaded with God to punish those responsible for the atrocity. But Antoine remained intrigued, busy opening cupboards, lifting furniture aside and even inspecting the inside of the chimney. They were a poor family, hardly rich pickings for thieves. And Antoine soon found what he was looking for. At the bottom of the wooden chest, he discovered the victims' heads, neatly aligned, a silver coin bearing the face of King Harold, lodged in each gouged-out eye socket…

Beyssac insisted decorum must be observed. He stood in the garden, looking up to a point in the sky beyond the tavern roof. His hat shielded his eyes. The words of his prayer dignified and perfectly appropriate.

"God our Father,
Your power brings us to birth,
Your providence guides our lives,
And by your command we return to dust.
In company with Christ,
Who died and now lives,
Let these murdered souls, rejoice in your kingdom,

Where all tears will be wiped away.

Unite them, together again in one family

To sing your praise, forever and ever. Amen."

They bowed their heads. Terror had given way to tranquillity. Beyssac struggled to maintain a turbulent calm. Life was simply a preparation for death. The purpose of life was to avoid sin, perform good works and follow the teaching of the Catholic Church. But these people had been murdered. They had not confessed their sins or received the last rites. A long stay in Purgatory or even Hell would await them. Beyssac struggled to control his anger.

"God, give you this day, sir."

A cheerful male voice diverted their thoughts. Smiling affably, a man was leaning against the side of their coach. He wore a reddish-brown tunic, brown leather boots and a red felt hat. A scabbard, holding a large dagger, hung from his belt. Stepping forward, he removed his hat.

"You look upon Tom Gascoigne, reeve and assistant to the bailiff at Eynsham. Not a rascal but engaged in law-abiding business as purposed."

Antoine could not hold back.

"Good sir. Your friendly face is contrary to our mood. God's mercy is absent today. We have seen their bodies. The proprietor of the Seven Stars and his family are murdered. Sorrow has master here."

Tom's smile melted into a frown. He could not believe it.

"All dead? No survivors?"

"All killed," said Beyssac.

"Slaughtered would be a more accurate description," said Jerome, the horrific scene in the tavern dominating his thoughts.

"Sacrificed is the word I would choose," said Antoine.

"That family was not just killed. Those people were tortured, offered up and sacrificed like animals. It was a pagan ritual."

"God is absolutely clear on this," said Beyssac earnestly. The Scriptures could not be challenged. They answered every question.

"What pagans sacrifice, they offer to demons and not God. Do not consort with demons."

Tom's anguished face reflected his distress.

"I must bear witness," he said abjectly. With slow, reluctant steps, he walked over to the tavern. He stopped outside the open door.

"However shocking this might be, I have a duty to this family. They were good people, Christians in the sight of God. I must see. I shall bear witness." Quietly, reverently, easing his way past the upturned tables, he disappeared inside.

An awkward silence. The road was deserted, the surrounding fields empty of crops or cattle. The countryside lapsed into a sun-filled stupor.

Antoine climbed into the coach. Sebastian needed to be fed. Jerome began to water the horses, stroking each one, whispering and acknowledging each horse's character. A mutual respect. Beyssac closed his eyes, enjoying the sun on his face. The events of the day had tested his faith.

After a few minutes, Tom came running out of the tavern. His face ashen, his jovial spirit crushed. Shaking with rage, he declared, "Thieving murderers. Robbery is a despicable crime. But why such violence? They will be caught. They will be hanged. There will be justice!"

Beyssac nodded.

"Immediately the horses are ready, we will leave. The perpetrators of this outrage may return. I don't think they are inclined to mercy. But on a more pleasant note, tonight I anticipate a cordial reception and Christian hospitality at our next spiritual stopping place. The renowned Eynsham Abbey."

Tom shook his head. He spoke slowly, firm deliberation in every word.

"Avoid Eynsham Abbey. Your life depends upon it. The Pestilence rages through the abbey like fire. Most of the monks are dead. Those who cling to life have no food except the flesh of cats and dogs. It is said, they are so desperate for food they are even eating birds' dung. Eynsham Abbey is doomed. God has forgotten that place."

Beyssac sighed.

"There will be an end to the misery of the English people. But they deserve God's wrath."

Tom was indignant.

"One day we will be free of the poisonous affliction which has dominion over us. I believe, with absolute certainty, God will liberate the English people from their oppression."

"If it is God's will, it will happen," said Beyssac sternly.

"You must accept that the Pestilence is God's vengeance against a sinful world. To question his justice is blasphemy. And a mortal sin itself."

"I am not privy to God's purposes," said Tom. "But the people of England are in thrall to a cancer — a pitiless, scourging cancer. The patience of the English people is not inexhaustible."

"True suffering will wash away the sins of mankind," said Beyssac. "Providence is lighting our way. We are Christian pilgrims on a journey to Hereford. I promise when we reach Hereford Cathedral, we will offer ardent prayers for the salvation of the English. But God's decree is final. He alone will decide this country's fate."

"I do not accept that," said Tom. "Fate is like a plodding carthorse. Sometimes it needs a good kick, if you want progress."

Beyssac was irked. His chest heaving. How could a reeve, an uneducated farmhand, have the impudence to question God's will? The Creator is not answerable to anyone. Beyssac cleared his throat. Boiling with anger, he was eager to berate Tom. But Jerome's conciliatory voice broke the tension.

"A horse is a beautiful, noble creature. No man has the right to vent his anger on the handiwork of God. God created the world, consequently, all that lives is inspired by God. All that lives is holy."

Jerome's gentle rebuke dissolved the argument. Beyssac was eager to continue their journey by heading straight for Witney. Tom was keen to reach his home village before dark.

"Take care on this road," Tom warned. "Evidently there are felons abroad who delight in murder. I wager, they would murder a stranger just for sport. Remember to say your prayers."

"My life is one long prayer," said Beyssac.

Tom bowed, flourished his hat, climbing nimbly over a stile. They watched him stride across the fields, his red hat bobbing up and down as he negotiated the steep ditches. Soon, he was a speck in the distance.

It was late afternoon and the sun was fading. They needed to continue their journey. Black-hearted murderers were in the vicinity. It would be prudent to set off.

Antoine noticed the tavern door and shutters were open. Animals would be attracted to the smell of decomposing bodies. Desperate for food, they would feast on cold, human flesh. Antoine was appalled by a vision of wild animals chewing, ripping and tearing at the corpses. He thought it morally wrong to turn his back on such a possibility. He ran back to the tavern, the ominous sweet smell, now stronger than before. He closed the shutters slowly, respecting the victims inside. The tavern had become a wattle and daub coffin. It would be indecent to leave it unsecured. With the shutters closed only the front door needed fastening. As Antoine pulled the handle, he glanced at a trestle table standing on its side.

In the middle of the table was a fresh incision. Wood shavings littered the floor. A figure carved into the grain. A winged, two-legged dragon with a barbed tail. Antoine recognised it straight away. It was a wyvern. Fresh blood dripped from its mouth.

Chapter Fourteen

The Blue Boar Inn, the most respected establishment in Witney, promised respite from murder and the horrors of the Pestilence.

A surfeit of hot food. Lamb, wild fowl, salmon, saltfish and eels being specialities of the house.

Beyssac's bedchamber was clean. The bed even had a straw mattress and muslin sheets. He need not share and his room was prestigious enough to possess a close stool for his private use. The cardinal's reluctance to spend more money, meant Antoine, Jerome and Sebastian were obliged to sleep in the coach.

Nevertheless, everyone's spirits were raised by the variety of wine on offer at the Blue Boar. Wine from Gascony, the vineyards of the River Rhine, Spain and Cyprus, were all to be had. The wine cellar was impressive.

After a brief deliberation, Beyssac, Antoine and Jerome decided to try them all. Sebastian's gurgling and burbling suggested he was content. Wine was not essential to his happiness.

So, after a belly-bursting supper, the evening dissolved into gentle carousing and eventually, well-earned sleep.

Jerome dreamed of wild Camargue horses galloping freely through the marshlands of the Rhone. Their bright, expressive eyes confirming a fierce spirit. The dream reflected Jerome's yearning for a life free from fear.

Antoine enjoyed a deep, wine-induced sleep. In his mind, he wandered the Land of Cockaigne. Food was abundant. The sky rained cheese. Cooked fish jumped out of rivers, ready to be eaten. Streams flowed with red wine. Beautiful women demanded immediate sexual satisfaction. Nobody grew old. Cardinals, reduced to the level of peasants, bent their backs tilling the soil. Antoine felt at home in this place.

In contrast, Beyssac dreamed of becoming Pope, Bishop of Rome, leader of the Catholic Church. A responsibility he would relish. As God's representative on Earth, kings and emperors would tremble when he spoke. The heady intoxication of power. Beyssac's flickering eyelids struggled to keep up with his ambition.

As for Sebastian, well fed and safe in Antoine's arms, he was fascinated by the vivid colours. Blue melted into yellow, orange transformed to green. These were the colours of the wine bottles, stacked inside the coach. Sebastian's settled sleep, proof of a contented baby.

But while they slept, forgetting their problems for a time, the Pestilence arrived. A malign presence, lethal and impossible to resist. The Angel of Death hid inside a farm cart taking bundles of cloth to Witney market.

After the plague's cold arrival, ragged clothes became shrouds and blankets turned into winding sheets. Witney was being punished. Within two weeks, the market in High Street would be abandoned. No one, would wish to attend.

But the guests at the Blue Boar slept soundly. A deep, untroubled sleep. Celebrating the first miracle of Jesus, left them exhausted and oblivious to the arrival of the plague. Full stomachs and comfortable beds encouraged them to remain in bed. They did not stir until the sun's rays illuminated the market cross and shouts, curses and raised voices made continued sleep impossible.

A hostile crowd had gathered at the end of Corn Street. A young woman wearing a blue tunic and an older man dressed in black were surrounded and could not escape. She was guilty of disturbing the king's peace.

Brutish cheers encouraged Mr Cooper, the bailiff, as he placed a yoke around the woman's neck, pushing her wrists through the smaller holes further down. Insistent on correct procedure, he brandished two iron padlocks, turning each key with an exaggerated gesture. The yoke of repentance proved popular entertainment.

Despite being unable to move, the woman was not subdued. As the second key turned, Roger and Elizabeth Barton resumed their dispute.

Roger took up the cudgels first, emphasising his words, hoping to garner the crowd's support.

"A true wife, church confirmed by God, must be ruled by her husband. A good woman should obey her husband's instructions."

Male voices bellowed support. Encouraged, Roger smirked triumphantly. His white hair and weather-beaten face suggesting sage-like wisdom.

Restricted by the yoke, Elizabeth could not shake her head in disagreement. Instead, she stuck out a contemptuous tongue.

"The selfish babble of an old man in his dotage. I am not content. Every circumstance of our marriage leaves me frustrated. I am not a mouse to be mastered by a drooling tom cat."

Some people in the crowd seized their opportunity. A discordant chorus of mews, yowls, screeches and squeaks filled the air. The people of Witney were unforgiving.

Watching from the elevated position of his room at the Blue Boar, Beyssac was dismissive. It was a trivial domestic squabble, provoked by an ill-disciplined wife. Although, Antoine and Jerome, standing on the box seat of the coach, had a difference perspective. They saw two actors playing heartfelt parts in an unfolding drama. The English had a way with words.

"Your shocking defiance has occasioned my humiliation," said Roger angrily. "Where is your gratitude? You have become a quarrelsome harpy. A scold, with a face as long as a serpent's tongue!"

Inspired by this rebuke, a few observers hissed like snakes, twisting and coiling around each other in a madcap dance. Others, exhilarated by the idea of more exotic beasts, flapped their arms in imitation of a dragon, breathing imaginary fire on anyone within reach.

Elizabeth remained undaunted. No rabble could bludgeon her spirit. Her dark eyes flashed contempt.

"Roger Barton. You are a feeble, spineless old man, set in your ways. My soul shrivels in your presence. You are hurtful to my faith. God knows you are a religious coward."

The crowd fell silent. The merrymaking stopped. Elizabeth had condemned Roger, casting aspersions on his faith. She questioned his loyalty to the Church. Denial of Roger's sincere beliefs could bring dire consequences for Elizabeth if proved against her. Yet, the defiant look on Elizabeth's face did not falter. Her eyes sparkled with dissent.

"Now, there's the marrow and meat of it," said Roger. "My wife denies the True Church. It's as plain as the nose on your face. This woman is a heretic."

Beyssac pushed back the shutters. His interest rekindled by hearing one, significant word. If Elizabeth was a religious renegade, as a cardinal, he must act. The Catholic Church — the bride of Christ — must be defended and avenged.

A few onlookers cursed; others muttered obscenities, but Elizabeth remained steadfast. She would speak out.

"I am schooled. I can read. Why do you forbid me to study the Scriptures in my own language?"

Roger sighed dismissively. Religious error must be corrected.

"The word of God is not a dog's bone to be served up on a platter, chewed over and digested by an ignorant woman. That would lead to error and fanciful beliefs. Leave Bible explanation to your priest. He is the intermediary between you and God."

Elizabeth would not accept criticism from a doddering old man. Her vehemence was palpable.

"Fraudsters and hypocrites! The teachings of Jesus are not the property of a privileged few but the birthright of all believers. Bloodsucking priests have turned the House of God into a house of ill repute!"

Beyssac watched in rapt silence, astonished by Elizabeth's attack on the Catholic Church. Every profane word tightened the noose around her neck. A blatant enemy of God, she must be confronted and punished. Those hostile to God must be destroyed.

Standing on the box seat of the coach, Antoine also witnessed Elizabeth's wild condemnation of the Church. But he was captivated. Her audacity was compelling. She spoke passionately and eloquently. An attractive young woman in a white bonnet and a long tunic. Beauty and danger. A heady combination. Though past experience had taught Antoine, beauty was seldom an indication of goodness.

Elizabeth's criticism plunged Roger into despair. What a fool he'd been to think he could turn Elizabeth into a dutiful wife! The prestige he enjoyed as a master glove maker, his money and his impressive house counted for nothing when suffering the anguish of a loveless marriage.

He was dull and insipid — a grey encumbrance in a world of vivid colours. Elizabeth had grown tired of his stultifying conformity and enervating routines. He despised himself. A gloomy old man, facing a bleak future. Elizabeth's criticism had broken him.

But Roger Barton was faithful. Loyalty to the Church was paramount. Elizabeth must be defeated. He remained resolute.

"You are wrong. The House of God is universally esteemed, abundant with virtue and furnished with charity. Everywhere..."

Elizabeth cut him dead.

"Yes, everywhere people are starving. Priests take their money and spend it on church decoration. Ten stained-glass windows are not worth the life of one child. You may have a magnificent church. But you do not have a magnificent religion."

"That's deep!" shouted an onlooker. Murmurings of agreement and supportive utterances were heard. Elizabeth had touched a nerve.

Roger bent his body and sat down. The burden of his conflict with Elizabeth weighed more heavily on him than the metal padlock.

He appeared a decrepit Methuselah, struggling to defend his beliefs. While Elizabeth, with her angry face, seemed cold-hearted, unmoved by the sight of her husband cowering in the marketplace.

But Elizabeth was upset. In the beginning, she had loved him. A pretty young girl, flattered by the attention of a charming older man. He offered security, social approval and the prospect of happiness. In a world fraught with danger, she would find safety within a sensible marriage. Unfortunately, Elizabeth's hopes had proved illusory.

Her simple English faith was suffocated by Roger's obedience to the universal Church. Bitter arguments followed. The tedium of a cold relationship eroded her spirit and crushed her desires. She considered Roger a pathetic old gentleman. Her love for him was long dead.

"You are bewildered," said Roger resignedly. "I will pray for you, attend mass every day and make pilgrimage to Canterbury. You are misguided and brimful of error. But every soul can be saved."

Elizabeth shook her head.

"Your whole life is an error," she said. "Pilgrimages and rituals don't bring salvation. You are duped. Priests are money grabbers. Their only concern is wealth."

Antoine was entranced. There was something alluring about a rebellious woman. Her zeal astonished him.

But not Beyssac. He was outraged by Elizabeth's denunciation of the Church and dismayed by the support she received from onlookers. Always vigilant, Beyssac sensed whispers of atheism in the comments he heard from those watching. To his mind, the people of Witney had a penchant for shameful behaviour.

News of Roger and Elizabeth's fiery altercation soon spread. Corn Street was growing into a mass of jeering, insulting and unruly townspeople. Mr Cooper, the bailiff, felt conspicuous and vulnerable. Perhaps this was a good time to set the prisoner free.

Still sitting on the ground, Roger took a deep breath. He would make one last attempt to rescue Elizabeth from her delusion. He must acknowledge her disquiet. Accepting her complaints would dissipate her anger. This was a trait he regarded peculiar to women.

"Why are you so unhappy? What is the wellspring of your distress?"

Elizabeth was not deceived by Roger's question. She knew it was a calculated attempt to persuade her to accept the blame for her own misery. It was, quite simply, a strategy designed to make her beg forgiveness. This was a trait she regarded peculiar to men.

Cautious and wary of the crowd's mood, Mr Cooper stepped forward, releasing Elizabeth from the yoke. She tilted her head, easing painful neck muscles back into place. Man and wife, yards apart in distance but a continent apart in affection. The crowd was silent.

"You ask me to explain my despondency. What a stupid question! The truth is my opinions are mocked and my faith ridiculed. I am confined, smothered and suffocated by your control. You are a prison warder, not a husband. In your presence, I am diminished!"

Antoine was enthralled. This woman was potent as English beer. A powerful and dangerous female — Antoine's definition of his ideal woman. Were all English women so fierce?

Out of sight, behind a half-closed shutter, Beyssac was watching the drama unfold. He did not admire Elizabeth. Now she was free, it was too late to step in and condemn her attack on the Church. Roger Barton was a good man but wanting in spirit. Elizabeth Barton was out of control.

Beyssac watched Roger unfurl the fingers of his right hand. In his palm, a gimmal ring, two hoops forming one complete marriage band.

"Whom God has joined together, let no man put asunder," said Roger solemnly. Elizabeth shook her head.

"I am the steadfast bride of my faith. No longer a cowed and dutiful wife. That ring is like the Eucharist. It is an imitation, a symbol. In reality, it is meaningless. I know where my heart really belongs."

Roger slumped to the ground. He could not believe Elizabeth's defiance.

The onlookers, the ordinary townspeople of Witney were shocked. And daunted. Open-mouthed, wide-eyed, they parted like the Red Sea, as Elizabeth strode purposefully through the crowd towards her house. The arrival of the Pestilence would ensure many of them would die. But at that moment, a darker, more tangible foreboding filled their hearts. In her fury, Elizabeth had demolished their faith in God.

That night, Elizabeth decided to leave. Smiling, filled with optimism, she stuffed a few clothes into a canvas bag. Deliberately and with gusto, she removed her bonnet, letting her long red hair hang loose.

Things would never be the same again. She was free. No longer under the control of the marital yoke. Now it was England's turn to be free.

She took a silver ring from her bodice, placing it on the fourth finger of her left hand. It bore the image of a dragon's head — a wyvern. In Hereford, back in the bosom of her family, she would be safe.

***

Once the commotion had died down, Beyssac and his entourage left Witney by a quiet back road, the wheels of the coach putting a safe distance between themselves and the volatile crowd.

The incident in Witney was scandalous. A woman had publicly dismissed her marriage, defied the law and most worrying of all, had denied the authority of the Church. What inspired such outrageous behaviour in an English woman, apparently enjoying a comfortable life alongside a wealthy and respected husband?

Beyssac scratched his head, unable to explain Elizabeth's anger. And Jerome, while quick to admit he understood horses, he confessed he could not understand women. Antoine smiled. He did understand Elizabeth's predicament. But he kept his thoughts to himself. Suppressed passion breeds resentment. Elizabeth was right to be angry.

Chapter Fifteen

Burford Priory, the Augustinian hospital, could not treat any more plague victims. The Black Friars could not cope with the number of people asking for help. Augustine of Hippo claimed, "Nothing conquers except truth." But the truth was cruel. The hospital was full of diseased patients certain to die.

Travellers on the road out of Burford reported the news. Beyssac conceded. Shelter at the priory was unrealistic. The Augustinians were too preoccupied with plague victims, to provide lodgings and food for pilgrims.

Therefore, that night, St John's Eve, Jerome stopped the coach on a causeway overlooking the River Windrush. Behind them, emanating Christian reassurance, stood the church of St John the Baptist. Its mission was explicit — to safeguard the spiritual life of Burford. The long shadows of twilight confirmed the church's authority.

As Jerome watered the horses, Antoine busied himself inside the coach preparing a meal of pain de mie and hard cheese dipped in honey. Antoine knew Beyssac would be delighted by his supper. Baby Sebastian eagerly chewed his portion, gurgling with satisfaction at its creamy taste. Antoine was certain, good foods encourage good moods

Suddenly, Beyssac opened the canvas at the rear of the coach, poking his head inside.

"Attend to this," he said. "The whole world is on fire."

Antoine jumped off the coach. On each side of the river, dozens of bonfires blazed fiercely. The Windrush glistened and rippled, flashing orange light. A smell of woodsmoke filled the air. The feast of St John's Eve had started.

"The bonfires will repel evil," said Beyssac sagely. "No demons, witches, imps or agents of Satan, can breach the ring of Christian fire which surrounds this town. The people of Burford are safe against sin."

"I've never seen so many fires," declared Antoine. "With this protection, the people here must be perfect saints. Thank God we can sleep easily for once."

Beyssac frowned.

"Always be on your guard. Corinthians tells us Satan can disguise himself as an angel of light."

Antoine nodded. Beyssac was ever watchful. Beyssac could discover evil in every nook and cranny of human existence. That was why he had reached such an exalted position within the Catholic Church.

The bonfires hissed and crackled. Burning wood splintered, snapped and fell deeper into the fire, sending red and blue sparks stretching up the river. Smoke billowed around the tower of St John's Church, hanging over the town like an ashen scroll. Burford seemed a friendly refuge in a hostile world.

Jerome thought otherwise. Coughing and spitting to clear his throat, he scrambled up the steep bank of the Windrush, clutching a bucket to his chest. Breathing deeply, he appeared flustered. He struggled to position the bucket of water under the coach. Black motes of soot dotted his face and arms. Wide eyes confirmed his astonishment.

"What in the name of hellfire, is going on?" asked Jerome, nervously rubbing his bald head.

"Be reassured. This is a hallowed place," insisted Beyssac. "The good people of this town, light fires to safeguard their souls. As certain as I am John the Baptist never sinned, I believe no demon could ever infiltrate this sanctuary."

Jerome's attention wandered. He could not believe his eyes. In front of him, a two-legged golden dragon, accompanied by screaming villagers chasing its tail, was winding its way along the high street, heading for the church.

"If what you say is true," declared Jerome, "explain that extraordinary creature!"

Fascinated, they watched the dragon roll across the churchyard wall, its undulating body swerving around gravestones, twisting past monuments before leaping over a grave-pit and coming to rest on the black marble lych stone.

The dragon's pursuers, men and women delighted by the opportunity to engage in legitimate violence, took it in turns to kick the dragon's tail. After a few minutes, the howling dragon collapsed, disabled by a barrage of painful blows. Robert of Burford, sneak thief and poacher had been punished.

Beyssac, who delighted in the ignorance of others, was eager to demonstrate his learning. His voice, charged with earnest authority, proclaimed:

"I assume this is a tradition whose origin is lost in the mists of time, allowing the townspeople to administer justice upon a local rogue. But how a dragon came to be involved, I cannot say."

Antoine nodded.

"Your explanation is plausible. But you are wrong concerning one important detail."

Angry at this challenge to his logic, Beyssac snapped back.

"As a chef, I value your opinion, but as a scholar I..."

Antoine would not be patronised. Beyssac must be told.

"That beast does have a dragon's head and wings and is covered in scales. But it is not a dragon. It's a wyvern."

Jerome looked puzzled.

"Whether it's a dragon or a wyvern, does it matter? We just witnessed a man get a good kicking. I wager he's more concerned about his broken ribs than debating the finer points of heraldry."

"All wrongdoers must be punished," said Beyssac. "But after deep consideration, I accept Antoine is correct. I have seen an illustration of a wyvern in a bestiary — a compendium of beasts — complied by Gervaise of Fontenai."

"And I saw a wyvern incised in a tabletop at the Seven Stars," said Antoine.

"How does a wyvern differ from a dragon?" asked Jerome.

Beyssac smiled, enjoying the moment, basking in his superior knowledge. It was an opportunity to outshine Antoine.

"A wyvern has two legs, whereas a dragon may have four legs or none at all. A wyvern is not as fierce as a dragon but it will not surrender and cornered, it will fight to the death. It was the old symbol of the kingdom of Wessex. The Bayeux Tapestry depicts King Harold fighting under a wyvern banner at the Battle of Hastings."

"A terrible defeat for the English," said Antoine, recalling his schooling.

"No. Rather a brilliant victory for a superior culture over brutish barbarism," Beyssac enthused. "Without the Normans, the English would be a nation of savages, wallowing in idiocy."

"And now?" asked Jerome, relishing the chance to pick the brains of a cardinal from Avignon.

Beyssac shook his head. "Still godless. Still barbarous. And still without shame. I find it hard to believe Christianity has reached this country."

A huge explosion. A red light lit up the sky, sending tongues of brilliant fire flashing over the church. They watched in wonder, as wild flames zigzagged through the darkness before crashing into the river. The firework display, unexpected and ear piercing, left them astounded.

As screaming fireballs flew overhead, they dived under the coach. Inside, unperturbed, Sebastian munched his pain de mie. The noise outside would not distract him from his cheese supper.

Exploding fireworks dazzled their senses. Acrid smoke swirled around the coach wheels, stinging eyes, leaving a sour taste in the mouth. Pungent vapours lodged in their noses making breathing difficult. A relentless barrage of cannon blasts assaulted their ears. St John's Church, shrouded in a blood-red mist, trembled as fireworks shattered its spiritual tranquillity. To Beyssac's mind, it was not a firework display but a demonic attack upon Burford's soul.

Gradually the pandemonium diminished. The display stopped. A fetid saltpetre and sulphur fog drifted across the river, fading into the trees. While Jerome checked the horses, Antoine scrubbed Sebastian and put him down to sleep. What is more appealing than a freshly washed baby? As Antoine cradled Sebastian, the sight of this little scrap of humanity filled him with awe. Antoine knew he would venture his life to protect this boy.

Beyssac too, was preoccupied by an extraordinary sight. Narrowing his eyes, he could not believe what he was seeing. Was it sorcery or zealotry? Were the participants devil worshippers or religious fanatics?

The bonfires had died down, leaving heaps of glowing embers. White-hot ashes smouldered and sputtered, sending minute splinters of charred wood spitting into the air.

Beyssac twisted his head to confirm the bizarre spectacle. He watched as men and women, hand in hand, walked over the hot cinders, seemingly unhurt or even indisposed. The Burford firewalkers were oblivious to pain.

Careful not to draw attention, Beyssac strolled over and joined the excited onlookers. Old men and women, middle-aged husbands and wives, young girls and their sweethearts, besides a few evidently unattached adults, all shouting, cheering, encouraging and coaxing, fully expecting each couple to walk safely across the hot ashes. An array of luminous faces, blazing with uninhibited energy. The spectators and firewalkers seemed hypnotised. Their beatific attitude at odds with the very real danger of being burned. To the cardinal's mind, it was an orgiastic pagan ritual. Beyssac loosened his collar.

"Walk with me," a female voice whispered in his ear.

Beyssac turned around. A flaxen-haired woman extended a hand towards him. A warm smile suggested she was not dangerous.

"Walk with me. I am alone." Her melancholy words sounding more like a summons than a request.

Beyssac knew the only woman's hand he had touched was his mother's. Still, this was an opportunity to ask questions of this woman and perhaps discover the purpose of the ritual. Beyssac weighed up the situation for a few seconds, before grabbing her hand.

A delicate hand, smooth skinned with long, exquisite nails. Not the hand of a working woman, but possibly the hand of a lady of noble birth or high social standing. An enamelled ring and eye-catching silk dress suggested she was a woman of exalted rank. Her name was Dionisia.

"Such a distinctive name," said Beyssac, genuine admiration in his voice.

"It means child of Dionysus," she said proudly. "I am privileged. I am named after a Greek god. The god of wine."

"I hope you have not inherited any of his evil proclivities," said Beyssac, smiling broadly,

"Not evil," said Dionisia. Her long nails dug into Beyssac's hand, her dark eyes seemed fixed on some distant object. "The word primeval would be a better description. Dionysus is also god of fertility and religious ecstasy. He inspires those who defy convention. He encourages chaos and danger. Dionysus represents powerful forces beyond our understanding. These forces are not evil. They are inherited. Generation to generation. In our blood."

Gently, imperceptibly, Beyssac tried to withdraw his hand from her grasp. Her fingers held firm. He realised he must gain her trust.

They walked hand in hand, following the path past the churchyard, along the riverbank and up towards another group of firewalkers. The spectators bellowed and cheered, while the firewalkers, absorbed by their task, appeared placid, indifferent to the blistering heat.

Her face beaming with admiration, Dionisia stopped to watch the firewalkers. Their eyes were closed, disdainfully ignoring the searing embers beneath them. Fascinated, she yearned to embrace the moment. But not yet.

"Why do they chance their lives? What is to be gained by taking part in a public display of stupidity?" Beyssac knitted his brows, perplexed by what he considered a collective penchant for immolation.

Dionisia frowned. What a disrespectful remark! This man was an outsider. He would never understand the time-forged elements which had shaped the English mind. His whole demeanour was alien to them. Like it or not. He must be shown the truth.

"Walk with me," she said meekly. "I will explain the purpose of this public display of stupidity."

Beyssac feared the bonfire. But Dionisia pulled him to the edge. His face felt hot. Dionisia grabbed both his hands, gazing with fanatic intent into his eyes.

"Firewalking is a test of faith. By overcoming the fire, true believers will overcome Satan. Fire cleanses and purifies. Consequently, firewalkers are absolved of all sin. With God's grace they return to that state of bliss which existed before the Great Affliction. Immaculate, pure and without sin. They achieve a wise innocence."

"The Great Affliction. A most perfect description of the Pestilence," said Beyssac. "It is without doubt, a malign presence, suffocating all and sundry, oppressing the spirit and destroying lives. The plague is a terrible affliction upon the people of this island."

Dionisia shook her head.

"I am talking about the French," she said coldly…

***

Sheltering under the coach, Jerome poured Antoine his third beer. Its buttery head rose like a bubbling spring, sealing the golden liquid underneath. Antoine adored its earthy bitterness. He relished its aroma of oven-fresh bread. Hell he defined, as any place beer was not available.

Beyssac was nowhere to be seen.

"I expect he is at the church, praying," Antoine mooted.

"Tomorrow is the Feast Day of John the Baptist. Although I've no desire to live on locusts and wild honey."

"Yes," said Antoine sipping his beer.

"I may be the voice of one crying in the wilderness but feed me English roast beef every time."

Jerome smiled, patting his head like a pastry chef preparing a cake. They were warm. They were safe. And they had plenty of food. The horses were rested and in good spirits. Burford with its fireworks and bonfires seemed an exuberant but friendly town. The River Windrush glistened under the moonlight, murmuring softly along its winding course.

"Such an engaging sight," Jerome enthused, captivated by the beauty of the river.

But Antoine's mind was elsewhere.

"Very alluring," replied Antoine, deliberately stressing his words.

Staring fixedly, his attention concentrated, Antoine crawled from under the coach. He had spotted another impressive scene. But one which promised more gratifying possibilities.

Nine young women stood at the water's edge, their hands raised in supplication. They were staring at the moon, singing a song in a language Antoine did not know. The rhythm and pattern of the words were strange, almost hypnotic. Words which awakened in Antoine, feelings he had long since subdued. The song rose and fell, eerie, unearthly cadences, beguiling his senses. Antoine felt elated. It was time to act.

Tapping Jerome on the shoulder, Antoine pointed.

"I need to investigate those women," said Antoine. Jerome was bemused. A few women, inspired by a beautiful evening, to sing a ditty, could not pose a threat to their safety. Antoine was too cynical. He seemed suspicious of everyone.

"They are just innocent maidens, enjoying a simple song," insisted Jerome.

"And you're a Frenchman who can't hold his beer," said Antoine. "Guard the coach and look after Sebastian. I'm going to find out what those women are up to. They might be planning to attack us. I've got no desire be humiliated by a gang of nubile young women. I know most men would agree with me."

Jerome shrugged his shoulders. Irony was beyond him. He watched as Antoine pushed through the long grass, walked over a slope and slid down an incline. The women stood in a circle holding hands. As the moon emerged from behind a black cloud, Jerome could see each woman's hair was crowned with flowers.

"Good ladies. I am Antoine, a pilgrim on the road to Hereford. I am ignorant of your customs. What is the purpose of your song? And why is each lady adorned with star flowers?"

A raven-haired woman spoke.

"Welcome, Monsieur Antoine. Your name betrays your birthplace. I am Edith, daughter of Eric, the wool merchant. But before I answer your questions…"

Whispering and simpering, playfully nudging each other, the women formed a tight circle around Antoine. He felt privileged not threatened by their presence. Being the sole object of their attention was flattering.

"Today, the 23rd June, is the eve of the Feast Day of John the Baptist. We are virtuous maidens, Burford born."

As she spoke, Edith pointed, singling out each woman.

"Elga, Rowena,Tayte, Beatrix, Hilda, Easter, Edwina and Ora. We wear pink daisies as a symbol of our progress from innocence to experience. It's not a melancholy farewell to our maidenhood but rather a joyous welcome to maturity."

Antoine wiped the sweat from his forehead. He had not expected a young woman to be so candid about losing her virginity.

"And the song?" asked Antoine.

"An old song. Passed from generation to generation. Perhaps a thousand years since its first recitation. It's an appeal for safe passage during our journey to an exalted state."

"An appeal to whom?" Antoine asked, genuinely ignorant.

"Dionysus," said Edith proudly…

***

"Walk with me," Dionisia insisted. Her eyes, reflecting the hot coals, glowing crimson. Her right hand clutched Beyssac's left hand in a pincer grip. Beyssac tried to extricate his fingers but to no avail. The beauty and grace of this young woman were appealing qualities. But in reality, she possessed the strength of an Amazon. More worrying was her remark about the French. It suggested she could be deranged. Or even worse, a zealot.

"Walk with me," she repeated.

Beyssac looked across to the coach but Antoine and Jerome were nowhere in sight. The spectators, a sea of twisted faces, shouted, wailed and shrieked, making rational thought impossible. Dionisia, an enchanting siren, luring him to destruction. A carpet of white ash stretched in front of him. Dionisia smiled.

"This is the ultimate test of your faith. Walk with me across the embers. This will be the true measure of your moral strength. If you falter, you will be burned and consumed by the fire. If your faith is steadfast, you will survive."

"Madness!" Beyssac shouted. "This ritual is a pagan descent into insanity. Let me be!"

That instant, a bull-necked man, wearing a red felt hat, lifted Beyssac clean out of his boots. He seemed familiar. But Beyssac had no time for cool remembrances. Dionisia screamed, determined to pull him across the embers. Beyssac yielded. He looked down. White smoke. His feet were beginning to shrivel.

Red-hot pain. The diminishing noise of the onlookers. Yes, his feet were burning but his faith burned stronger. Dionisia had doubted his courage, even his commitment to God.

Closing his eyes, Beyssac embraced his faith. The moment when Heaven and Earth connect and Man meets God. Like Jesus, "his face shining as the sun, his garments white as light," Beyssac was determined to survive. Suffering would strengthen his faith.

Dionisia seemed indifferent to the pain. She walked slowly, welcoming the opportunity to affirm her beliefs. Yes, her feet burned but her faith was strong. Completing the test would prove her loyalty to the cause.

She was surprised. She expected Beyssac to crumble and beg for his life. But he appeared resolute, almost serene. Hand in hand, walking confidently across the white ash, two traditions united in one fearsome test. Beyssac walked, praying earnestly, until he felt the cool grass soothe his blistered feet.

With God's help he had survived. He retrieved his boots and flopped down. The disappointed spectators drifted away. Their wish to see a cardinal burned to death remained unfulfilled. As Beyssac pulled on his boots, Dionisia stood over him, arms folded.

"I expected you to die," she said flatly. "I have betrayed the trust invested in me. Your faith has saved your life."

"Faith can move mountains," said Beyssac. "But keep things in perspective. This fire is not Nebuchadnezzar's furnace. Just part of a simple festival in a little English town. My faith was tested and by God's mercy, I passed muster."

Dionisia shrugged, pouting like a scolded pupil. A desolate look on her face, she stared at the ground, contemplating her next move.

"I gave my word. But I failed. I must suffer the consequences."

She seemed confused, her thinking muddled. Beyssac pondered whether the firewalk had damaged her reason rather than her feet.

With slow deliberation, she fell to her knees, holding her hands above her head in a submissive gesture. Without warning, she plunged her fingers deep into the ash.

Beyssac was astounded. This was the most appalling act of self-harm he had ever seen. But not a hint of pain or discomfort showed on her face.

Dionisia seemed disinterested in her fate. Beyssac was adamant the vile ritual must stop.

"No more. Please God, no more!" he implored.

Dionisia lifted her hands clear of the ash. Her palms were black. Her fingers blood red, skin hanging down in clumps, withered like autumn leaves.

"Walk with me," she insisted, her eyes closed, her mind preoccupied by a single thought.

"I have a task to complete."

Tentatively, uncertain of her reaction, Beyssac grasped her hand. She needed support, a sane way out of the madness which inspired her actions. No one is excluded from God's grace.

Smiling, she twisted the enamelled ring on her finger, pressing the hot metal into Beyssac's snow-white palm. She squeezed harder and harder still. A smell of scorched flesh.

Beyssac winced, instinctively pulling away his hand...

Burned into his skin, livid and wet with blood was the figure of a dragon — a wyvern.

Her face contorted, Dionisia laughed. Loud, insistent, maniacal laughter. She kept on laughing, until her heart, swollen with pride, burst...

***

Nearby, Antoine faced a different challenge. With a grin wider than a wheel of cheese, he felt ecstatic. It was not deceit but good luck which found him surrounded by nine beautiful women, all desperate to lose their virginity. A warm summer's evening. A bevy of voluptuous women and no Beyssac to check his lust. Burford was the most promiscuous town in England. And Burford men, the most fortunate.

Edith was happy to explain.

"Midnight is sacred. It is the moment of transition. When day vanquishes night. For us, it is the moment a maiden becomes a woman. At midnight each girl will remove her crown of flowers and cast it into the Windrush. Any man who succeeds in retrieving a crown from the

128

river can choose a girl as his prize. Each girl here is enthusiastic and obliging."

Antoine, although engorged with anticipation, remained puzzled.

"Where are your local men? They should be champing at the bit to be here!"

Easter, a pretty girl with braided brown tresses and a magnificent garland of pink daisies stepped forward. Her eyes fixed on Antoine, she pointed to the church. Licking her index finger, she ran it slowly around Antoine's lips.

"The ritual begins when the bell chimes midnight. Although I believe the o'clock can be brought forward if the right man becomes available."

Antoine fought hard to stifle a hallelujah. He considered how appropriate it was, the festival of Easter, was named after a Saxon goddess. Easter, with eyes black as opal stones, hair adorned with flowers and long, suggestive fingers, was definitely a goddess who deserved to be adored. His experience of England had felt like a long Lenten season of self-denial. Now Easter was here, it was time to celebrate. To Hell with those spineless milksops, too afraid to seize the day.

"I'm a good swimmer," said Antoine optimistically.

"And I'm a really bad thrower," said Easter, sliding the garland out of her braids, holding it at arms-length.

Edith led the girls down the slope and through the long grass before stopping at the water's edge. The Windrush trembled in the breeze. The water seemed pitch black. It was not the witching hour but the night was quiet. No noise of birds or animals. No human sounds coming from the town. It reminded Antoine of the respectful hush which descends upon onlookers before a man is hanged.

But danger was the last thing on Antoine's mind. The prospect of making love to Easter, filled his head with delicious images.

Exuberant, Antoine skipped along the riverbank, tearing at his clothes. In one, agitated minute, cassock, boots, cote hardie and doublet were discarded. Red-faced and breathing hard, Antoine completed his dishabille, by ripping off his leggings and throwing them in the river.

Antoine, the handsome gastronome, hands on hips, wearing only a loincloth, was now ready to prove his virility. Easter, eyes bulging in disbelief, noted the incredible extent of Antoine's anticipation.

Making the sign of the cross, each girl released the garland from her hair, throwing it into the dark water. Nine beautiful females, bathed in moonlight, reminiscent of pagan muses paying homage at an ancient shrine.

"Edith, ready for war."

"Helga, forever faithful."

"Rowena, eternally joyful."

"Beatrix, born for adventure."

"Hilda, battle ready."

"Ora, the golden child."

"Tayte, always cheerful."

"Edwina, harbinger of wealth."

"Easter, goddess of fertility."

Before Easter had finished speaking, Antoine dived into the Windrush. The water was cool. Just a few strokes and he would claim his prize. The prospect of unbridled intimacy with Easter, subdued his common sense, inspiring him to cut through the water like an erotic eel.

A perverse wind rolled across the surface of the river, making ripples, pushing the garlands just out of Antoine's reach. Now he would have to swim further and delay his lust. He imagined Easter, waiting on the riverbank, her body quivering with desire. He swam faster, trying to reach the garland before it floated downstream.

Mustering his energy, Antoine propelled himself through the water, seizing the garland with his teeth. At last! He had the damned flowers! A conceited smile spread across his face. His body may be cold but his desire was red-hot.

Treading water, he examined the daisies. Was this soggy mess, simply a crown of ruined flowers? Or a ticket to a liaison with an eager, insatiable goddess? Dreaming about Easter, Antoine did not feel the strong, female hands reaching from underwater, grabbing his legs.

The darkness engulfed him. No time for flailing arms or strangled cries. Just a cold, ominous descent into the gloomy clutches of the Windrush.

Confused, Antoine kicked out, trying to break free and reach the surface. But he was stuck. Tangled branches? A hole in the riverbed? No need to panic. The cold was beginning to numb his senses but it was not a calamity. He just needed to extricate himself from the hazard snaring his legs. That done, he could swim to the surface and claim his erotic prize. An expanse of cold river could not curb his lust.

Once again, Antoine pushed hard, attempting to propel himself upwards, away from the hazard holding him back. Yet, despite his best efforts, he did not move an inch. He grimaced, desperate for a mouthful of air. As an experienced swimmer, he could hold his breath. But now his stomach heaved and his lungs were empty. The cold was beginning to sap his strength.

Antoine braced himself for a supreme effort. Arching his back, he stretched his arms towards the surface. Raw, piercing pain coursed through him. He winced as human nails gouged furrows into his ankles.

The truth, too horrible to contemplate, chilled his heart. In the grip of female hands, he was deliberately being drowned…

Unaware of Antoine's plight and ignorant of Beyssac's fire-walking trauma, Jerome poured himself another beer. Eyes closed, mouth open, his face radiated alcoholic serenity. The horses were settled and baby Sebastian, his belly bursting with porridge, was asleep inside the coach.

Jerome relished English beer. Its buttery flavour caressed his taste buds, bringing him joy. A piquant seduction followed by a desired consummation. Drinking English beer, in a hospitable English town, alongside a magical English river, under a starlit, English sky. Could life get any better?

Jerome blinked, focusing his tired eyes. A group of young men, embellished to exaggerate their virility, were gathered in the churchyard, milling around, laughing, larking and taunting each other.

But Burford town was quiet. No lamps or candles could be seen. No smoke rising from cottage fires. No one moved along the streets. The tollbooth, where merchants haggled over wool prices, was silent. Even the animals seemed to have taken a vow of silence. Impressive bonfires collapsed into ashen heaps.

Languid, almost soporific, the Windrush appeared to be snoring, sending bubbles to the surface, like an old man sleeping in a comfortable bed. A bundle of discarded clothes drifted past, twisting aimlessly in the lazy current. Some hapless man had lost his underwear.

Jerome's beer pot slipped out of his hand. He scurried to the water's edge, darting to and fro. Trampling the rushes, splashing in the shallows. He hoped he was mistaken. It was almost midnight and quite dark but those leggings were familiar. He'd stitched them many times. Antoine was in the river. And probably dead.

Confused and cold, his arms heavy as millstones, Antoine closed his eyes. Sleep beckoned. But he would not take a breath. He would not submit. He had a life to live, dreams and ambitions to fulfil. Memories to hold fast.

Little Sebastian snuggled his head into Antoine's arms. He was warm and fragrant with the scent of a freshly washed baby. Antoine looked forward to teaching him the art of cookery. Perhaps one day, he would have the privilege of serving a king or even a cardinal.

Beyssac crossed himself. Antoine noticed an open wound on the palm of each of Beyssac's hands. Nail marks? Stigmata? Streams of blood trickled down his wrists, dripping on to his white cassock. Beyssac was a God-fearing, Christian cardinal but he needed to relax, to let himself go for once. A man unworthy of damnation, has not really lived.

Jerome swam into view. A spineless stable boy. A man with the vivacity of a sick, old horse — a nag only fit for its meat. Jerome was the antithesis of a knight in shining armour. Better to be dead than live an ordinary life.

Unconscious, delusional, occupied by elusive phantoms, Antoine did not feel Jerome pulling him out of the water. His loin-cloth was gone. A garland of pink daisies twisted around his groin.

An hour later, safe inside the coach, grim faces considered their predicament. The lantern cast an unearthly glow. Filled with shame, Antoine shook his head.

"I've been such a fool. A prisoner of lustful desires. Befuddled and bewitched. I let the promise of fornication cloud my common sense."

"Sins of the flesh are vile," said Beyssac sagely. "But spiritual sins are worse. Unbridled lust makes you the Devil's slave. Pride is the basis of all sin. Pride was the first sin and is the most difficult to subdue. Your desire to engage in erotic feasting is a mere blemish compared to pride, which cleaves a man's soul from God."

"Cleave is the right word," said Antoine, pointing to the bloody wounds on his ankles. "The girls enticed me into the river, to kill me. But why?"

Jerome shrugged his shoulders. Perhaps the English hated foreigners. And that was it. Or, more likely, fear of pestilence had made everyone wary of strangers. Their hostility was based on ignorance.

"Maybe, they think we are plague carriers, bringing more misery to Burford. If that's the case, I understand their aggression."

"No!" insisted Beyssac, waving a dismissive finger. "Tonight's events indicate we are the intended target of assassins. For some reason, they want to stop us reaching Hereford."

Beyssac held his hand under the lantern. The light revealed the outline of a dragon scorched deep in his flesh. Jerome closed his eyes, mumbling a prayer. Catching his breath, Antoine pointed at the wound.

"That abomination is identical to the emblem carved on the table at the Seven Stars tavern. When that dragon appears, people are murdered. You were assaulted tonight. Intoxicated by lust, I was not there to defend you. Please forgive me."

Beyssac smiled. He bore Antoine no bitterness. He judged the fire-walking to be a test of his faith. A test he passed, triumphantly. His burned feet and injured hand served only to strengthen his Christian beliefs. His distress had been a blessing in disguise.

"The exact details of my experience are not important. What matters is, I have learned from my encounter. I am stronger than yesterday. We will achieve our goal and reach Hereford. The Devil cannot thwart those engaged in God's work."

Resting on his bed, staring at the swinging lantern, Antoine reflected on the day's events. He acknowledged he was a numbskull, letting his passions dominate. In future, he would be more sensible in the presence of a pretty girl. Burford had taught him a lesson about the danger of unchecked lust.

Outside, sitting on the box seat, Jerome also considered Burford. He drove the horses hard, guided by the moonlight. It worried him Beyssac was convinced they were a target for murderers. It irritated him he had saved Antoine's life but received scant gratitude. And now, he was suffering a thumping hangover caused by too much beer. Looking back, the horrible events in Burford confirmed it as the most loathsome town in England. Christian Gloucester would be a more peaceful place.

Chapter Sixteen

Eyes sparkling with excitement, Beyssac could not wait to reach Gloucester. As a novice, he spent many hours poring over St Bede's 'History of the English People'. He recalled Bede's description of Gloucester as 'the most virtuous, loyal, and fervently Christian town in England'. For Beyssac, the visit to Gloucester was a pilgrimage, not just a search for lodgings.

During breakfast, as the coach travelled along almost deserted roads, Beyssac sat on his bed, taking occasional mouthfuls of bread and cheese whilst extolling the virtues of glorious Gloucester.

"We are spoiled for choice," Beyssac enthused. "The Abbey of St Peter, a Benedictine house, will provide wonderful hospitality. I have often corresponded with Abbot Horton. He is a devoted servant of our Church and a renowned scholar. His mind is fit to grapple with whole libraries."

"You mentioned a choice," said Antoine thinking quickly. The prospect of visiting another close-knit religious community, possibly riddled with plague, worried him.

Beyssac shrugged his shoulders. "Or we could call at St Oswald's Priory and pay homage to his relics. The prior, William Heved is famous for his piety."

Antoine frowned. Common sense suggested a community of monks, living together in a country overwhelmed by pestilence, would soon find themselves victims. Emanating unselfish insight, Antoine tried his luck.

"Considering the catastrophe which oppresses England, surely a tavern or hostelry would be a more sensible choice?"

Beyssac shook his head. "A tavern sells alcohol. Alcohol engenders lust. In Burford, wanton lust brought you to Death's door. Have I made my point?"

Confounded by Beyssac's perfect logic, Antoine nodded. Just occasionally, this disputatious cardinal did talk sense.

The Burford to Gloucester road was quiet. Jerome encountered no drovers bringing stock to market. He met no wagons carrying passengers or goods. They did pass a few footsore pilgrims eager to worship at King Edward's tomb but they were the exception. Fear of pestilence persuaded townspeople and villagers to stay put. As a consequence, strangers were feared.

The plight of every village showed the pitiless effect of the plague. In Northleach, the weekly market was abandoned, church services cancelled and outsiders refused charity. And Shipton became a ghost village, after the landlord of the Frog Mill Inn, his entire family and six guests were found dead in the tap room. In just one night, the Pestilence had ripped out Shipton's heart.

Furthermore, in Shurdington, there were so many plague victims, the door on the north side of St Paul's Church — used by pallbearers to carry out coffins — was left permanently open. The English countryside had become a vast garden of remembrance. But only a handful were left alive to do the remembering.

"My God!" gasped Jerome. On top of Gloucester's Southgate, a mutilated head, impaled on a pole, was staring at him. The man's face, livid with scarlet gashes, bore an astonished expression. His bemused eyes suggested a painful death. The Keepers of the Peace agreed, the spectacle of a villain's head had a salutary effect on those inclined to crime.

Suddenly, without warning, shouts and curses. Four burly watchmen, armed with halberds and daggers, sprang from a sally port in the wall, seizing the reins of the coach. The horses stopped.

"No one is allowed through here," the captain declared, pointing to the studded oak gates. "By the grace of God, Gloucester is free of pestilence. We do not want outsiders bringing corruption to our city."

Jerome could see the gates and the barbican were a formidable defence. But the Pestilence conquered by stealth. Stone walls and bolted gates were no barrier to malevolence.

Beyssac climbed into the box seat alongside Jerome. His heart was set on visiting Gloucester. The Venerable Bede called Gloucester the most blessed town in England. Now, these rustics were thwarting his ambition. Kettle helmets, iron breastplates and chain mail might make them look tough. But they had never faced an angry cardinal before. Beyssac exploded.

"Open the gate, you pompous, halfwit! I intend to visit the Abbey of St Peter this morning and the Priory of St Oswald this afternoon. I am on official business. No self-important, jumped-up armed guard, dare block my way. You have a lack of respect and a breathtaking lack of manners."

Beyssac scowled. That should do the trick.

"You're not coming in. It would be the same if you were Pope Urban himself. My orders are to prevent any living creature entering this town. The Pestilence has ravaged Bristol. Thousands of good people have perished. Go and find shelter elsewhere. We don't want plague-ridden foreigners here... And by the way, I have a degree in Moral Philosophy from Peterhouse, Cambridge. It is an esteemed seat of learning. Perhaps it is not known in your country."

Beyssac thought quickly. He was a cardinal. Equivocation came naturally to him.

"I use the word 'halfwit' in its positive sense. I can see you possess the simple, unaffected qualities of an apostle or more likely a saint. When I say 'halfwit' I actually mean a learned man, already halfway to God. You are clearly a disciple of..."

Captain Reeves pressed the blade of his halberd against Beyssac's throat.

"Stop your prattle. This coach is not passing through my gate. I will follow my orders. If you need lodgings, the Bell Tavern in South Gate Street, is respectable. It's clean and the landlord is honest. As a last resort, you might find refuge at St Kyneburgh's Chapel. It's a place conducive to Christian reflection."

"God be with you," Beyssac whispered. Captain Reeves had prevailed. A visit to Gloucester was not possible until the Pestilence had gone.

Without complaint, Jerome turned the coach around, heading back along South Gate Street towards St Kynburgh's Chapel. Beyssac's face oozed spiritual defeat. His authority crushed, he pondered the English and their disrespect. Culture and elegance were as alien to them as pearls before swine. The Normans had attempted to dispel English barbarism but to no avail. Deep-rooted Anglo-Saxon savagery, would take centuries to reverse.

Lost in reflection, Beyssac contemplated his dilemma. Ideas reverberated through his mind. He would not accept being humiliated by a student from an inferior university. Such disrespect was insulting. After much thought, logic provided the answer. He laughed exultantly before mellowing into a derisive smile. Peterhouse College? A university, morally degenerate, academically dubious and culturally decadent. Eyes twinkling like advent candles, Beyssac enjoyed his victory.

Jerome guided the horses along South Gate Street, carefully avoiding a deep pothole and skirting around a group of beggars, arguing over a rotting sheep's carcass. Another hundred yards on, he reined in the horses and stopped the coach. They were astonished by what they saw.

Set back from the street, behind a low wall, the sunshine revealed St Kyneburgh's Chapel. At its east end, a gold dome stretched towards the clouds. At right angles, the north and south walls formed a cross decorated with stained-glass windows celebrating St Kyneburgh's life. Inside the chapel, feminine voices confirmed the Dominican nuns were engaged in Holy Mass.

Entranced, Beyssac jumped down, rubbing his eyes in disbelief. Antoine and Jerome, perched on the box seat, sat in silence, mouths open. A chorus of exuberant birds reinforced the moment.

"We have found Eden," whispered Beyssac. "This must be the most peaceful place on Earth."

Beyssac took delight in sharing his knowledge. He could not restrain himself.

"Kyneburgh was a Saxon princess who fled from an arranged marriage. She found refuge in the home of a Gloucester baker. The baker's wife, jealous of Kyneburgh's piety, cut off Kyneburgh's head, throwing her body down a well. It is said, Kyneburgh's separated head spoke out, asking God to forgive the murderous wife. Her story teaches us to forgive our enemies, not destroy them. A salutary lesson for us all."

Beyssac stroked the palm of his scorched hand. It was raw. The wyvern burned into his skin seemed the grotesque symbol of an evil faction. But this was an idyllic spot. They were thirty miles from

Hereford. Two more days and they could celebrate Mass in Hereford Cathedral. At this moment, inspired by St Kyneburgh's, it was God's will he should be happy.

Throwing open the window of her study, Beatrice, the Dominican prioress of St Kyneburgh, was not happy. The plague had killed two sisters this week. Their deaths had caused much distress amongst the other nuns. Now, without her sanction, three men were sitting around a campfire on the chapel green, brazenly eating breakfast. Around their feet, a baby boy giggled and rolled in the grass. A coach was parked against the wall. Horses roamed freely around the green, grazing and emptying their bowels wherever they pleased.

This was an affront to her authority. Adjusting her scapular and smoothing her mantle, Beatrice threw open the door. Hospitality was a characteristic of the Dominicans but these strangers were downright rude. The chapel was a House of God, not a watering hole for reprobates.

Beatrice marched over, walking quickly, examining their faces and noting their clothes. Without doubt, foreigners. The little man with the broad-brimmed hat appeared to be in charge. The other two, wearing fake smiles, looked like common thieves, fresh out of prison. As for the baby, it was probably a waif or foundling. Beatrice fixed her eyes on Beyssac.

"You have no right to camp here. This is a religious community. Not a tavern or an area set aside for orgiastic debauchery. I advise you to leave immediately or I will call the nightwatchmen to eject you from this most holy place."

At that moment, pulling a determined face, Sebastian filled his nappy with the loudest, most foul-smelling explosion of faeces, those present had ever heard. Or smelled.

"Good boy," said Antoine proudly. "That'll be the pottage. Perhaps I included too much dandelion root but people say it prevents pestilence and promotes digestion. I won't add so much to our next meal."

Wallowing in his culinary expertise and impressed by Sebastian's noisy evacuation, Antoine picked up the baby, holding him at arm's length. Sebastian's nappy needed changing.

Horrified and nauseated by Sebastian's anal outrage, Beatrice, Beyssac and Jerome held their noses. Beyssac was reminded of the Bible's description of Hell as a lake of burning sulphur. Jerome recalled mucking out a particularly loathsome smelling stable. While Beatrice, shaking her head in disbelief, likened Sebastian's offering, to the putrid smell rising from a plague pit. A baby's bottom had polluted a holy place.

Beyssac stood up. Discourtesy was alien to him. A disarming smile billowed across his face.

"Jerome, miserable wretch. Restrain the horses and get them under harness. Those brutes should not be running wild. I do not want the prioress to think we are savages."

Beatrice relaxed. Her mood softened. Perhaps she misjudged the strangers. An articulate gentleman, accompanied by two servants with a coach and six horses. That did not suggest a gang of desperate cutthroats. They were visitors not vagabonds. Reassured, Beatrice smiled, her blue eyes sparkling like star sapphires.

Beyssac felt unusually flustered. Such a beatific expression, complemented by an angelic demeanour. It could only mean one thing. He was in the presence of a living saint.

"I am Beatrice, Prioress of St Kyneburgh. This is a Dominican convent, devoted to serving the people of Gloucester. We are friends to all who acknowledge Jesus as their saviour."

"Then you can be sure, that I, Cardinal Beyssac, confidante of Pope Innocent, is your friend. Thomas Aquinas reminds us friendship is the source of the greatest pleasure. For without friends, the most agreeable pursuits are tedious."

"You have studied Thomas Aquinas?"

"Like a ravenous man devouring food. As a novice, Thomas was my guiding light. Without him, Darkness would prevail."

Beatrice was impressed. Dismal experience persuaded her most men were heartless rogues. But Beyssac seemed different. He was authentic. His pomposity was genuine.

"Good sir. I was deluded as to your purpose. I judged your party to be miscreants, intent on felony. Unfortunately, the pestilence has undermined manners and boosted suspicion. Fear is now the people's currency."

"You have nothing to fear. We are pilgrims en route to Hereford, eager to worship at the tomb of St Thomas Cantilupe. We were forbidden to enter Gloucester so we made camp on chapel green. It's a location which animates the senses and enriches the soul. I do hope we have your permission to stay."

"Of course," said Beatrice warmly. "But on one condition. You must attend my study and take breakfast with me. I am keen to hear of your experiences in England... And keen to learn why you have a wyvern burned into your hand."

Beatrice turned, walking quickly back to the chapel. Beyssac followed a few steps behind. He sensed she had something important to say.

Morning sunlight flooded the room illuminating the stained glass, sending lustrous colours across the bookshelves. An aroma of vellum and old leather hung in the air. The wisdom of Aristotle, Ovid, Bede and Thomas Aquinas was all there. Beyssac considered he was in Paradise — an academic Elysium for scholars striving to understand the world.

Beatrice's study was a long table under a window in a corner of the scriptorium. Three rows of trestle tables and benches faced the door. Bookshelves and cupboards lined the walls. Goose quills, inks and pumice stones for smoothing parchment, were neatly arranged on a shelf.

Beyssac sat at the table, savouring his bread and Gloucester cheese. Beatrice sat opposite, picking at a crust of dark rye, occasionally slipping a nugget between her prim lips. She was eager to tell Beyssac what she knew. But decorum must be observed. She must wait until he was ready. Self-control came easily to her. She waited patiently, watching him enjoy his breakfast. Until at last, Beyssac scooped up the remaining crumbs of cheese, swallowed hard and wiped his mouth. Beatrice could not hold back.

"Let me see your wound," she said abruptly.

Beyssac pulled up his sleeve, stretching out his fingers to show the burned palm. Beatrice winced. There could be no doubt. Beyssac had been sentenced to death.

"The crude nature of your wound suggests it was inflicted and not received accidentally. I think you were assaulted and deliberately disfigured."

"Yes," said Beyssac. "Dionisia, the woman who did this, appeared unstable, almost delusional."

"Fanatical, would be a more accurate word," said Beatrice.

"Are you suggesting Dionisia was a zealot?"

"Absolutely," said Beatrice. Leaning forward, she pointed. "You have been targeted by the Wyvern Ring for execution. When they succeed, your head will be severed from your body and silver pennies placed on your eyelids. Decapitation is their trademark. Another corpse to add to the pile."

Gulping down a mouthful of water, Beyssac had time to make sense of Beatrice's revelation. He and his companions were being hunted by a clandestine sect, determined to kill them. The Wyvern Ring? Who were they? What was their motivation for a campaign of bloody murder? Beatrice looked so demure, virtually saint-like beneath her wimple. How did an innocent Dominican prioress acquire this knowledge? Despite the water, Beyssac's throat stayed dry.

"What do these people want?" said Beyssac bemusedly. "What could inspire such fury?"

Beatrice squeezed her hands together. The interwoven fingers confirmed her unease. Beyssac deserved an answer. Surrounded by books, heavy with the wisdom of great minds, she felt contemptible. It seemed improper to be the bearer of bleak tidings in this blessed place. But the truth must out. She spoke slowly, angrily.

"In 1066, Harold, the last Englishman to be king of England, was killed and this country colonised by invaders. Saxon culture was destroyed by a gang of mercenaries who made it viciously clear, they were now in charge. The English people were enslaved by a feudal system which kept them in thrall to a pitiless enemy. There seemed no likelihood the English could escape oppression. Only the prospect of endless servitude and exploitation… until, the Wyvern Ring."

Beyssac nodded. He had made the connection. "The movement took its name from the symbol on Harold's flag at Hastings. In 1066, the battle was lost. But for the Wyvern Ring, the war still goes on."

"Yes, until once again, an English king sits upon an English throne." Beatrice sounded wistful.

Beyssac narrowed his eyes. He was puzzled.

"What prompted the Wyvern Ring to resume its campaign?"

"England is in turmoil. The plague has demolished deference. Peasants openly defy their masters. In many places, law and order have completely broken down. The Wyvern Ring see England in 1360 as a country ready for revolution."

Beyssac considered for a moment, waving his hand dismissively.

"A gang of outlaws, deluded by a grandiose fantasy, cannot dethrone a monarch. King Edward is damnable but he holds supreme power in England. He is not in danger."

Beatrice rolled her eyes, piqued by Beyssac's disdain.

"You underestimate the Wyvern Ring. Its disciples are motivated by an inextinguishable hatred. They are utterly ruthless in pursuit of their prey. King Edward is marked for execution. Once a victim is selected for assassination, death is certain. The Wyvern Ring has a perfect record of dispatching its enemies. Thousands of foreigners and English collaborators have been killed. It is known ten kings of England, met their deaths at the hands of the Wyvern Ring."

Beyssac crossed his arms, shaking his head in disagreement. He had never heard such nonsense. Beatrice was the embodiment of Christian truth but the supposed murder of ten English kings by a fanatical Anglo-Saxon gang was clearly illogical. It was a fireside yarn, a flight of fancy dreamed up by impotent peasants yearning for their freedom. A prioress must be circumspect and not encourage such wild stories.

"A tale more mythical than rational," Beyssac insisted. "It reminds me of King Arthur and Robin Hood. The English have immersed themselves in legends to disguise their inferiority."

Beatrice scowled. Beyssac and his companions might be murdered at any moment. Pompous levity would not save their lives. Belittling the English was a stupid thing to do. Beyssac's comments demanded a rebuke.

"Do you regard the Venerable Bede, England's greatest historian, as inferior?"

"No."

"Or William of Malmesbury? Perhaps the most learned man in Christendom?"

"No."

"Just how inferior is Alexander Neckham? Many scholars consider him England's most distinguished thinker!"

Abashed, Beyssac shuffled in his seat. Maybe he had been disparaging but his analysis was correct.

"I admire those men and salute their achievements. My comment was a judgement on the dull-witted English multitude."

Beatrice gasped, amazed by the arrogance of this ignorant foreigner. He needed to be told.

"A multitude whose disciples are adept at murder and devious enough to assassinate ten kings of England. I think you should listen."

Beyssac leant forward, brow furrowed. A prioress had a right to be heard.

"For a time, Hereward led the resistance movement, killing many Normans, causing grievous destruction to the invaders. But it did not last. Betrayed by a collaborator, Hereward was butchered by a Norman death squad. All seemed lost, English hopes totally dashed until the emergence of a group of ardent patriots. The Wyvern Ring. William the Bastard was its first prominent victim."

"The Chronicles are adamant. William died in an accident, thrown from his horse."

"The Chronicles are false. They are lies to safeguard Williams legacy. Yes, William was thrown from his horse and was recovering. Until a disciple of the Wyvern Ring stepped in. William the Bastard, this country's most ferocious enemy, was strangled in his bed. He died at the convent of St Gervais in Rouen. His death was a day of rejoicing for the English. Without doubt, Hell was made more foul by his presence."

Beyssac folded his arms across his chest. He was not convinced by Beatrice's narrative. It sounded apocryphal. A story invented to please those who hated William. He had countless enemies. It was predictable such loathing would evolve into an old wives' tale.

"Your lips are silent but your eyes scream disbelief. Hear me out. Remember, it is the winners who write the Chronicles. Bear that in mind."

Beyssac nodded, breaking into a broad, engaging smile. Beatrice was providing him with an alternative education. This nonsense would allow him to dine out for years at no expense.

Beatrice returned his smile. Her enthusiastic account suggested support for the extremists. Beyssac quickly thrust the idea from his mind. Beatrice required his full attention. He leant forward.

"William Rufus did not die in a hunting accident. A monarch, bestial and abhorrent to God, he was executed by a disciple of the Wyvern Ring. A just reward for his immorality and abuse of the English people."

Beyssac bowed his head, encouraging Beatrice to continue her fantastic story. Her intensity seemed heartfelt.

"Food poisoning caused by eating a surfeit of lampreys? A Norman fabrication. Henry I, the most dissolute king ever inflicted upon England, was dispatched by a Saxon cook and a dish sprinkled with wolfsbane. It kills in seconds. Henry did not suffer. More's the pity."

Beyssac stroked his chin, mulling over Beatrice's lurid story. There was no disputing her sincerity. If her narrative was correct, the Wyvern Ring was prepared to eliminate any opponent. He needed to find out more.

"You mentioned ten kings?"

Beatrice shrugged her shoulders. It was a grim story but entirely true. Beatifically closing her eyes, she resumed her narrative.

"The Wyvern Ring has attempted many times to end Norman tyranny. Some kings, like John, have survived multiple assassination attempts. But in the end, all those sentenced to death by a native English court, have been executed."

So, England has two systems of justice?"

"Yes. Natural justice which protects the birthright of the righteous. And Norman justice which is designed to subjugate every Saxon and destroy liberty."

Eyes tightly shut, struggling to control her anger, Beatrice articulated her contempt.

"Forced to bow down before a 'sovereign', the English do not have a 'prayer'. 'Accused' of 'crime', they are 'sentenced' by a French judge and must submit to 'punishment'. English speakers cannot hope for 'mercy' or 'charity'. 'Obedience' is the name of the game."

"So it follows, the Norman kings, our oppressors, must forfeit their lives?"

"Yes. Absolutely. Let me complete the litany of executions. Then you will understand."

"You have my full attention," said Beyssac. She deserved to be indulged.

"Stephen, the most foolish king in Christendom, killed at Dover Priory. His throat slit. Henry II, murderer of Thomas Becket, poisoned… Richard, so called Lionheart. A man devoted to lustful abominations, dispatched by a crossbow bolt… John, confirmed atheist and cruel dictator, poisoned by English plums laced with wolfsbane… Henry III, blaspheming, Jew baiter, killed by a single sword thrust… Edward Longshanks, hard hearted, vicious tyrant, strangled in his bed… Edward II, a man consumed by abnormal passions, his body lies in Gloucester Abbey… skewered in his fundament. All decapitated, silver pennies left in their mutilated eye sockets… Just like Bishop Trilleck."

Beyssac gulped. His eyes widened. His mouth fell open. He must have misheard. Bishop Trilleck murdered? The sole purpoe of his mission to Hereford was to investigate Trilleck's conduct, censure him if necessary and re-establish the authority of the Catholic Church. Trilleck's ineptitude had turned the diocese of Hereford into a laughing stock. But murdered? The killing of a bishop not only marked the death of a pious man but was an assault on Christianity itself. The Christian religion was under attack from God's most vicious adversary. The Devil, in the guise of the Wyvern Ring.

"Bishop Trilleck murdered?" Beyssac's voice faltered. His throat, dry as parchment.

"Murdered in his own palace," said Beatrice, shaking her head resignedly. "Lewis Charleton has been nominated and accepted. Hereford will have a new bishop very soon."

Beyssac looked away, running his eyes along the bookshelves. *A Life of Saint Wilfrid.* Numerous works by the Venerable Bede. Aristotle's *Categories. The Riddles of Aldhel. The Story of Eadric Silvaticus.* The chapel was a place, brimful with the wisdom of great minds. But immune from the actual concerns of everyday life. Beyond its precincts, lay a world ravaged by pestilence and murder.

Beyssac turned to face Beatrice. Such a compelling countenance. He must ask.

"Your familiarity with the activities of the Wyvern Ring, a group swathed in secrecy and violence, seems rather astonishing for a prioress leading a Christian community. How did you acquire this intimate knowledge?"

Beatrice, eyes burning like star sapphire, leant forward, clasping Beyssac's wounded hand. Sharp fingernails pierced the healing flesh. Beyssac winced. Beatrice exhaled deeply.

"My knowledge is based on abject experience. I have kept this secret for nearly twenty years. I've lost count of the nights I cried myself to sleep or whispered prayers to an indifferent God. I have to tell you now. I was once a trusted disciple... of the Wyvern Ring."

In an instant, Heaven became Hell. Demons filled St Kyneburgh. Beyssac dreaded the unquenchable fire which he knew would descend upon the chapel, devouring the whole community. As a Catholic cardinal, Beyssac was fixed in his belief, a murderer cannot gain eternal life. Beatrice was damned.

She sobbed. Impious tears rolled down her face, splashing onto the table. She wept, gasping intermittently, struggling to explain the circumstances which brought her to this crisis.

"My father, Morcar, is an elder of the Wyvern Ring. A member of the Inner Council. I was brought up to despise our oppressors. Every day, I watched them imperiously looking down on the subjugated English from the walls of their confiscated manor houses. My hatred was nurtured, shaped, polished to perfection. I killed Normans, mutilated them, waded in their blood. My conscience was clear. I slept the sleep of the righteous. Until one day I was ordered to execute a collaborator, a Benedictine monk, living at Leominster Priory. He begged for his life. In all my dreams, I see his pleading face. The blade of an axe sent him to God's embrace. That murder changed everything. I became repulsed by the bloodletting. I fled from my family and eventually found solace at St Kyneburgh. My father has disowned me. He considers me as good as dead. In his eyes, I have been lifted out of the stream of life. Will God forgive me?"

Petite hands covering her face, overwhelmed by memories. Beatrice retreated into the nightmare swirling around in her head. Steeped in pity for a lost soul, Beyssac stood up.

"Only God can forgive you. I am a man of God, not God himself. Confess your sins, follow the example of St Dominic and pray with unrelenting determination. God always listens. But He does not always answer."

Beyssac left the scriptorium, quietly closing the heavy door behind him. He did not see Beatrice reach into the cupboard on the wall. A lead crucifix and a small, green bottle. The vial containing wolfsbane was there. She grasped the bottle. Now, she would find peace.

Antoine and Jerome were stunned by Beyssac's revelation. St Kyneburgh seemed an idyllic spot. The gold dome promised protection and peace. Beyssac had yearned for a profound experience, to find spiritual nourishment amidst the devastation of the Pestilence.

As Jerome steered the coach on to South Gate Street, Beyssac struggled with regrets. They were forbidden to visit the abbey of St Peter and denied the privilege of worshipping at St Oswald's Priory. Most of all, he regretted his encounter with Beatrice. He knew he could not help her.

Chapter Seventeen

Butcher's Row, Hereford. A dark, cloudless night. The third- floor meeting room is bolted from inside. Wulfstan, the Black Monk, stands, his back against the door. He holds a candle, revealing a room packed with disciples of the Wyvern Ring. Wulfstan licks his lips, impatient to speak.

"Saxons. Today, on the anniversary of his death, we celebrate the life of Eadric Silvaticus, the brave earldorman who masterminded the uprising and refused to yield to Norman iniquity. This is the man whose army stormed Hereford Castle. A potent symbol of foreign oppression. This is the man who burned Shrewsbury to the ground in a fight to the death with our enemies. And this is the man murdered by Normans. Does he deserve our respect?"

"Yes!" roared a hundred voices. A crescendo of approval, nods of assent, cheers, handclaps, gruff voices gushing praise, stamping feet, a tumult of reverence. The room shook. Adulation reverberated around the walls like thunder. Eadric, an inspirational beacon of resistance. In the hearts and minds of the Wyvern Ring, only Harold deserved more esteem.

Wulfstan beamed, elated by the reaction to his speech. Zealots united in a common cause. A powerful movement, impossible to stop. Morcar nodded in appreciation, acknowledging Wulfstan's oratory. Now, it was Morcar's turn. Wulfstan handed him the candle. In seconds, the room was silent. Morcar eager to castigate the enemy.

"An indomitable spirit. Courage. Cunning. Vigilance. And in the end. Adamantine resolve. These are the qualities I demand of each of you in this room. Our moment has arrived. God's chosen people are ready to destroy their oppressors. The Pestilence has made England ungovernable. Norman law and order cannot be enforced. Hereford is in turmoil. Bishop Trilleck, the Norman sycophant, has been hurried to Hell by an English axe. Now, our agents report Cardinal Beyssac will arrive in Hereford in two days. Let him come. The execution of a cardinal will be palpable evidence of our power. All English men and women will rise up and support our cause. Beyssac's death will affirm our freedom. And astonish the world!"

The candle flame lit up the room. But the fire in Morcar's words ignited an inferno. The Wyvern Ring seemed unstoppable. With one voice, its disciples rejoiced.

"When God wills, may the end be good. Rise up and drench our land with Norman blood!"

Morcar resumed the council of war. Only when dawn broke, sending shafts of sunlight into every secret place, did the disciples slip out of the meeting room and head home. All the disciples, except for Alitha.

Six watchmen patrolled the area between Butcher's Row and the Castle Ditch. Not wishing to be stopped and face awkward questions, Alitha remained alert, dodging into doorways, skilfully concealing herself from prying eyes. Silent as cats' paws, she tiptoed along Cabbage Lane before sprinting down Canons Street and crossing over to St Ethelbert's Well. No one had seen her. Hereford, in the grip of pestilence, was quiet as a pauper's grave.

Alitha knelt down beside the well. Scooping up a handful of water, she sipped. Cold and clear. It quenched her thirst. But strengthened her resolve. This was a hallowed place — a fitting tribute to a martyred Saxon king. Unlike Hereford Cathedral, a mansion of superstition, an intimidating symbol of Norman rule.

Alitha kissed her amethyst ring. She would kill Beyssac. She craved the honour. Beyssac stood for everything she despised. Her personified Norman tyranny. His death would enable the English to break free and regain their birthright. It would be a privilege to be his executioner.

She pulled up her hood, gathering her distinctive red hair to the nape of her neck. Her face could not be seen. Intense brown eyes surveyed the streets for signs of life. Hereford was still asleep. It would not take long to reach the Saracen's Head and slip quietly into bed.

Chapter Eighteen

Cardinal Beyssac closed his eyes. It was warm inside the coach but the constant jolting made sleep impossible. Besides, he had too much on his mind, to relax. He and his companions were the target of a cabal of merciless killers. Now, every stranger was a potential assassin. The milestone indicated Hereford was just twenty miles away. A short journey. But one likely to be fraught with danger and dark predicaments.

The plan was to avoid Newent and spend the night in Gorsley. Jerome heard Newent was overwhelmed by pestilence. Hundreds of townspeople had died and the Benedictines at St Mary's Church had run away certain Newent was being punished for its wickedness. A night spent in Gorsley would circumvent the Pestilence and allow them to arrive in Hereford the next day.

But their plan to reach Hereford assumed Jerome would find the most straightforward route. By steering clear of Newent, Jerome inadvertently guided the coach into a labyrinth of bridleways, trails and faint tracks. Dense woodland and impenetrable gorse bush made progress frustratingly slow.

By early evening, after crossing the Ell Brook three times via the same ford, Jerome admitted he was lost. Worried about what to do next, he did not notice the dark figure hiding amongst the ash trees. Nor did he catch sight of the raised dagger, gleaming in the twilight.

Antoine lifted the canopy. Jerome had stopped the coach. A worried look etched on his face. Jerome let the reins slip from his grasp, nervously rubbing his head. Aware of Jerome's distress, Antoine sat alongside him on the box seat. Berating Jerome would only make matters worse. After overcoming so many dangers, it would be stupid to start bickering. Antoine smiled, squeezing Jerome's arm.

"We can rest here and have supper. Blundering around these woods at night, is foolhardy. I'll whip up a stew while you tend to the horses. The cardinal can change Sebastian's nappy. In view of our situation, wiping a baby's bottom is not beneath his dignity. It's a rite of back passage, so to speak."

A diffident smile. A nod of warm gratitude. Jerome jumped off the coach and began to inspect the horses. They were tired and mud splashed. But thankfully, no injuries.

Whereas, events inside the coach had become perilous. Beyssac's cultured world of theological argument and papal politics was falling apart, undermined by the Herculean task of changing a nappy.

Sebastian understood the rules. The more he twisted, turned and flailed his arms, the more the man in the big hat shouted and became exasperated. It was good fun. Sebastian even heard words he did not know existed.

Frustrated and ham fisted, Beyssac's spiritual realm of cold celibacy had not prepared him for the real world. Nevertheless, once he reminded himself he was a cardinal of the Catholic Church, he continued unabashed.

"Keep those legs still!" he barked. "You are headstrong and disobliging. There is no place in Heaven for a naughty child."

Outside the coach, Antoine crouched by the fire, sprinkling herbs into the pot, mixing the stew with a spoon. Jerome was brushing the horses and inspecting their hooves. But whenever their eyes met, they collapsed, clutching their bellies, convulsed with laughter. Beyssac's logic versus Sebastian's high spirits was not an even contest. Beyssac didn't stand a chance.

"Fiend! Consider your predicament! You must submit to my wishes or remain naked before God. Why are you so defiant?"

Sebastian exhaled, blowing bubbles of saliva into the air. He watched them float around the coach before they burst, showering Beyssac's face with a veil of slobber.

"Hell hound! You will not get the better of me!"

With a prodigious effort, Beyssac avoided Sebastian's flailing arms and kicking feet, managing to wrap a cloth around his groin. Sebastian whimpered, upset at being outsmarted by the fat man in the big hat.

"Now, you little goblin. I order you to go straight to sleep. Your obstinacy has left me drained. In truth, I have cast out devils from a Mother Superior and exorcised spirits from a demon-infested cathedral.

But neither caused me as much distress as your nappy. Close your eyes and pray to God to spare your soul. I believe you are possessed by a malevolent spirit."

As Beyssac emerged from the coach, he vowed he would never again attempt to change a nappy. It was undignified and degrading for a man of his importance to engage in such activity. Nowhere in Holy Writ does it state Jesus saw fit to clothe a baby's bottom. So, why should a cardinal? Beyssac held up his bowl. Antoine filled it with warm, vegetable stew. The seasoning — parsley, bay and thyme — reminded Beyssac of home.

Antoine's stew was delicious. Beyssac's mood improved. Antoine believed that enjoying good food, on a summer's evening, would provide fulfilment for even the most jaded palate.

When he had finished, Beyssac put down his bowl, patting his stomach contentedly.

"Antoine. That was wonderful. A whole chapter in *Le Viandier* should be devoted to your epicurean cooking. That was the best meal I've ever had."

Antoine stopped eating. "That sounds like a compliment. I'll take it as such. But what is *Le Viandier*?

Beyssac's lips curled into a smile. The condescending look of the haughty academic.

"*Le Viandier* is the most celebrated cookbook in the world. Its author, Guillaume Tirel, is a close friend of mine. The Duke of Normandy will not eat a meal unless it is prepared by Tirel. On our return to France, I will take you to meet him."

Jerome monitored their conversation. He was being ignored, excluded as usual, from cheerful matters. Had they forgotten, if it wasn't for him, the expedition would have ended in disaster months ago?

"What about me?" asked Jerome. "I would also like to meet Monsieur Tirel. My culinary skills are basic. I would value his instruction."

"Yes," said Beyssac. "You can join us. I'm sure his book includes an excellent recipe for horsemeat."

Antoine dropped his bowl, staring at Beyssac in astonishment. What a cruel thing to say to a man who loved horses and had devoted his life to them. Undoubtedly Beyssac was studious and academic. But at times, he was just plain stupid.

Jerome stood up. His mood darker than the shadows enveloping the wood. Tears in his eyes, he trudged off into the night.

Antoine watched Jerome until he was out of sight, swallowed by the trees. Deep in the wood, a resentful owl screeched in defence of its territory. Antoine turned, gesturing with his spoon.

"Cardinal, I must speak. Jerome may be timid and deferential. But he is a good man. Moreover, he loves horses and is superb at handling them. Your remark about horsemeat caused him much pain. Can't you see his distress?"

Beyssac would not accept being scolded. Least of all by Antoine. A mere cook! The cardinal folded his arms, narrowing his eyes into a scowl.

"Heed the Scriptures! God insists human beings have dominion over all creatures on Earth. Are you denying the word of God?"

"No," said Antoine quickly. Beyssac was devious. In any dispute, if victory was in doubt, he would counter-attack with an insinuation of atheism. It was a master stroke. It guaranteed he always won the argument.

"I would never contradict God. I just want you to understand how Jerome feels. The idea of consuming a Camargue or banqueting on a Barb, is repulsive to him. It would break his heart to think of a horse as the main ingredient of a casserole."

Beyssac shook his head. "Jerome is too thin skinned. But on reflection… and we must have a coach driver… I concede my comment was somewhat indelicate. When he returns, I will extend him my wise counsel. I do not expect him to grovel. An apology will do. The sooner, the better."

Beyond the warmth of the fire, past the boundary of its burning light, creatures of the wood moved stealthily, stalking their prey. The darkness concealed a multitude of vicious presences. But only one was wearing a red hat and carrying a dagger.

The moonlight confirmed the horses were safe. Estienne, the chestnut was asleep, whickering and twitching, dreaming of mountains of hay and buckets of juicy apples. Hippocrates, astute as ever, was wide awake on guard.

154

Jerome ran his fingers down Hippocrates' neck. Beyssac had made a thoughtless remark. Killing a horse was tantamount to murder. But to eat the flesh was an act of utter depravity. The behaviour of a blood-swilling savage. He had changed his mind. He did not want to meet Monsieur Tirel. That man was an advocate of equine slaughter!

Jerome continued to stroke Hippocrates' neck. Each delicate caress repaid by a warm tongue licking the top of his bald head. Jerome relaxed, nuzzling closer to Hippocrates, mulling over possibilities, trying to decide what to do next. 'All shall be well, all shall be well and all manner of things shall be well.' Comforting words from his childhood. Jerome decided to act.

Quick as a whip, Jerome unhitched the halter, leading Hippocrates through the trees, past the overhanging branches, in the direction of their camp. Beyssac must be made to respect horses and understand their temperament. One day, a horse might earn his esteem.

Jerome stopped. He pulled Hippocrates close. Raised voices. The smell of Antoine's vegetable stew. A baby whimpering. The blade of a knife glinting in the moonlight. Jerome dropped behind a bush. Hippocrates stood still, silent and obedient. Both transfixed by what they saw.

The campfire revealed a nightmarish sight. Antoine and Beyssac, heads bowed, hands tied behind their back, were kneeling in front of the coach. A powerfully built man, brandishing a dagger, stood over them. His face gnarled with scorn, he taunted his prisoners, pinching their noses, pulling their ears and repeatedly drawing his dagger across their throats. Sebastian, bewildered and afraid, was crawling under the coach.

Tom Gascoigne pointed with his dagger. His voice was cold, matter of fact.

"You have been found guilty by a People's Court and sentenced to death."

Antoine raised his head.

"Guilty of what crime?"

"The subjugation of the English people. You support and are complicit in, persecution and oppression. Your presence in this country is a threat to our cause. Therefore, you must be eliminated. I will be your executioner."

155

Beyssac winced, aghast at his cruel logic.

"You are a member of the Wyvern Ring?"

"A disciple. Our cause is holy. You will depart this life knowing you were dispatched by an elite organisation."

Antoine nodded derisively.

"An amoral gang of murderers, would be a better description. Did you kill the family at the Seven Stars tavern?"

Tom ran his finger along the blade of his dagger. Drops of blood splashed onto his boots.

"The plan was to ambush you at the tavern. The landlord and his family were an obstacle to my preparations. They deserved their fate. They were collaborators, sycophantic to the Normans. Traitors to their own country."

The wound on Beyssac's palm was still sore. The dragon red and vexatious. He yearned to know.

"Dionisia. Is she a disciple?"

Tom closed his eyes.

"She was a disciple. But she failed our cause. It was fitting she took her own life."

Desolate, Beyssac whispered a silent prayer, asking God to forgive Dionisia and Beatrice, two hapless women caught up in evil beyond their control. They needed Beyssac's ministration not condemnation. Now, only God could help them. Surely, He would judge their mental instability to be an affliction, not a sin?

Antoine's thoughts were not so exalted, twisting his hands behind his back, straining to break free. Common sense suggested, to stay alive, they must keep Tom talking. But they were powerless. At the mercy of a maniac, hell-bent on cutting off their heads. His serrated dagger, blood trickling down its blade, was a gruesome sight. Neither Antoine or Beyssac, were ready to die. And more importantly, nor was Sebastian.

Drained by the journey and his battle with Beyssac, Sebastian was sleeping under the coach. His stomach gurgled. He sniffed, wrinkling his nose. A robin, perched high up in the trees, performed an insistent lullaby. Sebastian was enjoying the blissful sleep of a tired baby.

"And Sebastian?" asked Antoine. "Is he also on your death list?"

Solemn faced, Tom shook his head. He considered himself a specialist in assassination, a legitimate agent of retribution, not an amateur ready to kill anyone who crossed his path. Antoine didn't understand.

"Sebastian is a Saxon baby. Not a wretched, Norman waif. He will be spared and given to an English family to raise as their own. Little ones like him are this country's future. I wish him no harm. But as for you, Cardinal Beyssac, it is now the appointed time."

Holding his dagger with two hands, Tom positioned the blade against Beyssac's neck. Finding the most propitious place on the neck, to sever the head from the body, was important. Multiple blows would be messy. As Beyssac closed his eyes, Antoine fixed his gaze on Sebastian. At least the baby would survive.

Jerome rubbed his head vigorously as he watched the atrocious scene unfold. His legs were paralysed. But his mind was racing. Antoine and Beyssac were about to be murdered. If he did not run away, he would be next.

He could not abandon his friends. Yes, he loved Hippocrates and could boast of a unique bond with horses. But the pilgrimage to Hereford had fostered in him a compassion for humans as well as animals. He had witnessed too much suffering to remain unmoved. St Jerome, after whom he was named, had gained the trust of a lion by healing its paw. Faith had conquered fear. God had promised believers, "Do not be frightened. Do not be dismayed. For I am always with you.'

Jerome stopped rubbing his head. Now was the moment. Clicking his tongue, Jerome stroked Hippocrates neck, pulling down on the halter. Stretching up, he whispered the words confirming their friendship. "Two into one."

Hippocrates raised his head, flattening his ears, fixing his eyes on Tom Gascoigne. Jerome jumped on Hippocrates' back, controlling him with his legs. Two into one, determined on a single purpose. Nostrils flaring, Hippocrates charged.

Hooves pounding, branches snapping, a black, snorting silhouette, rearing and trampling, eyes rolling white, strong teeth biting, frothing at the mouth.

A resisting arm, raised but broken like a twig. Screams and gasps. Red hooves stamping on bones cracking beneath the onslaught. A torn, red felt hat. A bloody body, trodden into the forest floor.

Tom Gascoigne, his face smashed beyond recognition, was dead. The contented robin, satisfied the clamour had ended, resumed his song. Jerome, boots and hands blotched with blood, slumped down onto the warm, wet grass. Hippocrates stood quite still. His champagne coat, now a different colour.

Chapter Nineteen

The Pestilence killed thousands. People died in agony, unable to make sense of their fate. Death made no distinction. The anguish was indiscriminate. Dispirited and heartbroken, good people felt forsaken by their God.

As more plague pits were dug and more corpses buried, many citizens were convinced Hereford had reached the lowest point of its suffering. They were certain it was not possible to endure more horror. But they were wrong. In the first week of August, hot, oppressive days, followed by stifling, suffocating nights, Hereford was overwhelmed by a campaign of unbridled murder.

The decapitated head of High Sheriff, Richard Bere, was discovered wedged in the privy at Kinnersley Castle. His body found floating in the fish pond.

Henry Catchpole, MP, was missing from home for two days before a Benedictine monk found Catchpole's head staring at him from amongst the white carnations decorating St Thomas' tomb. Silver pennies replacing his gouged eyes.

But it was the killing of Bartholomew Clerk, the bailiff, which left an indelible impression. His murder passed into folklore, the remembrance of which was used by parents to discipline naughty children.

Bartholomew Clerk, bailiff and principal tax collector, was a middle-aged man of immense girth and even greater wealth. A model of rectitude, apart from insatiable sexual desires which made him a customer of every whorehouse in Hereford. Indeed, on the night he disappeared, he was seen arm in arm with a red- haired woman, sauntering along Widemarsh Street, towards the bowling green. In a city afflicted by pestilence, morality was a subject open to negotiation.

The following day, as dawn threw its first light across the bowling green, players from the two teams walked briskly onto the playing surface. Some were chatting, shielding their eyes or blinking against the sunlight. Others were quiet, determined, full of serious intent. Two teams. The Worshipful Company of Vintners versus the Worshipful Company of Woolmen. The prize? A sumptuous meal at the Green Man tavern.

Then… the horror. As the players selected their bowling balls from the pyramid-shaped pile, one ball fell. But did not roll. It seemed misshapen. Open mouthed, astonished, the severed head of Bartholomew Clerk looked up at the sun. In his eye sockets, two silver pennies reflected the breaking light.

***

The sunlight flooding through the stained-glass windows of the deanery, found Lewis Charleton, bishop designate, kneeling on the floor of his office, eyes closed. Prima, the First Hour, a fixed time of prayer, a confirmation of faith.

"And they that have done good, shall have everlasting life. And they that have done evil, will be thrown into everlasting fire."

Hereford was dissolving into chaos. Its citizens dying in droves, tortured by a pitiless disease. Fervent prayer, the only consolation for those who had lost hope.

Lewis Charleton stood up, eyes still closed. The deep lines etched on his face, testimony to years of despair. He steepled his hands, tapping his lips, considering his situation. There was much to be anxious about.

The Pestilence terrified him. Anyone might fall victim. An exemplary life of pious devotion was no guarantee of immunity. Thousands of dutiful Christians had died. He was worried an attempt might be made to kill him. The Church had tried to conceal the circumstances of Bishop Trilleck's death but the truth had got out. A gang of assassins murdered Trilleck and were now busy slaughtering Hereford's most esteemed citizens. Who was next?

But most of all, he was worried about the fragility of people's faith. Unable to defeat the Pestilence, the Church appeared impotent, almost irrelevant. The authority of the Catholic Church had collapsed. Profanity and atheism were widespread and growing in strength. Without the guidance of the Church, millions would go straight to Hell. God had punished Sodom and Gomorrah for iniquity. Why should Hereford be spared?

For centuries, the cathedral was revered as the heart of a thriving Christian community. A precious stone set in a Catholic see. But now, too feeble to resist the Pestilence, the Catholic faith was being criticised. Rejected by many as powerless. Moreover, the impending arrival of the Pope's envoy, Cardinal Beyssac, only added to Charleton's agitation. A coach emblazoned with a golden lion, had been seen in Mordiford, four miles from the city. No doubt, Beyssac would blame him for Hereford's descent into chaos. Beyssac might even stop him becoming bishop.

Fretting like a condemned man standing under the gallows, Charleton wheezed, his stomach heaving as anxiety knotted his insides. He coughed, trying to clear his throat. With painstaking deliberation, he smoothed the creases from his cassock and wiped the sweat off his tonsured head. In all his sixty years, he had never felt so tense.

He stopped, listening hard. Outside, an escalating commotion. Raised voices. Footsteps rapidly approaching. Protocol consigned to Hell, Beyssac flung open the door, shouting and waving his arms, a raging red tempest in carmine silk.

"God's judgement names you, Canon Charlatan! Hereford is doomed! Its citizens heading for perdition. You alone, are responsible!"

A furious face, irate eyes, wounding words. A barrage of accusations.

"Thousands of Christians face eternal damnation because of your incompetence! Corruption rules here! Such depravity is impossible to match!"

Stunned by Beyssac's whirlwind, Charleton staggered across the room, wringing his hands. Dazed and bewildered, he slumped into a chair. He had expected a squabble, perhaps a difference of opinion. But not this maelstrom of invective.

"You have abdicated your moral duty. This city is rotten to the core. It is lax in faith. And now under threat from a nest of murdering vipers. Remember, Lucifer was banished from Heaven and consigned to Hell for his betrayal. I consider your betrayal, worse!"

Beyssac placed a chair opposite Charleton. Eyeball to eyeball. Knees almost touching. Hereford's bishop designate trembled. His Oxford education, his degree in Theology and his doctorate in Law, hallmarks of distinction behind which he usually felt secure, were no deterrent to Beyssac. The cardinal removed his hat, throwing it on the floor. This theatrical gesture, a sign of his authority. Beyssac wanted the truth.

Charleton shuffled in his chair. It was impossible to find a comfortable position. Beyssac, sitting in silence and staring at him, did not help. Charleton felt like an imprisoned heretic, waiting to be interrogated or even tortured. Beyssac narrowed his eyes.

"The Holy Father is angry. Hereford is not under his control. Citizens are defiant and obstinate in faith. Lollardy and atheism are widespread. John Trilleck, appointed bishop by God, is murdered. These abominations, a source of distress to Pope Innocent and offensive to God, must stop! Tell me, what have you done to defend our Church against wickedness?"

Sweating profusely, Charleton felt ill used. Beyssac's criticism was unfair. The awful situation in Hereford was not his fault. God had unleashed the Pestilence to punish a sinful world. Therefore, a bishop designate could not defeat the Pestilence unless God willed it. And he was not privy to God's wishes. Beyssac's question was unethical. It suggested he lacked moral courage. That was an unforgivable insult.

"Your Eminence. I have done as much as any man," said Charleton timidly.

"What!" Beyssac shouted, wrinkling his nose in disgust. "Bishop Trilleck was incompetent. But he lost his life while engaged upon God's business. He has earned our compassion. There is a place in Heaven reserved for him. I ask you again, what have you done to defend our faith against the dark depravity engulfing this city?"

Charleton raised his eyes to the ceiling.

"I have prayed hard and prayed stubbornly. Every day, I take a moment to implore God to spare this city from the Pestilence and the brutality of those taking advantage of the disorder."

Beyssac shook his head.

"That is not good enough! Your whole life should be one long prayer. Psalm thirty-four tells us, when the righteous cry for help, the Lord will take away their troubles. So, why is the Lord deaf to your cries for help? Simple. Because you are not righteous! I see no light of God in you. I discern only utter corruption."

Charleton closed his eyes. He was reluctant to contradict a cardinal but such scorn was unwarranted. Beyssac needed to be put right.

"Your Eminence. The Christian religion is safe in this city. Moreover, there are more than thirty religious houses in this diocese. The Benedictines have ten, including Leominster Priory, a most holy place, England's own Jerusalem. The Augustinians have eight, with Wigmore much celebrated for its charity. There are Cluniacs at Clifford. The Dominicans and Franciscans have well respected houses not a mile from the cathedral. There are Carmelites and Austin Friars in Ludlow. Is this not proof Hereford remains in awe of God? Does it not confirm, this is an area where virtue prevails?"

Charleton opened his eyes, smiling nervously. Without doubt, the facts confirmed Hereford to be a Christian community. Most people were righteous, striving hard to please God. The cardinal was ignorant.

Beyssac leant forward, shaking his head.

"No! Your words are specious. The evidence you present is a gutless attempt to avoid the truth. Your argument is as diaphanous as a whore's bodice. You leave me no alternative."

Squirming in his chair, Charleton struggled to speak.

"What are you going to do?"

"I have decided to take charge of the cathedral, your errant House of God. You have one hour to convene a meeting of important cathedral officials. This will take place at St Thomas' tomb. I wish to interview the archdeacon, the chancellor, the dean, the precentor, the treasurer and all the canons. I will lead the prayers... And take delight in telling those impostors, they have neglected their duty. As a consequence, God has consigned them all... to the fires of Hell."

"But your Eminence. You are not being fair."

***

The Saracen's Head was noisy, crowded with exuberant drinkers. Fear of the Pestilence had not discouraged those who habitually enjoyed alcoholic refreshment. In fact, the number of customers increased dramatically when the Pestilence got worse.

On this warm, August afternoon, Hereford's most popular tavern was so packed, it was difficult to find a seat. But after some jostling, many oaths and a few icy stares from the regulars, Antoine, Jerome and Sebastian found an empty bench to sit down on.

Brow furrowed, mind absorbed, Antoine considered the matter deeply. He pondered all possibilities and analysed all aspects. He evaluated every opinion and appraised every potential problem. It was a profound truth beyond debate by learned scholars. English beer... and especially that produced by Christian brothers in their abbey brewhouses... was the most sublime liquid with which to satisfy a thirst. Paradise gained for the price of one penny.

Mindful of all the hardships they endured on the journey to Hereford, Antoine vowed to make merry and enjoy his beer. Avoiding summary execution did sharpen one's appetite for life and its pleasures. Undoubtedly, Beyssac would bring the incompetent clergy into line and restore the authority of the Church. The Wyvern Ring had failed in its mission and God willing would never be heard of again. Welcoming and convivial, Antoine considered the Saracen's Head, a happy refuge from a dangerous world.

A woman holding a jug of beer emerged from the throng. Antoine felt an instant attraction. She seemed the epitome of an English rose. Luxuriant red hair, cascading down on to exposed shoulders. And perfect creamy skin, radiant in the afternoon sunlight. She reminded Antoine of a woman he had encountered before. But he could not remember where.

An effortless transformation. Alitha yields to Alice.

"Gentlemen, I see three empty cups, devoid of England's finest brew. This is an immoral act, offensive to God. Are you willing to expiate your sins by consuming prodigious amounts of Benedictine beer?"

"Yes!" said Antoine and Jerome.

"Yeb!" gurgled Sebastian, twisting and wriggling, trying to escape Jerome's grasp.

Alice filled the cups to overflowing. A dark, raisin-coloured brew, its buttery tan head, spuming over the rim of each cup. It smelled like plum pudding.

"This is Hereford's most beautiful beverage," Alice enthused. "Expertly crafted by the monks of St Guthlac's Priory. And only available in this tavern! A divine drink. A restorative, rejuvenating, refreshment. Good enough for anyone. Even foreigners, like you."

A brief moment. Scarcely time to take a breath. Yet time enough for Antoine to sense hostility concealed behind a cheerful façade. Alice smiled. Antoine's insight dimmed, dissolved and vanished. The moment had passed. This lady demanded his attention. Antoine nodded, raising his cup.

"We are pilgrims, keen to worship at the tomb of St Thomas."

"And the baby?"

Jerome held Sebastian close. "This is Sebastian, an English boy rescued from the plague house in Wycombe. His mother is dead."

"English? That is interesting," Alice murmured, lost in thought. "An innocent English baby. And you have travelled from?"

"The court of Pope Innocent at Avignon," proclaimed Antoine, smiling broadly, hoping this beautiful woman would be impressed by his connection to the papacy. Experience had taught him women like to be dazzled.

Alice turned, tilting her head to one side, eyes fixed on Antoine, absorbed by his presence. Gently biting her lips, she smiled.

"Pope Innocent is indeed God's man on Earth. And his cardinals are comrades-in-arms against Satan. I admire any man who devotes his life to the Church and achieves high office. Such men inspire me. I am fascinated by them."

For Antoine, this was an opportunity too good to miss. With dramatic deliberation, he stroked his chin, a caricature of the powerful man mulling over his options, cogitating, deciding what to do. Antoine closed his eyes. But opened them again instantly. A brilliant idea had come to mind. He must share it with her.

"Madame. You have the advantage of me."

"My name is Alice. It's a Celtic name. It means woman of noble birth."

"Madame Alice, noble Alice. I am Antoine and this is my friend Jerome. We are professional gentlemen in the employ of Cardinal Beyssac."

Alice bit her lip, her eyes scrutinising the ceiling in disbelief. She topped up their beer, oblivious to the spillage frothing across the bench.

"So, Cardinal Beyssac is here in Hereford?"

"Yes. At this very moment, he is presiding over a high-level conclave. I'm sure I can arrange for you to meet him. He relies on me for sage advice. In fact, many of my recommendations have been accepted by the Pope himself. I have inspired much papal bull."

"I'm sure you have," Alice nodded. "And if you could arrange a meeting with the cardinal, I would be grateful to you in my own, practical way. Is it wrong, I expect you to satisfy my needs?"

"No. Not at all!" spluttered Antoine, almost choking on his beer.

"No," chimed Sebastian, giggling and kicking his legs.

"No," said Jerome, overwrought, struggling to keep Sebastian under control.

Alice stepped up on to a bench. She surveyed the tavern, the red-haired queen of her kingdom, examining all the faces, taking stock of each group, scowling at those who continued their discussions, frowning at those who dared to maintain whispered exchanges. Silence soon prevailed.

"Ladies and gentlemen. Stay your merrymaking. Today, we are joined in our temple of refreshment, by three pilgrims eager to visit the tomb of St Thomas. They are Antoine, Jerome and baby Sebastian. Their home is Avignon. I'm sure you will afford our guests a genuine Hereford welcome."

Standing up for a better view, the customers' gaze fixed on Antoine, Jerome and Sebastian. A crowd of inquisitive men and women. An array of seemingly friendly faces, all weighing up the foreigners who had the gall to set foot in Hereford's most alcoholic, holy of holies. Alice knew this was not the moment for retribution. Beyssac's head was the real prize.

Alice leapt from the bench onto a table, a mischievous smile dancing across her face. She acknowledged the sea of upturned faces. The usual customers. Although, one regular, a man with a special place in her heart, was not present. To her audience, she appeared confident, self-assured, her normal self. But the charade was a burden, a struggle becoming more onerous. Time to raise everyone's spirits.

"To ensure our friends from Avignon do enjoy their sojourn in our celebrated city, I promise for the next hour, until the bells of All Saints sound two o'clock, all beer served in this tavern… is free!"

A round of applause, strangled cheers, stools quickly shoved aside. A mad rush towards the serving hatch. Cups and mugs held tightly in excited hands, overfilled, overflowing with buttery Benedictine beer. Mellow, contented customers.

Leaning against the wall to support unsteady legs, Magnus raised his cup, saluting Antoine and Jerome.

"Thank you, gentlemen from France. May your visit be a life-changing experience."

"Bless you," said Antoine.

Determined not to be outdone, Leofgar stood up.

"And with the guidance of St Thomas, may you find the peace which passeth all understanding."

"Bless you, kind sir," said Jerome.

Deep in thought, Hengist stayed seated, rubbing the knuckles of his right hand under his chin, lifting the hairs of his beard. He had heard enough.

"My friends, as a soldier who fought at Crecy, surviving many horrific wounds, I know I am blessed. I hope you understand what you are doing. Remember, the living know they will die. But those already dead, know nothing."

An enigmatic smile lightening up his face, Hengist shuffled out of the door, into the street. Antoine and Jerome were bewildered.

"Bleth you," Sebastian gurgled, sprinkling customers near him with milky bubbles of baby saliva. Most, too busy enjoying their beer, did not notice.

Twisting the cup between his fingertips, Antoine inspected his beer. He held it to his nose, sniffing the beverage, delighting in its piquant fragrance. An epicurean with sophisticated tastes, he considered the beer to be pleasing to the eye, aromatic to the nose, irresistibly seductive and a stimulant to his extremities. In essence, a potent brew. Just like Alice.

Relishing their beer, Antoine and Jerome were blissfully unaware of the danger they were in. For, if ordered, every customer drinking at the Saracen's Head, on that warm August afternoon, was prepared to kill them.

A dark shape appeared, a silhouette defined by the sunlight flooding through the window.

"I see you are a man who appreciates the finer things in life," observed the stranger.

His thoughts interrupted, Antoine looked up. A dark-haired man, with tired, melancholy eyes, pulled up a stool. His cassock and boots were caked in mud. His chin unshaven. His careworn face suggested a lack of sleep. John Dornell was grieving for his son.

"Too right," Antoine said. "I hope you don't mind plain speaking. In a country engulfed by pestilence and inhabited by criminal gangs, your delicious English beer is something to cherish. Of course, there are also English women. They are beautiful. But they can be cruel."

The stranger nodded, picking up an abandoned cup, gulping down the dregs without stopping. Antoine recognised a man tumbling into a black abyss. He understood. He had been there himself.

Jerome shifted Sebastian across his knee. Now he could examine the stranger more closely. His black cassock indicated a position in the Church although his hair was not tonsured. Perhaps he belonged to an obscure English sect. The Pestilence had encouraged an increase in extreme religious groups across Europe. There was no reason why Hereford should be exempt.

"I can stand you a beer," said Jerome. "If you don't finish it, this little guzzler certainly will."

Right on cue, Sebastian exhaled, blowing a staccato string of beery bubbles into the air.

John Dornell smiled. It was the first light-hearted moment he had experienced in weeks. A glimmer of light at the end of the tunnel.

"That would be…"

"Out of the question!" insisted an angry, female voice.

Alice was standing behind him, fists clenched, disdain etched into her face. What a shameless, arrogant, bastard! After sending her that letter, he had no right to come within a hundred miles of her tavern. If he refused to leave, she knew her customers would take violent pleasure in throwing him out.

"There's the door," she said icily. "Leave!"

John stood up. He didn't want to cause a scene. This tavern was a place of many happy memories. Alice's face remained hard. Her arms folded. Strange how quickly a warm embrace can turn into a cold rebuke.

Unperturbed, the customers continued to make merry, enjoying their free beer. A compliant drunkard being ejected from a tavern was nothing unusual.

John headed for the open door. The smell of the street, a heady mixture of rotting food and animal waste. He stopped. He must ask her.

"That letter you sent. Why did you say such cruel things?"

Alice was bemused. Shaking her head, she stretched out her arms.

"I don't understand. It was I who received a letter from you! A horrible, humiliating, letter of rejection. You made it crystal clear, my only function was to be a mare to your stallion. You told me I was your summer slut. I burned that degrading epistle as soon as I'd read it!"

John shook his head, perplexed by Alice's vehemence. "I have not sent you a letter. But I do have the one you sent me."

John reached inside his cassock, retrieving a folded piece of paper.

"Shall I read it out loud?"

"No. Not here. This is between us. The barrel room would be a good place to talk."

John sat on the barrel room floor, beneath the lantern. There was sufficient light to read. Alice, perched on a hogshead of beer, smoothed down the creases of her dress. She appeared unmoved, indifferent to his words. But in reality, she felt forlorn. She remembered a time when the sound of his voice would make her heart beat faster. It seemed so long ago.

John read the letter out loud. His tone was matter of fact, cold.

"Mr Dornell,

After much consideration, I have decided to end our relationship. I do not wish to talk to you or meet with you, ever again.

On reflection, it is clear, you have corrupted my morals and directed my life towards wickedness. You disgust me. Is it any wonder God has sought to punish you by taking away your son?

To relieve this regrettable situation, I urge you to leave Hereford and forget me.

Alice."

Alice was in turmoil. She did not write that letter. But it was obvious to her who had. Morcar, her father, had always hated John. A simple exchange of letters and her father had destroyed their relationship. She felt humiliated. A woman unable to make her own choices.

And yet. The sacred cause, an issue more important than the life of any individual, still remained unfulfilled. John had captured her heart. But from the day she was born, the Wyvern Ring possessed her soul.

John looked up at the vaulted ceiling. Raised voices, loud laughter, the sound of beer mugs banging on tables. Customers enjoying their beer.

Alice looked down at the rush-strewn floor. The smell of beer. Pungent yet appealing. An awkward silence. Like an unwieldy piece of furniture, refusing to be moved. The bells of All Saints sounded three o'clock. Alice lowered herself to the floor.

"I'm sorry your son passed away. He was a good, English boy."

"Passed away! I'm convinced he was murdered. Poisoned by someone who wanted to punish me!"

"You're overwrought, John. Not thinking straight. In the life of the nation, one individual does not matter. What's important, is the nation prevails."

John jumped to his feet, dumbfounded by her lack of compassion.

"Do you really believe that? It's utter nonsense. You're like two people in one. Sometimes loving. Other times hard hearted. I don't think I know you. I don't think I ever knew you!"

"Then you should leave," said Alice, pointing to the door. "My loyalty and my devotion are elsewhere. My devotion extends far beyond the love of one man."

Shaking his head, John ran upstairs and out into the street. He did not look back.

Alice unhooked the lantern, holding it above her head, searching the room until she found the barrel she wanted. Saltpetre, a mash used to preserve food during the winter. Alice knew saltpetre had another use. Hard as she could, she hurled the lantern at the barrel. It caught fire, lifting blue flames towards the ceiling.

Chapter Twenty

The cathedral clergy, grey-haired brothers in Christ, were shocked by Beyssac's criticism. A few senior officials, more used to being admired than admonished, broke down in tears. Others, too afraid to draw attention to themselves, sat in rigid silence. Not one of them could escape the cardinal's wrath.

His conclusions were damning: Lewis Charleton was an utter charlatan; the regular canons were regular idiots; the archdeacon was more wicked than the archfiend; the chancellor, focus of academic attainment, was actually illiterate; the dean could direct a cup of wine to his mouth but he could not direct the clergy; while the treasurer was so ill suited to his role, he regularly forgot to buy candles for the cathedral. He was also hindered by a debilitating phobia. An irrational fear of stained glass.

Beyssac's tirade lasted an hour. Until, crushed by his denunciation, a shuffling line of humiliated Christians stumbled out of the cathedral door. Beyssac knew he could whip Hereford into shape and return it to the Catholic fold.

As Beyssac congratulated himself, two hundred feet above his head, John Dornell took another mouthful of beer before slumping down on the roof of the central tower. Beer helped him think straight.

Time to weigh up the situation. He closed his eyes. His wife was dead. His son was dead. His relationship with Alice, dead. Fear of the Pestilence had forced the cathedral school to close and cost him his job. His purse contained just a few pennies. Maybe enough for one last slap-up meal. Hereford remained in the grip of a virulent disease. Plague pits, overflowing with corpses were everywhere.

John opened his eyes, gulping down more beer. Below him, strident voices, echoing through the streets, confirmed Hereford was still alive. Leaning over the parapet, he contemplated the city and its struggle to survive.

A few people hurried along Broad Street, knocking on doors, looking to buy food from shops which might be open. But most shops were closed. Their owners were either dead or run away to the countryside to escape the horror.

Looking down from his vantage point, the people resembled tiny insects, scurrying along a dusty path, searching for anything to dispel their hunger. St Nicholas' Church, burned, razed to the ground, reminded him of the bones of carrion. Shaking his head, John turned, looking towards the graveyard and the Cathedral Close.

Beyond the tombs and the headstones, Canon Street was deserted, except for one black dog, chasing its tail, spinning around, running back and forth before sticking its nose into a dunghill.

In Cabbage Lane, every shop was boarded up. John squinted. Only High Street seemed busy. He watched a stream of men and women running towards the guildhall, accompanied by clouds of silver smoke. A fire had taken hold somewhere. The hot summer made every wooden building, tinder dry. A dropped candle or spilled lantern could bring disaster.

A smell of burning wood. John swigged more beer from his flask. Smoke particles were irritating his throat.

High Street. The Saracen's Head. Alice. Her face filled his head. Why was she so aggressive? How could such an intense relationship fall apart so quickly? Passionate feelings transformed into hatred in the blink of an eye.

Beautiful, confident, joyfully physical, Alice filled the void left by his wife's death. She had become a second mother to William. Her presence enriched their lives. With her, the family was once again complete. But their relationship was over. She had rejected him. Her heart lay elsewhere.

Wisps of acrid smoke blew across John's face. He wheezed, banging his chest, gasping for air over the edge of the parapet. A mouthful of beer would clear his lungs. And help him forget.

**

In stark contrast, Cardinal Beyssac could not dismiss his troubles. Laying on his bed, under the coach awning, he was certain the Wyvern Ring would make another attempt to kill him. In view of that terrible prospect, common sense suggested it would be wise to spend the night away from Hereford. A city full of pestilence and swarming with potential murderers.

On the advice of Lewis Charleton, they made their way to Mordiford, a village, four miles east of Hereford. A village free from disease and noted for the piety of its inhabitants. The plan was to spend the night encamped near to the Church of the Holy Rood, before returning to Hereford the next day. A man on a mission, Beyssac was impatient to resume his investigation.

After crossing the River Lugg via Mordiford Bridge, Jerome guided the coach along a stone pathway bordered by yew trees. It was ominously quiet. Even the birds had stopped singing. A church. Five cottages. And a fishpond. This was the village of Mordiford.

Pleased to leave Hereford behind, Jerome halted the coach at the lychgate. The church tower, supporting a huge wooden crucifix, dominated the village. It seemed too magnificent for such a little church. Captivated by the face of Jesus, Jerome felt a lump in his throat. It was a sight which would persuade Lucifer to change his ways. A spectacle to stir the darkest soul.

"Where's the tavern?" asked Antoine, jumping off the box seat. "Where's the inn? Or the beer house? Whoever heard of an English village without a drinking den?"

Dressed in his red cardinal suit, Beyssac emerged from the coach. To Antoine, always intolerant of pomposity, Beyssac's magnificent clothing seemed ridiculous. But experience had taught him not to comment. Beyssac felt he needed to put Antoine in his place.

"I'm pleased to say, there's no alcohol to be found here. This village is a model of abstinence and sobriety."

Antoine frowned. "Sobriety is overrated. Zealots are always sober. They luxuriate in their virtue."

Beyssac shook his head dismissively.

"Remember Burford?"

Antoine winced. Beyssac had seized the righteous high ground.

"I was convinced Burford had taught you to curb your desires. In a corrupt world, we must strive for moral excellence. Virtue cannot be overrated. Jesus had no vices. He was virtuous. Are you saying the Son of God, mankind's only hope of salvation, is overrated?"

Once again, Beyssac had skilfully turned an innocent discussion into an insinuation of atheism.

Antoine retreated into himself.

"No. Please forgive my nonsense. Hunger has made me stupid. By your leave, I'll shut my mouth and get on with our supper."

Beyssac smiled. Depravity had been defeated. Antoine was teetering on the edge of the everlasting bonfire. He needed an occasional reprimand to keep him on the straight and narrow. Besides, it was important to remind his companions who was in charge.

As night closed in, they rested by the fire, enjoying a meal of rabbit, breadcrumbs and white beans. It was eerily quiet. The only sound was the scraping of food bowls and the crackle of burning twigs. The village appeared abandoned by all living things.

Antoine twisted his head, searching the darkness. Behind them, illuminated by the silver moonlight, the Church of the Holy Rood. In front, black and impenetrable Haugh Wood. A perplexity of rowan trees.

"Why is it so quiet?" Jerome whispered.

Beyssac shrugged his shoulders. "This village has a good reputation. I expect all God-fearing people are tucked up in bed."

Antoine rubbed his whiskers. He still felt uneasy. "That would account for the locals. But why can't we hear a single animal or bird? Tonight's supper was a coney I trapped in Gorsley almost a week ago."

Beyssac took off his hat and scratched his head. There was no rational explanation. The silence was unnatural. Almost oppressive. But in Mordiford they were safe. Out of reach of the Pestilence and the Wyvern Ring.

Beyssac stood up. "I suggest we retire for the night. This silence should allow us to enjoy a good sleep. In the morning, I will continue my investigation into Trilleck's murder. Those lily- livered Hereford clergymen won't know what's hit them. Furthermore, tomorrow after vespers, I will install Lewis Charleton as the new Bishop of Hereford."

While Antoine damped down the fire, Jerome tethered the horses. No more chores. In ten minutes, they were all asleep, except for Sebastian. He lay still. And listened.

The chink of dangling swords and heavy shields. Determined footsteps. The groan of an oak door pulled back. Low, furtive voices demanding loyalty to the cause. Sputtering tallow candles held tightly. A hundred disciples, fanatics, breathing hard, pledging their lives in snatched whispers. A turbulent calm.

Sitting up in his cot, Sebastian strained to hear what was happening. Above his head, the canvas awning rippled in the breeze. The Church of the Holy Rood was full.

Astonishing and terrible, the Mordiford dragon maintained its vigil. The flickering candlelight revealed its eyes. Jagged red jewels, threatening and deadly. An elongated, twisting, glittering head. A mouth dripping blood. A lascivious forked tongue, hanging down, hinting at unspoken corruptions. Uplifted wings adorned with green and gold scales, stretched across the west gable. The Mordiford dragon, imperious and pagan, ready to strike. Morcar raised a hand. The disciples listened.

"Tomorrow will be the most glorious day in England's history. For the next thousand years, proud parents will tell their children how we secured their liberty. Tomorrow will be the day our oppressors are destroyed. A day of national renewal. The day of reckoning for Norman tyranny. The first day of a free, reborn, England!"

A tumult. Shouting, cheering, swords banged against shields, the stamping of feet, sinister threats, oaths and brutal promises of violence. A hundred disciples, hell-bent on revenge, unable to be stopped. In the flickering candlelight, the stained glass seemed to ooze blood. Morcar was happy.

"No mercy!" Leofgar shouted, waving his sword above his head. "Kill all who stand in our way!"

"Extermination will bring liberation!" yelled Magnus, intoxicated by the mood.

Edwin raised a fist, wild eyes staring. "Death to our enemies. We will obliterate them!"

Wulfstan, the Black Monk, threw back his hood. An inscrutable face, disguising a bitter, black heart. His words, deep as gashes.

175

"An eye for an eye, a tooth for a tooth. A hand for a hand, a foot for a foot. A wound for a wound, a stripe for a stripe. The Scriptures show us the way. The Normans are doomed!"

Yelling and blaspheming, Wulfstan's words gave voice to the mood. Morcar raised his hand, an open palm facing downwards, reasserting his authority. Instant silence. He pointed at the font. A carving of St Michael battling a dragon.

"We cannot be stopped. We cannot be defeated. Providence has decreed we will win. The dragon is destined to destroy its enemies. Unfortunately, there are some God has not chosen to share our victory. Tom Burgoyne is murdered. His death will be avenged. And Hengist, the warrior, taken by the Pestilence. His indomitable spirit will be missed. They were true Englishmen. But tomorrow, the world will turn upside down. Yes, there will be bloodshed. Blood must flow. We must wade through blood to achieve victory. This is not the time for scruples. The knowledge our cause is right, will confirm your decency, however many you kill. When the history books are written you will be acclaimed heroes.

"The Pestilence has made England ungovernable. Easy prey for an organised force, determined to succeed. That force is the Wyvern Ring. But we must be patient. The execution of Cardinal Beyssac and counterfeit Bishop Charleton will signal the start. All over the country, our disciples will rise up and slit Norman throats. Alitha is granted the honour of beheading the cardinal. And nailing his head to the cathedral door. Sic semper tyrannis!"

Morcar smiled, cruel eyes, sparkling like blue sapphires. Quietly, almost imperceptibly, he began the entreaty.

"When God wills, may the end be good. Rise up and drench our land with Norman blood."

A solemn promise, confirmed by a hundred assassins. Inspired, they filed out of the church, melting into the night.

Stillness. A few hours later, as the first rays of sunlight broke through the clouds, Mordiford regained its heart. An inquisitive robin hopped through the open door of the church and began to sing. Slowly, frightened animals returned to their familiar haunts.

Restless, muttering to himself, Sebastian rolled over in his sleep. He dreamed he saw Beyssac's head, nailed to the cathedral door. Each eye socket contained a silver penny. Unable to come to terms with such humiliation, Beyssac's face wore a look of idiotic disbelief.

Chapter Twenty-one

Elizabeth stopped, letting the bag slip from her grasp. Senlac House. Four storeys high, surrounded by rose gardens. Considered by many, the most magnificent house in Hereford. But to Elizabeth, it meant only one thing. Home.

The journey from Witney to Hereford had been difficult. Wagon drivers and carters were willing to offer a woman a ride but they expected more in return than a handful of groats. Undaunted, Elizabeth knew she could look after herself.

The indecent suggestions of a carter from Pershore made her particularly angry. After repeated warnings, which he ignored, she left him without a head, buried at the bottom of his own dung cart. Similarly, a Gloucester wagon driver, transporting wine, got what he deserved, after putting his hand up her skirt. She castrated him. Washing her hands in wine proved an effective way to remove blood. Her only concern was the delay to the journey.

Now Elizabeth was home. Inside the house, sitting on a stool by the fire, Alitha was stirring the contents of a large pot. Lamb stew. The smell was unmistakable. The ecstasy of childhood, rekindled in an instant.

A footstep. Alitha turned. Startled eyes and a beaming smile confirmed her joy. Elizabeth, her twin sister, was home.

They embraced, almost squeezing the life out of each other, excited by the empathy only sisters understand. Teary-eyed and bemused, Alitha finally managed to speak.

"Why are you here? Why have you returned to Hereford? You are married to a wealthy businessman. You are obliged to him. Is he ill? Or God forbid, dead?"

Elizabeth shook her head, throwing off her cloak.

"Mr Barton breathes. He eats. He sleeps. He makes money. But it is not a life. It is only an existence. He has no spirit. No expectation of happiness or excitement. No passion or fire. I lived in a dark place, never feeling the warmth of the sun. I have abandoned my marriage to save my sanity and my soul. To remain in Witney would be to accept a life of cold duty. I will never deny my true self."

Alitha smiled resignedly. She was proud of Elizabeth's determination but unsure what the future held for such a high-spirited woman.

Smoothing down her dress, Alitha returned to her stool, motioning Elizabeth to sit on the bench opposite. The stew could wait. There was much to discuss.

"Remember when we were little girls and everyone said we were so alike, they couldn't tell us apart?"

"Yes," said Elizabeth wistfully. "And nothing has changed. Looking at you is like holding up a mirror. Most people can't separate us. As a child, I rejoiced in our opportunities for devilment."

"It's more than looks," said Alitha, grasping Elizabeth's hands. "Our kinship is profound. Our principles the same. Our attitudes and beliefs drawn from a single well. We share the same triumphs and endure the same misfortunes. So, I have to tell you… I have ended my relationship with John Dornell… Have I done the right thing?"

Elizabeth closed her eyes, tapping her lips with a forefinger, pondering. She shrugged her shoulders.

"You have made the right decision. He is a drunkard, wallowing in alcoholic self-pity. I never liked him. For your own sake, you must ban him from your tavern."

"Yes," said Alitha, her mind's eye conjuring up an image of the Saracen's Head, ablaze from doorway to roof, flames engulfing its timbers.

Elizabeth leant forward, stroking Alitha's face. Alitha shook her head, returning to the moment.

"Forget John Dornell," said Elizabeth. "Whether he lives or dies is of no consequence. I have more melancholy news. Our sister Beatrice, God rest her soul… is dead."

Alitha felt faint. Her heart and mind, a confusion of emotions. Anger and sorrow combined in the instant it takes a tear to fall.

"No. You are mistaken. She resides at Kyneburgh Abbey, committed to a life of quiet devotion."

Knowing Beatrice's fate, Elizabeth had already decided what to do. Her grief had evolved into a need for revenge. She had no tears left.

"Beatrice did not suffer," said Elizabeth. "She was in full control, right to the end."

"Definitely dead?"

"Yes. Definitely dead. Our disciples in Gloucester confirmed the circumstances. She died by her own hand. A vial of henbane ended her suffering."

"Father is responsible," said Alitha bitterly. "If he had not rejected her, she would be here now, safe in the bosom of her family."

"No!" said Elizabeth abruptly. "You must not rewrite the truth according to your mood. Beatrice lost her nerve. She abandoned our cause. Be mindful of our creed. The individual does not matter. It is the nation which must prevail. The destruction of Norman rule is of more consequence than the life of one person."

Alitha nodded. Her misery was raw and very real. But Elizabeth's resolve was impossible to contradict. Her passion was a force of nature.

Elizabeth reached down, pulling a knife from inside her boot. A silver knife with a red handle. A wyvern dragon, etched into the metal, wound its way along the blade. Its barbed tail defining the knife edge. Elizabeth plunged the knife into the bench. She seemed preoccupied with matters beyond the kitchen.

"On the day of her suicide, Beatrice received a visit from a French cardinal. She killed herself soon after he left. When I find him, I will cut off his head."

"Do you know this man's name?"

Alitha shook her head, gasping in disbelief.

"His name is Beyssac."

Alitha grabbed the knife. It rested comfortably in her palm.

"Cardinal Beyssac is already here. Tomorrow he intends to install Lewis Charleton as bishop. I will be Beyssac's executioner. His death will begin a nationwide uprising against our oppressors. The day of retribution will have arrived."

Elizabeth's eyes sparkled.

"Providence has returned me to Hereford at the most important moment in our history. This knife will not be sheathed until every Norman is in Hell. Take me to Father. I'm sure he will be happy to see I'm back."

Chapter Twenty-two

The smell of woodsmoke intensified Antoine's mood. The charred timbers confirmed the tittle-tattle. The Saracen's Head, Hereford's happiest watering hole, was burned down. Antoine hoped Alice, the proprietor, had survived.

"This is Purgatory," Antoine declared, he twisted in anguish. "I enjoy beer. But I must be punished. Made to suffer for my wickedness. God has denied me access to refreshment."

"Don't exaggerate," chided Jerome. "You have to be dead to enter Purgatory. And be warned. Sneering at tenets of the Catholic faith will lead to trouble."

"My epicurean taste buds are frustrated," Antoine lamented. "And I can't think of a worse torture for a bon viveur."

Shaking his head, Jerome released Sebastian from his grasp, setting him down inside the tavern's blackened shell. Straight away, Sebastian picked up a piece of burned wood, put it in his mouth and began chewing. Cutting milk teeth was painful. Gnawing on charred timber might help.

Exasperated, Antoine continued his rant.

"Tonight, Lewis Charleton will be consecrated Bishop of Hereford. I put on my best shirt for the occasion. Yet, I can't celebrate because there is nowhere in this alcohol-forsaken city to buy a drink!"

"You're wrong," proclaimed a cheerful voice. "There are hogsheads of beer up at the castle."

Thomas the watchman approached, pulling a cart piled high with corpses. The Pestilence still raged, merciless in its choice of victims.

Jerome, noticing a baby's body sticking out of the heap, grabbed Sebastian, holding him close. Thomas stopped his cart.

"You bring wonderful tidings," said Antoine. "But I don't think the castle steward would consider our needs. Knights and soldiers must come first. Fighting men are always thirsty."

Thomas looked puzzled.

"There be no soldiers or knights at the castle. The garrison is away in the service of King Edward. There is no steward, or constable or marshal. Only me and Peter. He's a scholar. He's read a book. He's real deep. He has a notion my good looks and noble head rival the best features of a castle."

Jerome smiled.

"Yes, I can see it. You inspire confidence. You're strong. And come what may, always safe and secure."

"No," said Thomas. "He says my head is solid. But empty. And my body is like a besieged castle. Much damaged. Almost ruined. Peter is usually right."

Antoine's gut feeling was Thomas might be a madman or a criminal. Better indulge him. It seemed reasonable to conclude that a man, wandering around the streets, pulling a cartload of dead bodies and claiming to command a castle was not sane.

"I'd be obliged if you would take me straight to the beer," said Antoine. "We must make haste. I don't think your passengers will complain if they experience a bumpy ride."

As Thomas hauled his cargo through the winding streets, up the hill towards Hereford Castle, Antoine, Jerome and Sebastian followed at a stench-free distance.

To passers-by, their progress seemed a preposterous funeral cortège. Sebastian's relentless chuckling confirmed it.

Hereford Castle stood on a hill, overlooking the river. On first sight, a stone-walled fortress, built by the Normans to intimidate the locals and monitor the traffic on the Wye. An impregnable stronghold, capable of repulsing the most ferocious assault.

But as Thomas wheeled his cart under the gatehouse, across the bailey towards the keep, it became evident, this imposing citadel was actually a caricature of a castle. Surrounded by dilapidated buildings, crumbling walls and heaps of rubble, Hereford Castle was a grandiose ruin.

A creaking hinge. To their left, a man emerged from the chapel, closing the door behind him. Peter, the watchman. Jerome noticed he seemed flustered, slipping a ring off his finger and pocketing it, before walking over. His trousers, leather jerkin and boots were bloodstained. A small knife dangled from his waistband. His hands were red.

"Welcome to Hereford Castle," said Peter, smiling broadly.

Thomas scratched his whiskered chin.

"These gentlemen are thirsty. Thirst deep as a castle well. They want to buy beer."

Peter nodded. "The soldiers have gone to join the king's army. They left behind an ocean of beer. Enough beer to drown every priest in England and choke every foreigner. Of course, we're not a charity."

Antoine and Jerome exchanged a knowing glance. Sebastian, safe in Jerome's arms, closed his eyes and fell asleep.

"I would pay any price for good beer," said Antoine.

"The buttery is where our beer is kept. Follow me," said Peter, pointing at a stairwell, leading underground.

A dozen tall candles, impaled on stands, provided brilliant light. Barrels and hogsheads of English beer were stacked high, against the walls. It was very cold. Awestruck, Antoine became a pilgrim, kneeling before a shrine.

Thomas, ascetic in spirit, was dubious.

"My doctor despises beer. He told me it causes bad breath and rots the teeth. It fills the stomach with poisonous fumes and muddles the brain. Worst of all, it provokes detumescence. And that's not good."

Antoine and Jerome laughed. Peter looked at Thomas with disdain.

"I believe that's a problem you stopped worrying about years ago," said Peter, shaking his head. "Gentlemen, you wanted beer?"

Antoine placed Sebastian on top of a barrel, using his coat as a pillow. He was sound asleep.

All smiles, Peter rubbed his hands together in exaggerated anticipation. Now he could watch Antoine and Jerome while they were off guard. He drew a quick breath.

"We have sundry English beers awaiting your taste buds. Name your poison."

"What have you got?" asked Jerome.

Peter listed the beers, counting them off on his fingers.

"For your delectation we have: god ale; posset ale; carrot ale and fruit ale; small beer; table beer; honey beer and bramble beer. There's

Druid Fluid and Jerusalem Juice. Liquor from Ledbury and Wibbly Wobbly from wonderful Weobley. We have white wine from Lugwardine and red wine from Bredwardine. And for the discerning drinker, there's a Cistercian version from Dore Abbey and a Benedictine brew from St Devereux. Each, an exquisite beverage."

An alcoholic idyll. Antoine beamed with apparent delight.

"We'll work our way through as many as we can," said Antoine cordially. He motioned to Peter and Thomas.

"Will you accompany us on our sacred quest?"

Thomas shook his head, a serious look on his face.

"I have a cartload of decaying corpses to take care of. Unless I attend to them right away, they'll slide off the cart."

Jerome grimaced. The thought of human bodies turning to jelly, made him feel sick.

"It must be an onerous job having to lay those wretched people to rest," remarked Jerome.

Peter shrugged his shoulders.

"We can't bury them. Every graveyard and burial ground in the city, is full. I've seen dogs scratching in the soil, looking for flesh. If a corpse is not at least six feet under, a dog will dig it up and eat it."

"If you can't bury them, how do you dispose of them?" asked Antoine.

Peter and Thomas looked at each other. Shadows from the candles twisting their faces into conspiratorial masks.

"We bequeath the corpses to the River Wye," said Peter solemnly. "The Scriptures speak about the Water of Life, bright as crystal, floating from God's throne. It is not disrespectful or insulting to their memory. Dignified and at peace, they proceed serenely downstream into the bosom of the Almighty."

Jerome stopped trembling. He imagined the deceased, each one secure in their covenant with God, soothed and protected by the benevolent waters of the River Wye, held safe in the arms of the comforting current, full of hope, on a blissful journey to Heaven.

Giving voice to his thoughts, Jerome looked directly at Peter and Thomas.

"I can picture you on the riverbank, kneeling in respectful silence. A gentle push. Each soul en route to God."

A pause.

"No. It's not like that," said Peter in a business-like tone.

"We drop each one, head first down the castle privy. The water is quite deep at the bottom. They disappear. Job done."

Antoine stepped back, open-mouthed. Jerome, holding a hand to his mouth, froze. Wide, staring eyes and palpitating hearts. Both men were appalled.

"I would start with the Cistercian," said Peter. "Each coat of arms is branded on the barrel. Help yourself to whichever you want. There are cups by the stool. You must excuse us while we attend to those rotting bodies."

Climbing the stairs with hurried footsteps, Peter and Thomas were gone. Silence echoed around the buttery. Antoine and Jerome were in shock.

A whimper. Sebastian was awake. Jerome lifted him off the barrel. Curious, Sebastian raised his head, looking around to see what was happening. Unimpressed, he closed his eyes, snuggling into Jerome's shoulder.

"He's having a bad dream," whispered Jerome.

"I know the feeling," Antoine retorted. "From day one, this expedition has been a nightmare. Thomas is a harmless fool. But I don't trust Peter. Did you see the blood on his hands and clothes? What is he up to? I suggest we limit ourselves to one drink and leave *tout de suite*."

Jerome cradled Sebastian. A sleeping baby would make it easier to slip away from the castle unobserved.

"I agree," said Jerome firmly. "This place exudes evil."

Antoine poured two cups of Cistercian beer. A dark brown brew, boasting a creamy white head, spumed over the rim of the cup.

Antoine took a mouthful.

"Aromas of dried fruits, raisins and possibly cinnamon," he said sagely.

"Quite sweet," said Jerome, running the beer around his tongue and shifting Sebastian onto his hip.

186

"The nose is definitely dried fruits. I also detect plums. In truth, a complex beer. And absolutely delicious. Sebastian doesn't know what he's missing."

Antoine drained his cup.

"You finish yours while I find out what Peter and Thomas are up to. If the coast is clear, we should leave immediately."

The castle appeared deserted. The cart was gone. Thomas and Peter were nowhere to be seen. Antoine crouched on the top step of the stairwell, scanning each building, looking for signs of life.

The keep, a black silhouette against the sun, was quiet. The barracks, usually swarming with roistering soldiers, was silent. The Great Hall, focus of castle life, was empty.

No guards stood to attention at the gatehouse. No cooks or servants or scullions were raising a commotion in the kitchen. Hereford Castle seemed dead. Except, that is, for the shouts, expletives and atrocious threats to life, emanating from the chapel.

Antoine hunched down, watching. A group of men, armed with swords and axes, sidled out of the chapel and assembled in the bailey. Antoine recognised Garth, Leofgar, Edmund and Wulfstan, customers of the Saracen's Head. Peter the watchman was leading. His voice strident. His words, chilling.

"Today, England is reborn. God's chosen people will destroy their oppressors and regain freedom. All foreigners will be killed. Tonight, Cardinal Beyssac will die. But first we must eliminate his odious entourage. As I speak, Antoine and Jerome are drinking themselves into oblivion. Five more minutes and they will fall on our swords. Do not harm the baby. He is a Saxon child. He is destined to…"

Antoine could not wait any longer. Racing downstairs, he grabbed Jerome's arm.

"We must leave this instant," Antoine panted. "The Wyvern Ring are outside. They will kill us on sight. We must leave now or be butchered!"

Jerome winced, aghast at Antoine's news. Sebastian remained motionless, eyes closed, sleeping innocently.

"There's a door behind the stairwell," said Jerome, holding Sebastian, whilst gesturing with his head. "It might lead to the kitchen. In any case, I'm not going up those stairs."

Footsteps. The jangle of weapons knocking against armour. Angry, resolute voices.

Antoine opened the door. Two sinks, a barrel filled with fetid dishwater, cooking pots, pans, plates and a broken washing paddle. An abandoned room. Antoine felt insulted. A scullery was not the place for a last stand.

A red curtain, embroidered with a golden sun, divided the scullery. As Antoine bolted the door, Jerome drew back the curtain. The castle kitchen seemed frozen in time.

The departing soldiers had removed most of the kitchen equipment. But not all. Sunlight streaming through the windows, revealed a trestle table complete with chopping blocks, knives and a brutal-looking cleaver. A blackened spit, stretched across the fireplace. Two frying pans rested on a shelf. A mallet, hung down from a meat hook. On the earth floor, a discarded apron and a pair of trousers, indicated the soldiers had left in a hurry.

Fists, boots and sword hilts, pounded the scullery door. An axe blade shattered the wood, sending splinters into the air. Antoine grabbed the cleaver and mallet, a weapon in each hand.

For a moment, Antoine stood defiant, puffing out his chest, steadfast as Samson facing the Philistines. He considered the wonderful nobility of a fight to the death. But Antoine knew he was no warrior. Jerome, Sebastian in his arms, had already fled.

In fear of their lives, they dashed across the kitchen, scrambling up the stairs, winding frantically round and round before stumbling into an empty room. The Lord's bedchamber, stripped bare. Nothing left but undraped walls and a simple privy.

An open, nail-studded door. Breathing hard, relieved he had not thrown his life away in a futile gesture, Antoine slammed the door shut, turning the key with a flourish.

"We're trapped," said Jerome gloomily. "Once they break down the door, you and I will be killed. Take Sebastian. I need to prepare myself to meet Jesus."

Antoine dropped his weapons, taking Sebastian in his arms. There was no way out.

Clasping his hands, Jerome knelt down, closing his eyes. He appeared reconciled to death.

"O most merciful Jesus, I pray Thee by the agony of Thy most Sacred Heart and by the sorrows of Thy Immaculate Mother…"

Antoine opened the window shutter and looked out. There were armed men everywhere. The gatehouse was guarded by a hooded man, wielding a poleaxe. A dozen Wyvern Ring disciples, weapons glinting in the sunlight, stood outside the chapel. They were taking orders from a red-haired woman. She pointed a knife towards the Great Hall.

Peter the watchman dragged a body across the bailey towards the death cart. Antoine narrowed his eyes. It was Thomas. Covered in blood. His throat slashed.

Jerome's prayer was almost finished.

"Wash in Thy blood, the sinners of the whole world, who are agonised and ready to die this day…"

Hammering on the door. Crashing of weapons against the wood. Dreadful oaths. Profane threats. A hinge, buckled and snapped. Antoine knew what to do.

With loving respect, he laid Sebastian down, gently kissing his forehead. Jerome's voice diminished to a whisper.

"Jesus, I live for Thee, Jesus I die for Thee, Jesus, I am thine in life and death…"

The door crashed open. A horde of disciples lusting for blood, burst into the room.

Antoine seized Jerome's hands, still clasped in prayer, throwing him headfirst down the privy. Scooping up Sebastian, he followed, tumbling down into utter darkness. The River Wye beckoned.

"Good God," gasped Jerome.

Chapter Twenty-three

His eyelids flickered. He didn't know where he was. A blue sky. Fleeting clouds. He seemed to be floating, spinning in the gentle current of a river.

He could not feel his arms or legs. The mellow serenity of alcoholic bliss. But the booze was wearing off. After a night of excessive drinking, John Dornell woke with a start.

He sat up, rubbing his legs, squeezing the stiffness out of his limbs. The roof of Hereford Cathedral was an appropriate place for a Christian to sleep. Not comfortable but safe. Neither the Pestilence nor the murder gang terrorising Hereford could reach him here.

John looked up. A silhouette cloaked him in shadow. His musing stopped. A dark figure, outlined against the sun, stood over him. Despite the long cloak and raised hood, John instantly recognised his visitor. Alice.

"You look wretched," she said, stretching out a hand, helping him up. "I knew you would sleep off your hangover in your regular refuge. Your clothes are filthy. You're unshaven. And you smell. But you are alive."

John tried to smooth the creases from his cassock but to no avail. He had not washed or trimmed his beard for two days. Alice was right. He did smell. He exuded a heavy scent of beer and sweat.

"Why are you here?" he asked peevishly. "The last time we met, you said you never wanted to see me again."

"Nothing has changed," said Alice. "I regret our relationship. It was a time of my life frittered away in sinful indulgence. Your lust eroded my principles and corrupted my faith. You diverted me away from my real passion."

John shook his head.

"If you regard our relationship as time wasted, why have you climbed two hundred steps to the roof of the cathedral to tell me?"

Alice's expression softened. John discerned shards of suppressed affection. She stretched out an arm and pointed.

"Today, here in Hereford, a momentous event will take place. An action so significant, it will alter the course of history forever."

John smiled.

"The installation of a new bishop is an important occasion. But I doubt it will alter the course of history forever."

"Don't ridicule me!" Alice snarled, biting her lip, glaring at him. "I'm here, against my better judgement, to advise you not to attend Lewis Charleton's consecration."

"Why?"

Alice shrugged her shoulders.

"His appointment will bring conflict. The people are angry with the Church for its feeble response to the Pestilence. They blame Charleton for the collapse of law and order in the city. I am certain there will be violence."

"And?"

"You will be caught up in it. And not survive."

John looked over the parapet. Hereford was waking up. A few people ambled along Broad Street. Smoke rose from the blacksmith's stable and the fishmonger's yard in Pipewell Street. The garden of the Bishop's Palace swarmed with monks, priests and various church officials, scurrying to and fro, preparing for the appointment of a new bishop.

The wind gained strength. John swept the hair back off his face. Looking at Alice, pouting and angry, he doubted she had ever looked more beautiful.

"The fact you sought me out, is proof you still love me," said John softly.

"No!" said Alice. "I pity you. I don't love you. Don't confuse sympathy with affection. Your wife died. Your son needed a woman to care for him during his early years. I shouldered the burden. Our relationship was no more than that."

"Burden!" John's face twisted in despair. A hurtful remark from a woman he still loved.

He remembered that afternoon at Hay Bluff. Sharing a meal of bread and cheese; speaking in whispers; awestruck by the Black Mountains; laughing; defying a teeming rainstorm; rolling head over heels down a gully before collapsing in each other's arms. And the intimacy. Just being together. It was most important thing in the world.

"So your passion was a deceit? All those nights carousing at the Saracen's Head meant nothing to you?"

"Yes," said Alice. "It was an arrangement not a relationship. We fulfilled each other's needs. You supplied the sex and I dispensed the beer. Those days are long gone. Now, my tavern is destroyed, I can stop pretending."

Astonished, John looked down at his boots, taking shallow breaths, trying to remain calm.

"Are you telling me the Saracen's Head is gone?"

"Yes, I was furious with you. And with someone else. My anger got the better of me. I burnt it down."

The tavern was your livelihood. You are the most esteemed proprietress in the county. How…"

"You are wrong. I did not own the Saracen's Head. I managed it on behalf of a businessman and his friends. My presence there, like my friendship with you, was simply an expedient, meaning I could pursue a more profound obligation. At last, I can be myself."

Bemused, John ran his fingers through his hair. Was Alice suggesting her life was an elaborate deception? Had she tricked him into loving her? Had lust addled his reason to such an extent, he never discerned the real Alice?

She turned to go, raising her hood to cover her face.

"I have warned you to avoid Lewis Charleton's consecration. If you ignore me, your life will be in danger. That is the only reason I sought you out."

The wind had grown stronger, gusting around the cathedral tower, making John arch his back, to retain his footing. Alice stood unperturbed. John knew he must ask her.

"Wait. I will heed your advice to steer clear of the ceremony. But, what did you mean when you spoke of your 'profound obligation'?"

Alice sighed.

"My birth name is Alitha. I have been chosen to realise a most illustrious endeavour. Tonight, I will kill Cardinal Beyssac and Lewis Charleton. Their assassination will herald the dawning of a golden age for the English nation."

The gusting wind knocked John back. He caught his breath. Alice's confession left him stupefied. His legs were unsteady, his mind dizzy with violent images, struggling to come to terms with a new reality. The woman standing in front of him was not Alice but Alitha. Not the woman with whom he had enjoyed an affair. But in truth, a cold-blooded fanatic, obsessed with murder.

Alitha stared hard at John, granting him a perfunctory nod.

"You seem surprised by my honesty."

"I thought I knew you. Obviously, I was wrong."

"You knew Alice. You did not know me. My friends and I are the vanguard of an unstoppable movement."

"The Wyvern Ring? The gang who caused such mayhem?"

"Yes. The Wyvern Ring. But the word mayhem is an insult. All our actions are elements of a stratagem, designed to destroy Norman power and liberate the English people. Are you so cowardly you accept the yoke around your neck without complaint?"

"I hate injustice as much as any man but I yield to the law. To oppose the powers that be, is a recipe for disaster."

Alitha curled her hands into fists, speaking through gritted teeth.

"You are in thrall to a foreign power. You are a slave. We are ruled by a king who does not speak English. Every archbishop, judge, lord mayor, tax collector and wealthy landowner is French. The English people are an underclass, struggling to retain their identity and to survive. To accept servitude without complaint, proves you are a coward. Our freedom must be wrested from the bloodstained hands of the oppressors."

John bowed his head. Thoughts racing through his mind. Alitha's rant confirmed she was a zealot. Militant, opposed to any belief except her own. And without question, prepared to kill.

John wiped his forehead. Could Alitha's ferocity be a weakness and not a strength? Even the hardest heart has its limitations.

Blowing a farewell kiss, John bowed exaggeratedly, waving his hand with a theatrical flourish.

"Don't delay. I believe you are en route to a murder?"

"Not a murder. An execution. Beyssac and Charleton are sentenced to death. I relish the opportunity to consign those criminals to the dung heap of history."

"And will that be the end of the killing?"

"No. Their demise will signal a nationwide uprising. Blood must flow if England is to be free."

"Innocent blood?"

There is no such thing as an innocent Frenchman. It is a contradiction in terms. All those complicit in the subjugation of the English people, are guilty of a heinous crime. They must be dealt with accordingly."

"And those English people who consorted with the oppressors. What will happen to them?"

"All collaborators should expect immediate execution. Colluding with the enemy is treachery against one's own people."

"What about the elderly? Or women? Or children? What will happen if they are judged to have consorted with the enemy? Must they also die?"

Alitha averted her eyes, looking across the cathedral rooftop into the distance. A blustery wind filled the silence. It was the first time she had failed to respond. Evidently, John had touched a nerve. Her hands were locked together as if in prayer. On her ring finger, a wyvern dragon bared its teeth.

"Well?" John insisted, exasperated by her silence. "Must those people also die?"

"Yes!" thundered a female voice. "And I would wield the knife."

"Good God!" John exclaimed "What Devil's work is this?"

Astonished, he watched in disbelief, a red-haired woman, jumping from the top step of the cathedral tower and sprint across the roof, before falling into Alitha's arms. They embraced warmly.

The two women, indistinguishable in looks and apparel, stared at John. Ravenous wolves, contemplating a kill.

"Am I witched?" asked John. "Or my brain overheated? I see two, where before, there was one."

Alitha seemed amused.

"Not the Devil's work. Rather a gift from God. Elizabeth and I are twins."

Elizabeth strolled slowly towards John, coquettishly swinging her hips, pouting and smiling. Before grabbing his hair and tilting his head against the parapet.

She examined his face. Rubbing the whiskers on his chin, pulling down his eyelids and looking in his mouth to assess his teeth.

"He's a prize pig," said Elizabeth. "But not as handsome as you claimed."

One more intimidating look into his eyes, before releasing her grip and returning to Alitha.

John got to his feet, shaking his head in disbelief, trying hard to understand. The Saracen's Head was destroyed. Alice was not the genial hostess she had pretended to be. In reality, she belonged to a murder gang, intent on killing Cardinal Beyssac and Lewis Charleton. As for Elizabeth, she was clearly deranged.

Elizabeth stared at John with disdain. This was her opportunity to take revenge against the man who caused Alitha so much distress. She hated him.

"It's hard to believe my sister allowed you to corrupt her innocence. You strike me as a pathetic drunk, wallowing in your own misery. Your whiskers are deceptive. You resemble a man but in truth you are really just a quivering milksop. The world will be made more tolerable by your removal from it."

"My death would not hinder your intentions. But it would place an extra burden on your conscience."

"Conscience?" said Elizabeth scornfully. "I don't have a conscience. I have a mission which must be completed. Life is too short for scruples. Moreover, I find the prospect of your demise excites me."

Alitha blanched. She had spilt much blood at the behest of The Wyvern Ring without any qualms. But the thought of John's death did upset her. She despised him and loved him in the same moment. Dark anxiety engulfed her. She did not want him to die.

John sensed Alitha's misgivings. He noticed the colour drain from her face. Perhaps she retained a scrap of compassion. After all, in happier times, they were lovers.

But in engaging with Elizabeth, John realised he was arguing for his life. He knew he must appear calm. Holding out his hands, he looked directly into her eyes.

"The Scriptures say, you must not pollute the land in which you live. Spilled blood will pollute the land. By rights it must be possible to improve the plight of the English without recourse to mass killing?"

"No!" shrieked Elizabeth. "You still don't understand. This is the time of reckoning. Scores will be settled. Enemies of the people will receive their just desserts. For too long, the English have been slaves. Today, that vile imposition will end. The liberation of the people means we must wade through blood."

John winced. Pitiless and immoral, Elizabeth was the consummate assassin.

"Your insanity conceals an ironic truth. Here you are, rejoicing at the prospect of slaughter while standing on top of the house of God. Of course, I shouldn't expect you to be aware of such profanity."

Elizabeth shook her head dismissively. Her patience was exhausted. She had indulged John for too long. His criticism of the Wyvern Ring was not acceptable. It was clear evidence of his cloying sentimentality. Besides, she wanted to kill him. Experience had proved a quick death was less messy.

She stood for a few seconds, eyes closed. Then with practiced expertise, she fastened her arms around his neck, throwing him face down. A knee in the small of his back prevented escape.

Elizabeth nodded in acknowledgement as Alitha drew her knife, ready to assist the execution. John, his head pressed against the cathedral roof, muttered an incoherent prayer.

Looking up to the sky, Elizabeth raised her knife.

"Do you not know, I must be about my father's business? Therefore, must all traitors…"

"Die," whispered Alitha, plunging her knife into Elizabeth's neck, twisting the blade like a key.

Unaware what had happened, John rolled over. He was astounded by what he saw.

Alitha, hands covered in blood, stood rigid, wild-eyed, aghast at what she had done. Elizabeth, blood dripping from her lips, was stumbling across the rooftop, towards the parapet.

Breathing hard, Elizabeth rested against a wall, looking over the city, drawing comfort from the familiar streets below. The wind blew in gusts, coiling her hair, fashioning it into a plaited red wreath.

A knowing glance between the sisters. Then Elizabeth stepped over the parapet. The Pestilence was still rampant. Another corpse on the streets of Hereford was not news.

Chapter Twenty-four

Beyssac rolled his eyes, stomping back and forth, calling out, lifting the awning, searching behind the wheels and scrabbling in the strong box. The money was there, not a single penny missing. His companions had not absconded. The horses, placid and indifferent, rested on the pathway between the yew trees. Mordiford village was quiet. Still as a stained-glass saint.

Where could they be? It was disrespectful to expect him to prepare his own breakfast, dress himself and attend to his appearance. His responsibility was to appoint a bishop!

He must appear cultured and well groomed. A man of high station, worthy of respect. Although, he did admit to himself, the demeanour he desired might be impossible to achieve. Irked by the absence of his companions, Beyssac decided to make a determined effort to look good.

Scowling like a felon, Beyssac held up the mirror. He grimaced, stroking the skin with his fingers, trying to massage away the bags under his eyes.

The expedition had forced him to endure many horrible moments and witness many loathsome sights. These incidents had aged him. But he was alive and still determined to impose God's will on Hereford. To this end, he decided to begin the day with a prayer of petition in Mordiford Church.

A warm, sunlit morning. Resplendent in scarlet from head to foot, Beyssac strolled down the pathway to the church, swinging an incense burner from side to side. The fragrant smoke would confirm his status and serve as a bulwark against evil.

The fumes stung his eyes. Red-faced, tears rolling down, he coughed and coughed, desperately trying to clear his throat. A silent prayer. And a pinched nose allowed him to regain composure.

Arriving at the church door, Beyssac dropped the burner and removed his hat. Mordiford Church deserved respect. Lifting the latch, he went in.

Groups of worshippers, mainly men, were at prayer, kneeling in huddles along the nave, whispering devotions, pleading for God's help. The atmosphere was purposeful. Christians in defiant mood. Standing under the west gable, hands together, Beyssac listened.

"Whoever is born of God, will overcome the world. Our faith will bring us victory."

A rather loose quotation from John. But Byssac knew he must be tolerant. It would be unfair to expect English peasants to have any knowledge of the Scriptures.

"He will trample down our enemies."

Beyssac recognised a section of Psalm 108. And, of course, the words of Timothy, Paul's most loyal friend.

"I have fought the good fight, I have finished the race, I have kept the faith."

Moved by the spirituality of the Christian souls around him, Beyssac raised his gaze to Heaven, yearning to contact God, to share the simple joy of these country folk…

But what he saw, turned his blood to ice. On the gable above his head, the Mordiford dragon maintained its unrelenting vigil. The flickering candlelight dilated its eyes. Jagged red jewels, threatening and deadly. An elongated, twisting, glittering head. A mouth dripping blood. A lascivious forked tongue hanging down, hinting at unspoken corruptions. Uplifted wings, adorned with green and gold scales, stretched across the gable. The Mordiford dragon poised to strike.

Beyssac gasped. Rough hands slipped quickly around his throat. He could not move. A trenchant voice, seething with anger, spoke. Pitiless blue eyes, held him rigid.

"Disciples of the Wyvern Ring. I introduce Cardinal Beyssac, senior leader of the Catholic Church in Avignon, Prince of the Holy Faith, papal legate and personal assistant to Pope Innocent VI… A man whose presence in England is a dagger across our throats! He is an outsider, a foreign oppressor, a meddling fool and an enemy of God's own people. Cardinal Beyssac. Welcome to Hell!"

Searing pain pierced Beyssac's hand. He grimaced. The sleeping dragon, burned in his flesh, appeared to rouse and waken. The circumstance he dreaded most, had come to pass. He was prisoner of the Wyvern Ring.

Besieged by aggressive faces, Beyssac closed his eyes. A sword pommel smashed his back. Impatient fingers grabbing, clawing at his clothes, scratching his face, clutching his arms and legs, pressing him face down on the church floor. A crime, unpunished for three centuries, soon to be avenged.

Yet, although resigned to death, Beyssac was not despondent. His place in Heaven assured, the Wyvern Ring would hasten his arrival in Paradise. As a Christian, he knew his life on Earth was merely preparation for the afterlife.

Dragged into the churchyard, Beyssac blinked against the sunlight. His red hat, stamped on by heavy boots, lay trampled. His torn clothes now more reminiscent of a pauper than a papal official.

A noose was thrown over his head. Ropes tied under his armpits.

Morcar smiled. Freedom was the prize. It was time for decisive action. For everything there is a season and a time for every matter under Heaven. A time to be born. And a time to die.

Deep in thought, Morcar surveyed the churchyard and the village, turning his head from side to side, inspecting every grave, scrutinising every monument. His eyes focused on the village cross. It seemed appropriate. An ideal place for a cardinal to die. After a few moments of reflection, Morcar came to his decision.

"Beyssac, know this. Your death and that of Lewis Charleton will set in motion the end of Norman tyranny. As Jesus is your role model and the lifeblood of your faith, it's fitting you follow his example. I have made up my mind. You will be crucified. The Saxon cross in the centre of the village, will be your Calvary. We must all die. But to die magnificently, is a privilege afforded to very few."

Kneeling on the grass, held by two disciples in a vice-like grip, Beyssac could only raise his head.

"You are Antichrist."

"No," said Morcar, waving his hand dismissively.

"Just Anti-French."

Chapter Twenty-five

With deferential respect, Nicholas set down his coffin at the water's edge. He did not need a boat. The river journey to Mordiford would be difficult. But his faith was unshakeable. 'When you pass through the waters, I will be with you.' Nicholas trusted the Scriptures. God promises everlasting life for those who believe. Thus, Nicholas was confident.

Unlike John, who was convinced the day would bring bloodshed and chaos, culminating in the destruction of England. John did not have a plan but he did have a score to settle. He must reach Mordiford. Journeying there by river would be quick and discreet. Travelling by road would increase the risk of being intercepted.

The cathedral bells announced midday as John pushed his coracle into the river. He was troubled. Dark, disturbing thoughts occupied his mind. Distressing memories like wounds which never heal.

After Elizabeth's death, amidst floods of tears and outbursts of self-loathing, Alitha confirmed John's worst fears. Her father was the leader of the Wyvern Ring, an underground movement based in Mordiford, the lair of the wyvern dragon. The Wyvern Ring was responsible for hundreds of killings and acts of brutality. Alitha's father murdered John's son as revenge for John's supposed indecency. Next to die, would be Lewis Charleton and Cardinal Beyssac. Their murder would spark an uprising by the English against their Norman oppressors. England would once again, be free.

John shook his head. An intoxicating madness was about to deluge England. The slaughter would be terrible.

Digging his paddle into the mud, John pushed hard and set off. He followed Nicholas, who sitting astride his coffin, was content to let the current direct his progress.

John had convinced Nicholas the Day of Judgement was imminent. Evil would triumph unless they could reach Mordiford and stop the Wyvern Ring. A foot soldier of Christ, armed with a potent faith,

201

Nicholas needed no persuasion to fight the good fight. He insisted the dragon must be slain.

"We should stay together," John shouted. "This river is dangerous. Not a day goes by without a drowning or a body found entangled in the weeds. The Pestilence has made the river a convenient place to dispose of the dead. It's a depot of the deceased."

Nicholas was not listening. Exhilarated by the righteousness of his mission and emboldened by the sluggish current, he stood on the coffin, hands raised to Heaven, an evangelist preaching from a moving pulpit, capturing the attention of a herd of cows and a donkey. To Nicholas, this was not just a journey to Mordiford but a life and death quest to save the world from the Devil. Nicholas' words thundered across the river like cannon fire.

"Behold. This is the river of the water of life, bright as crystal, flowing from the throne of God, surging through the heart of the holy city."

"Sit down, Nicholas!" John yelled, paddling furiously in an attempt to steer his coracle alongside the coffin. The Wye was deep and they were midstream, well away from the bank. If Nicholas tumbled into the river, he would drown. John had no time for a gallant rescue. He must reach Mordiford as quickly as possible.

Despite John's plea, Nicholas ignored him. He was certain, an honest soul, engaged upon God's work, was entirely safe. This enterprise would test his faith and prove his mettle. The River Wye was his Sea of Galilee.

Reconciled to his decision, Nicholas unbuttoned his jerkin, throwing it overboard. It twisted in the water, spinning around, before disappearing below the surface. His boots followed. Decency prevented him removing his trousers. Fearing the worst, John covered his eyes with his hands.

Ominous whispers, a prayer concluded, a mellow voice, commending himself to God.

"Do not be conformed to this world but be transformed by the renewal of your mind. For by testing, you will discover the will of God."

Nicholas took the first step, convinced he could walk on water. John was convinced, he would drown…

Chapter Twenty-six

Bedraggled but thankful to be alive, Antoine and Jerome spurred their horses along the road to Mordiford. Every so often, when Sebastian peeped over the top of Antoine's saddlebag, they slowed, not wishing to send him flying through the air like a cherub.

His mind full of dragons, Jerome reined in his horse, stopping abruptly. He rubbed his head, trying to calm his nerves. The experience at Hereford Castle was a nightmare. He knew Cardinal Beyssac was a target for the Wyvern Ring. The cardinal was alone, unguarded and probably stomping around the coach, flailing his arms and raging against he and Antoine.

The distance between Hereford and Mordiford was only four miles, yet the clatter of hooves, crashed around Jerome's head like a war hammer beating against armour. Jerome was at the end of his tether.

Antoine slowed, wheeling his horse around. The cardinal was in mortal danger. They must keep going. Frustrated by the delay, he was ready to raise hell, until he saw the look of dejection on Jerome's face. Jerome was in a state. Antoine's anger evaporated.

"We're not too far away. Perhaps one more mile. When we get there, I'll prepare a venison stew. It will take your taste buds to the promised land. Good food always leads to a good mood."

Jerome looked down, shaking his head, remaining silent. The promise of an excellent meal did not excite him. Day after day of unremitting anxiety had eroded his spirit, leaving him desolate. He was drained by constant worry and tired of fearing every stranger. Unceasing vigilance had made him cynical. The human race was a bad lot. Only the rustle of yew trees, bowing to the wind, broke the silence.

Antoine racked his brains, desperate for a solution. Time was of the essence. The had to reach Mordiford and rescue the cardinal before the Wyvern Ring found him. They had delayed long enough. Antoine was resolute. Jerome's black mood needed to be purged. He must be encouraged to vent his spleen.

A whinny, followed by a snort. Ears forward, tail high, Antoine's horse, a skittish dapple grey, whimpered, shaking its head in frustration at the hold-up.

"Easy, my beautiful girl," whispered Antoine, stroking the horse's neck like a father soothing a frightened child. He knew Jerome was watching.

"I hope you realise the Wyvern Ring will murder the Cardinal if they find him. And we will be killed if they capture us. But that would just be the start."

Jerome nodded.

"Lewis Charleton is high on their death list along with anyone they decide is an enemy. The Wyvern Ring are everywhere. I don't have the will to resist any more. I want to return to Avignon and look after horses."

This was Antoine's moment.

"Of course, once we're dead, they will butcher the horses. And bearing in mind, the English are not known for their epicurean palates, very likely, eat them. The English love meat pies. In their eyes, Hippocrates would provide enough meat to feed a regiment."

Jerome bit his lip, appalled by the idea of a meal of horse flesh. It seemed cruelty came easily to most human beings.

At that moment, prompted by hunger rather than moral outrage, Sebastian, cosseted in Antoine's saddlebag, began to wail. His sobbing made the horses shudder. Hanging on desperately, Antoine reined in his horse, hoping it would calm down. Jerome, with easy expertise, stroked the withers of his chestnut horse, repeating the words of the Lord's Prayer. The chestnut was soon compliant. Antoine had never seen a more biddable beast.

As Sebastian's weeping decreased to a grizzle, Jerome's distress ebbed away. The prospect of Hippocrates' death, transformed his anguish into anger. His wretchedness developed into wrath. No more brooding. Mordiford was quite near. The bridge was in view.

Jerome spurred his horse into a gallop, kicking up dust in his wake.

"Make haste!" Jerome shouted. "We must fulfil the orders of our Holy Father."

Smirking, Antoine raced after Jerome. He had shocked Jerome out of his torpor, inspiring him in to action. His clever stratagem had lifted Jerome's despair. He felt pleased.

But Antoine's conceit was foolish. Hiding amongst the yew trees, Garth, Edmund and Leofgar had tracked Antoine and Jerome all the way from Hereford. They had seen and heard everything. The ambush would take place at Mordiford Bridge.

Chapter Twenty-seven

Try as she might, Alitha could not remove Elizabeth's blood from her fingers. Red smears, claret confirmation of Alitha's crime. Neither washing in scalding water nor scouring with pumice would make the stains go away. They seemed indelible, an affliction, marking her out, cursed by God.

Walking along Wyebridge Street, Alitha kept her hands inside her coat pockets. Elizabeth's death had left her confused. Perhaps it was not sensible to dwell on things. Better to throw oneself into a cause more important than personal happiness. The journey to Mordiford would only take an hour.

A brilliant, sun-filled day, distracted the few people left in Hereford from worrying about the Pestilence. Not a cloud in the sky. Nor a bird.

On the Wye Bridge, a cadaverous woman, clutching a dead baby to her chest, stuck out a hand, pleading for money. Her sunken eyes and ragged clothes, evidence of a life hanging in the balance.

Without stopping, Alitha placed a silver penny in the woman's palm. A silver penny would buy a lot of food. The king's head shimmered in the sunlight, illuminating the woman's face. A hero reaching down the centuries. Just for a moment, Harold appeared to smile.

As did Alitha, when she recalled her mission. Her task was straightforward. She must execute Cardinal Beyssac. His death would signal the beginning of a campaign of mass murder which would destroy the Norman oppressors once and for all. The English people would rise up, taking control of their own country for the first time in three hundred years. The English, God's chosen people, would be free. Morcar's plan was foolproof.

But if the plan was to succeed, it required discretion. Alitha felt the dagger in her pocket. Its blade was throat-sharp. She must not attract attention or share her purpose with anyone. By avoiding the road and journeying across country, she would reach Mordiford more quickly.

A deserted landscape. So many peasants had died of pestilence, the population had fallen by a third and food production virtually ceased. Those still living, were afraid to leave their homes.

Skirting around Putson village, Alitha met no one. In front of her, only blighted fields of grey barley. While outside the old Bishop's Palace, flax plants struggled to survive, their tall stems withered, their brittle blue flowers, crumbling in the wind. Untended fields and neglected crops, hard evidence of the suffering caused by the Pestilence.

Alitha's journey would remain discreet. She knew the secret way. An invisible high road across Herefordshire, established by the Black Monks. A pilgrim's way to a holy destination.

A mile further on, as Alitha caught sight of Rotherwas Chapel, her mood changed. To her mind, 'Our Lady of the Assumption' was a travesty of a church. A huge deception inflicted upon the English by their oppressors.

Hands on hips, derisively shaking her head, Alitha inspected the exterior. Her conscience would not allow her to go in. It was a Norman church, owned by the De La Barre family. A house of God, forbidden to the English. But the time of reckoning was near. Blood would be the measure. Alitha took a last look, her face twisted with contempt. Dinedor Hill, breathtaking under the sunlight, beckoned.

She pressed on eagerly, convinced this day would mark a turning point in history. But she could not leave Rotherwas without saluting the dragon. Only a privileged few, who understood the invisible high road, knew where to find it.

At the foot of Dinedor Hill, hidden behind a scattering of ancient yew trees, Alitha knelt down to pray, calling on Providence to grant her success. As she spoke, the eyes of the dragon fixed on her. To an unbeliever, it was merely the skeleton of an animal long extinct. But to Alitha, it was an opportunity to receive benediction. Only God's blessing could purge her guilt. If that failed, the yew tree leaves in her pocket promised a way out.

Alitha found Dinedor Hill an easy climb. From her vantage point on the top, she could see for miles in each direction. She ran around the summit, giggling like a child, stopping every so often to scan the horizon for familiar landmarks.

To the south, Gloucester and the wooded slopes of Yarleton Hill. White sunlight, breaking through the clouds, transforming the hill into an angry man with a silver beard. The image of her father. While to the west, the Black Mountains reared up, armed warriors standing guard. Mordiford, at the junction of two rivers, lay a mile to the east. She could see the Church of the Holy Rood. A group of men were standing around the village cross. A line of soldiers blocked the bridge. An ordinary English village. But in reality, the heart of English resistance. Alitha gritted her teeth.

With foreboding, she turned north. Plague-ridden Hereford. The River Wye cutting through the city like blood oozing from a severed vein.

In contrast, the cathedral seemed steadfast, aloof from the horror outside its precincts. Constant as a loving sister. Persistent as intrusive thoughts. Alitha's sanity had started to unravel. She examined her fingers, holding them up to the sky, twisting her wrists around front and back, digging nail under nail, searching for traces of red. What she found made her hate herself even more. Hands, bone dry and scarlet as berries, encrusted with Elizabeth's blood.

She set off down the hill, running as fast as she could, dodging in and out of trees, falling over bushes, stumbling over stones, trampling a path through a carpet of bluebells, cursing loudly and breathing hard. A release of stifled feelings. A desperate attempt to expunge guilt. Alitha did not stop running until she reached the riverbank at Even Pits.

Here, at the crossing, a short distance from Mordiford, the River Wye ran shallow. It would be easy to wade across and follow the secret high road through West Wood up to Mordiford Church. There, at the appropriate time, she could take revenge.

As Alitha entered the water, the bitter taste of yew tree leaves, made her feel sick.

Chapter Twenty-eight

Antoine reined in his horse, signalling Jerome to stop. They pulled off the road and dismounted, leading their horses into a thicket. Mordiford Bridge was a hundred yards away. The sun was high in the sky. A beguiling summer's day in Mordiford.

Turning away from the sunlight, Jerome held Sebastian, rocking him, stopping every so often to feed him a gobbet of bread. Sebastian chewed his food, rotating his jaw like a goat. While Sebastian feasted, Jerome listened to Antoine's plan.

"The Wyvern Ring are merciless killers. We've seen what they do to their enemies. Remember those corpses at the Seven Stars tavern?"

Jerome nodded. It was a sight burned into his mind's eye. Killing came easy to them. If they were not stopped, what more torment would they unleash?

"We must defeat them," Jerome whispered, his head full of nauseating images.

Antoine shrugged his shoulders.

"I am a cook. You are a groom. We can't hope to defeat them by force. But I am certain, we can put the fear of God into them and save the cardinal. Our French wits should prevail over their English weapons. While I gather berries, I want you to scratch your face. And your head. Never mind the pain. The more weals you raise, the better. No sane person will approach a bunch of notorious sinners, cast out by God and universally feared. From this moment, you and I are lepers."

A few minutes later, a bell was heard echoing across the river. The guards on Mordiford Bridge held their weapons close. Two dishevelled and manifestly diseased creatures approached, their flesh purple, their faces disfigured by weeping sores. They dragged their feet, moaning and waving their arms like broken birds struggling to fly. Lepers. Such creatures were not human. The Church regarded them as devils, too obscene even for Hell.

The first brute sounded the bell. His gnarled and scaly hands resembling the skin of a tortoise. He shouted something unintelligible. Every so often, he stooped down to kiss the road.

The second leper glared at the guards, looking fixedly at each man, selecting his next victim. His wild eyes searching for prey. But what this monster carried, made the guards tremble and doubt their senses.

He was clutching a saddlebag. Emerging slowly from it, scabrous and despicable, red from head to foot, came a child of the Devil, an imp in human form, an entity known to Christians as a Fiend. A foul stench attended its appearance.

Antoine sensed this was the crucial moment. The guards seemed on the verge of panic. Antoine raised his arms to Heaven, in an emotional cry from the heart. "My friends, we seek only your goodwill. We bear no malice towards you. Yes, we are enfants perdus, miserable wretches, who could infect you with a single exhalation. All we want is food and a bed in which to rest. St Giles Hospital in Hereford is closed. Its staff are all dead, victims of the Pestilence. Common report states, the people of Mordiford have offered to care for the stricken. The patients of St Giles know this. My companion and I are here to assess your hospitality. What paradise we have discovered! Just an hour behind us are scores of contagious, incurably sick outcasts, looking to make this beautiful village their home. I know you will welcome them with open arms. What a joyful prospect!"

Garth, Leofgar, Edmund and Magnus looked at each other, open-mouthed, uncertain what to do. They were brave men who did not fear death. But the life of a leper was one of unremitting misery. Cursed by God, condemned to everlasting punishment in Hell, they would be rejected by everyone, even by their own wives and children.

Anxious faces confirmed an unspoken decision. Sheathing their swords, the dispirited guards quit their post, running up the hill towards the crossroads. An errant cloud drifted across the sun, darkening the sky.

Antoine and Jerome embraced, dancing up and down the road, celebrating their guile and revelling in their acting talent. Unacknowledged for his part in the drama and still confined to the saddlebag, Sebastian shrieked fiendlike. The brutes halted their celebration.

Grinning like a schoolboy, Antoine reached into his pocket, pulling out a handful of berries.

"Blackthorn, spindle berry and dogwood. We defied the Wyvern Ring by using our brains and some fruit."

Unconvinced, Jerome shook his head. Chasing the guards off the bridge could not alter the fact they were still in mortal danger. Indeed, the cardinal might already be dead.

"We returned to this village to find Cardinal Beyssac. Not to pick fruit," said Jerome derisively.

"Of course, you're right," said Antoine, chastened by Jerome's words. He was conscious their triumph was negligible compared to the demands of the task ahead.

"The river is under our noses. Let's wash off these false colours and get going. Lewis Charleton expects to be ordained bishop tonight. If the cardinal does not attend the cathedral, the ceremony can't take place. I didn't put on a clean shirt for…"

Nonplussed, Antoine stopped mid-sentence, staring at the river in disbelief, eyes wide as horseshoes. With a trembling finger he pointed.

Jerome clamped his hand over his mouth, watching the miraculous scene from behind a tree.

Two men were preaching, impassioned voices, crying out to an imaginary audience.

"When you pass through the waters, I will be with you. And the rivers shall not overwhelm you."

Inspirational words and a heartfelt performance. But it was their emulation of Christ, which made the spectacle astonishing. Both men, smiling and unperturbed, were walking on the water.

Chapter Twenty-nine

Antoine leant over the parapet to get a better view. The river rippled and sparkled. Two shadowy figures silhouetted against the light.

He soon relaxed, breathing a sigh of relief. Taut muscles became loose. He recognised John. They had shared beer in the Saracen's Head before it burned down. It was not a miracle. There was a more banal explanation.

Jerome perceived Antoine's mood. Taking slow, reticent steps, Jerome and Sebastian joined him on the bridge.

John looked up, waving his hand to attract attention. The people on the bridge were savages. Human beings are not purple. But they were at a safe distance and he needed their help.

"Good sirs. We have journeyed from Hereford. Our destination is Mordiford where urgent business commands our attention. Have we arrived at that melancholy place?"

Jerome's curiosity subdued his fear. He must know.

"Yes. This is Mordiford. You have reached your destination. But tell me. Did you walk the whole way?"

"No!" said John. Although my companion aspired to do so. We are standing on a coffin. It's not a conventional vessel but it saved us from drowning. The point is we are here and hope to forestall a horrible crime. Are you acquainted with Cardinal Beyssac?"

Antoine and Jerome nodded. Between the four of them, there was much to discuss.

While Antoine and Jerome bathed in the river, trying to wash off the berry juice, John and Nicholas sat on the bank, recounting what they knew about the Wyvern Ring. Baby Sebastian, scrubbed clean and unfiended, lay naked on the coffin lid, drying himself under the heat of the sun.

John's narrative was chilling. The Wyvern Ring, already responsible for hundreds of murders, intended to kill Cardinal Beyssac and Lewis

Charleton. Their deaths would initiate an assassination campaign, targeting Normans, those of French descent and English collaborators. It would be slaughter on an unimaginable scale.

The network of Wyvern Ring disciples, embraced all of England. It had even penetrated King Edward's court. The king, his wife and children and all his mistresses would be murdered. England would become a sea of blood. The carnage would begin with the first thrust of Alitha's knife. How could the Wyvern Ring be stopped?

Only partially cleansed but thoroughly exhausted, Antoine and Jerome sat with John and Nicholas to plan a strategy. John shook his head in disbelief. It was difficult to engage in a serious discussion with purple-coloured men.

Sebastian, fast asleep under the branches of a yew tree, babbled and burbled, making more noise than the ebb and flow of the river, slapping against the arches of the bridge.

Nicholas raised his voice. Well versed in the Scriptures, he knew God had shown him the way to defeat the Wyvern Ring. The answer was simple.

"Without bloodshed, there is no remission of sin. God is telling us the Wyvern Ring must be annihilated. Every one of its disciples killed. Only the shedding of blood will atone for its iniquity."

John was not convinced.

"No!" he said firmly. "We cannot hope to fight the Wyvern Ring and win. Your suggestion is a recipe for an early grave."

Enthused by his beliefs, Nicholas remained adamant.

"O ye of little faith! Be zealous! Under the direction of the Lord of Hosts and reinforced by His prodigious army, equipped with celestial fire, victory will be ours. Be joyful. Make ready your sword of righteousness. Put on your armour of valour. The Son of God will obliterate the forces of Darkness. Our faith will make us invincible!"

Always distrustful of fanatics, Antoine shook his head. Religious ardour often concealed a desire for martyrdom. He was not ready for that.

"No!" said Antoine sharply. "John is right. An attack on the Wyvern Ring would be futile. But we must do something. And quickly, or it will be too late for Cardinal Beyssac… and England."

Jerome exhaled, massaging his head in the hope it might stimulate his brain to find a solution to their problems.

Gradually, an idea began to fall into place. Unhurriedly, little by little, like small pieces added to a mosaic, Jerome conceived of a way to stop the Wyvern Ring. The reaction of the guards on the bridge when confronted by he and Antoine indicated a way out of their predicament.

Jerome stretched, making himself as tall as possible, palms down, ensuring he had attention. He was sure Antoine would be impressed.

"If we are to save the day, I know what we must do."

John, Nicholas and Antoine, bereft of any ideas, shielded their eyes from the sun and listened. Antoine wanted Jerome to contribute. On occasions, he could be insightful.

All attention on Jerome, no one noticed the shimmering black shape, knife in hand, standing behind him. Tousled red hair, tears trickling down flushed cheeks. A familiar, female voice.

"Idiots! Don't you realise the die is cast? Look at my knife. Remember no human can escape the Angel of Death. Your demise is assured. Make haste. Cardinal Beyssac is impatient to reunite with his companions. A single execution is a mere diversion. A massacre will be much more entertaining."

Sebastian giggled as Jerome held him in his arms. Stony-faced, Alitha shepherded her captives down the path, through the churchyard towards the crossroads. On reaching the crossroads, they were stupefied by what they saw.

Chapter Thirty

Split lips, dripping blood, Beyssac was tied by his wrists and ankles to the village cross. His head bent to one side, Christ like. His scarlet vestments were ripped and stained. Shallow breathing confirmed he was alive.

Deeply moved, Antoine considered Beyssac's humiliation the most miserable sight he had ever seen. Although Morcar, directing events sitting astride a golden courser, regarded Beyssac's fate as poetic justice, long overdue.

Their faces twisted with hate, the disciples parted ranks, allowing Alitha to lead her captives to the base of the cross. Garth and Edmund exchanged worried glances while Leofgar and Magnus blanched before merging into the throng.

The sun was oppressive. Sweating profusely, John realised the vicious comments aimed at he and his companions, pointed to a quick and bloody death. Alitha had an appalling propensity for violence. And the attitude of the disciples suggested they would not be merciful.

Morcar dismounted, thrusting his riding crop under Beyssac's chin. Beyssac winced. The disciples were jubilant, cheering and punching the air, exulting in Beyssac's suffering.

"Oh, how are the mighty fallen," said Morcar scornfully. "Today, you and the tyranny you represent will be destroyed. And England will revert to the Garden of Eden it used to be before the catastrophe of 1066."

Intimidated by the noise, Antoine shuddered. The disciples shouted their approval, in a discordant tribute to Morcar. They were under his spell, mesmerised by his promise of a glorious future for England. Beguiled by his cold blue eyes, hypnotic and compelling but devoid of pity.

All, except Alitha. Antoine noticed she stood apart from the throng, not joining in the adulation. Her eyes seemed glazed, their ferocity subdued. She hunched her shoulders, mumbling under her breath. Every so often she pulled a wad of leaves from her pocket, placing them on her tongue, chewing determinedly.

Antoine shook his head in disbelief. They were yew tree leaves, poisonous and deadly. It seemed Alitha wanted to die.

Morcar raised a hand, demanding silence. The disciples obeyed. They were impatient. The wanted to see Cardinal Beyssac killed.

Morcar stroked Alitha's hair. She drew back a fraction. Antoine sensed her subtle disapproval. Determined on revenge, Morcar was too preoccupied to notice.

"Soon Alitha will return this cardinal to Hell. His death will signal the start of the uprising. Those who come after us, will regard today as the greatest moment in England's history. Never again will a Norman look down on an Englishman. Plucking out their eyes, demonstrates our refusal to accept slavery and subjugation."

Beyssac began to recite the Lord's Prayer. John, Jerome and Nicholas fell to their knees, refusing to watch the gruesome scene unfold. Even Sebastian, discerning the mood, held his hands over his eyes. The disciples, keen to see a cardinal die, jostled and elbowed each other, trying to make room for a better view.

Antoine felt outraged but knew he was powerless to save Beyssac. They would all be executed. Perhaps even Sebastian. Antoine was determined Sebastian should not be harmed. Riddled with guilt, he decided he must act. His voice was loud and lucid.

"I will pluck out the cardinal's eyes."

The disciples were shocked. Incredulous gasps and astonished whispers, confirmed their surprise. A diseased creature, prepared to mutilate his master. Undeniable evidence, lepers were immoral villains, cursed by God. And Norman lepers were even worse. Antoine's request appeared loathsome. But knowing Antoine well, Jerome recognised a subterfuge.

"Why should I let you?" asked Morcar.

"Because I hate him!" said Antoine. "For years, he has treated me like a slave, bullying me and intimidating me, making my life a living hell. I swore, before I die, I would get revenge. I don't need a weapon. I will use my fingers to remove his eyeballs. When that's done, I will die a happy man."

216

"Proceed," said Morcar.

The disciples fell silent. Clenching his fists, Antoine held them up to Beyssac's face, extending his thumbs like gimlets. The cardinal was not frightened. Just disappointed by Antoine's disloyalty.

"God will forgive you," said Beyssac meekly.

"He will," said Antoine irreverently. "That's His job."

Antoine pushed his thumbs into Beyssac's eye sockets and squeezed, sharp fingernails punching deep wounds into his hooded eyelids. Blood trickled across Antoine's knuckles, running down his arm in rivulets.

"Father, forgive them, they know not what they do." A humble appeal to God. Eye sockets transformed into blood-filled, black holes. The disciples were hushed.

Beyssac screamed, straining at his bonds, attempting to alleviate his suffering. He screamed again, writhing and grinding his teeth, as his eyeballs felt the pressure and were crushed. A torrent of red, spongy tissue, spurted between Antoine's fingers, splashing his face. Beyssac's breathing faltered.

Pleased with his work, Antoine raised his head, licking the ejected matter from around his mouth like a dog. Only a whit of blood. The bitter-sweet flavour of Spindle berry was not to his taste.

"It's done. His eyes are destroyed. I have consigned him to permanent darkness. That is sufficient. His death would be a victory over you. But as a blind man, he would pose no threat."

"An engaging spectacle," said Morcar, scanning the disciples' faces, trying to locate Elizabeth. "Although, it will not save the cardinal's life. My daughter must fulfil her duty. The cardinal's suffering will be brief."

Alitha stepped forward, grabbing Beyssac's hair, deftly tipping his head back to expose his throat. Raising her knife, she scored a shallow incision across his windpipe. The mark would facilitate the quick removal of Beyssac's head. The cardinal would not survive. Antoine was crestfallen. His ruse had failed.

Morcar raised a hand, motioning her to stop. He seemed annoyed.

"Where is your sister? Her presence is essential to our success. I rely on her implicitly."

Alitha moved the knife away from Beyssac's throat. Her eyes were listless, her manner, oddly defiant. She sighed wearily, struggling to control her rage.

"Beatrice will not attend today. Her heart lies elsewhere."

Morcar waved a dismissive hand.

"I don't wish to see her. Beatrice is a traitor. Her name is abhorrent to me. The day she rejected our noble cause was the day she ceased to be my daughter."

Alitha shook her head. Despite everything, her love for Beatrice remained constant. Beatrice was not a traitor but a devoted older sister with whom she shared a special bond. Her father's opinion was heartless, almost inhuman.

"She was your first child. My older sister. You disowned her when you decided she was of no further use."

"She banished herself," said Morcar derisively. "Beatrice questioned our cause. She admitted she was no longer prepared to kill. She could not understand an individual life does not matter. It is the nation which must prevail. Her dissent was a betrayal of the English people. Such a crime deserves to be punished by more than exile. It demands a salutary execution in a public place. She was lucky to escape harsh punishment."

"Beatrice is dead," said Alitha, her voice deadpan, her gaze fixed on some distant, unspecified point. She was cold and her head felt heavy. With chilling certainty, the lethal leaves of the yew tree coiled around Alitha's heart, cutting off her lifeblood, making her breathing difficult. The news of Beatrice's death left Morcar unmoved. He nodded his approval. Beatrice was a traitor. She had received her just desserts. As for Alitha, Morcar considered her defiance the obstinacy of an emotional female.

The disciples milling around Mordiford crossroads, were frustrated. They enjoyed watching Beyssac suffer and anticipated his decapitation. But Beyssac was still alive and they did not appreciate the delay. A hundred fanatics, armed to the teeth and bent on extreme violence, were not impressed by their leader bickering with his daughter. They wanted blood.

Antoine and his companions were waiting to die. Escape was impossible. Antoine wanted to live but was resigned to death. Jerome was also reconciled to his demise. He hoped it would be quick. In contrast, Nicholas felt elated, convinced his martyrdom would speed him to Heaven. Only John was thinking hard, racking his brains to devise a plan for their survival. The conversation between Morcar and Alitha seemed to him, to suggest a way out.

Morcar wiped his forehead. He considered Alitha's affection for Beatrice, contemptible.

"The death of a traitor must improve the world. Forget Beatrice, her name pollutes our discourse. Of more importance, where is Elizabeth?"

Alitha stared at the ground, her face careworn. She struggled to clear her throat, reluctant to give voice to such painful news.

"Elizabeth remains in Hereford. I believe she will not leave it ever again."

Morcar grimaced, puzzled by the news.

"Why stay in Hereford? She is obliged to be here."

Alitha seemed exhausted, disinclined to speak.

"Her support for our cause is unwavering. But she will not come to Mordiford today."

Listening intently, John waited for the right moment to speak. He sensed his life and the lives of his companions depended on the outcome of Morcar and Alitha's conversation. Morcar was furious.

"Why?" Morcar demanded.

"She cannot come," said Alitha penitently.

"Why not?"

"It's not possible. It cannot be done."

"You speak in riddles. Explain to me why Elizabeth will not come to Mordiford?"

Tortured by remorse, Alitha was loath to speak the truth. Her conscience made the words stick in her throat. The look on her face convinced John his moment had arrived.

"Alitha. Tell your father the truth." John's distinct voice quietened the disciples, concentrating their attention.

Morcar seemed bemused. Alitha shook her head, warm tears splashing down on the cold road stones.

"Tell him the truth," John insisted. "Or I will."

Alitha raised her head, stung by John's ultimatum. Her joints were sore and her limbs heavy. But while Alitha had breath in her body, she could tell the truth.

"And you will know the truth and the truth shall set you free." Her voice was subdued.

Morcar's anger exploded, rolling like thunder over Mordiford.

"What is it? I must know!"

Alitha spoke freely. A dying woman has no need to lie. The disciples, standing, waiting for their orders, watched and listened in disbelief. Alitha's behaviour made no sense.

"My entire life had been directed by you. I have obeyed your commands, followed your orders, listened to your instructions and submitted to your desires. I have endured an existence, not a life. Alice was a mask you forced me to wear, a semblance which eroded my spirit, making deceit second nature to me. Now, deceit is all I have left."

Morcar smiled disdainfully. Alitha was not thinking straight.

"What really possesses you, are the wild imaginings of a deluded mind. John Dornell's corruption runs deeper than I thought. I will take particular delight in protracting his death."

Alitha closed her eyes, a momentous recollection of a happier time, long since past.

"John is the only man I've ever loved. You killed our relationship just as you killed his son. Just as you killed Beatrice by forsaking her when she needed your support. A father who disowns his daughter, plunges a knife into her heart. Such a crime demands a reckoning. I killed Elizabeth to escape from your control. Now Beatrice can rest in peace. I know, I never will."

A confused silence. Some disciples, bewildered by Alitha's confession, put aside their weapons and knelt in prayer. Others, too astonished to talk, gathered in huddles, drawing strength from the presence of comrades. But the prisoners, paralysed with fear, were convinced death had been delayed, not prevented.

Morcar's eyes were filled with contempt. Despite Elizabeth's demise, the guiding principle of his life remained unaltered. Every individual must die. But the nation is supreme and will endure. True kinship was not based on family ties but on communion with England. Elizabeth's death was of no consequence. It was the disciples who deserved his attention.

Holding his sword above his head, Morcar sought to rally his men.

"Grief is a luxury, an affectation designed to impress others. Elizabeth has gone, consigned to oblivion. Now, there is a task ahead of us which demands all our energies. It is easier to shed Norman blood than to tolerate English tears."

Alitha stepped closer to her father, reaching in her pocket. His eyes sparkled with disdain. She was furious. Outraged by his dismissal of Elizabeth's life and appalled by his cold heart. With one thrust, she buried her knife deep in Morcar's chest.

He fell backwards, lifeless. For a few seconds, nobody moved, transfixed by the sight of Morcar, a knife protruding from his chest, his white shirt rapidly turning red.

Instantly, Antoine assessed their situation. He remembered the terrified faces of the guards on the bridge when faced by purple-skinned lepers. The idea of being cursed by God and stricken with leprosy was too awful to contemplate. In the minds of the guards, running away was the sensible thing to do.

Antoine grabbed Jerome's shoulder.

"This is our chance. A headless dragon is harmless. Seek out the guards we met on the bridge. Remind them St Giles Hospital has closed. The patients are grateful Mordiford has promised them respite. Tell them, at any moment, hundreds of plague victims and lepers will descend on Mordiford expecting a warm welcome. Encourage the disciples to be optimistic. There are some patients whose illness is not virulent."

Jerome nodded. He knew exactly what to do. Without hesitating, he barged straight into the midst of the disciples. Once again, the purple-faced brute was on the rampage.

Garth and Leofgar recoiled in horror. Magnus, frozen with fear, dropped his sword. Edmund, less devoted to the cause, envisaged a life of physical torment, shunned by his wife and despised by society. Beset by these certainties, Edmund sidled away from the throng and ran.

Walking quickly, Antoine was pleased to see the disciples shrink away when he or Jerome approached. These fighting men did not fear death but were horrified by the thought of contracting leprosy. They considered the life of a leper, a living death. Hell itself could not be more terrible.

Speaking with a strident voice, Antoine delighted in explaining the hideous details.

"Those arriving here today, in search of respite, may be leprous or pestilential, poisonous, incurable and monstrous to behold. But they are desperate for your friendship. See beyond their ulcerating sores and weeping lesions. Embrace each one as a brother. Welcome them into the bosom of your family. Do not forget, inside each pustuled body is a man given life by God. I challenge you to make light of the leprous blight."

Leaderless and confused, the disciples began to break ranks and leave. By the time Nicholas had finished reciting the Lord's Prayer at the top of his voice, all the disciples had gone.

Jubilant, Antoine untied Beyssac's bonds freeing him from the cross.

"Cardinal. You can open your eyes now," said Antoine.

Wary of the strong sunlight, Beyssac rolled his eyes. Dried blood crusted the eyelids. His eyes were sore but his vision, undamaged. The sight of Morcar's body elicited an inward prayer.

"You played your part brilliantly," said Antoine. "Your screams could wake the dead!"

"Digging your fingernails into my eyelids and pinching chunks of skin was very painful. Such torment made screaming easy," said Beyssac, ruefully rubbing his eyes. "But a few superficial wounds are inconsequential when I know you saved my eyesight. Squirting the pulp from the berries, convinced the disciples you had blinded me."

Gathered around Beyssac, Antoine, Jerome and Nicholas forgot Alitha. But John did not. As Beyssac sat Sebastian on his knee, delivering an embellished account of his experiences in England, John lifted Alitha into his arms. Her skin was cold, her face pale. Her red hair, shining golden in the afternoon light. She was quiet, her breathing shallow. It was obvious she was dying.

John carried her down the path to Mordiford Church. God's house seemed the most appropriate place for a person close to death. Perhaps she would find solace and reconcile herself to God before it was too late.

With tender hands, John laid her down on the stone floor. Who was she really? Was it Alice or Alitha he had loved?

She opened her eyes. The Mordiford dragon, imperious and pagan, looked down ready to strike. A single tear splashed on to Alitha's dress. John looked up, searching confusedly to find who had shed the tear.

But the Mordiford dragon had gone, tumbling and spinning down into the darkness of the bottomless pit, shut in and sealed, not to be free for a thousand years. The deceiver of the world had been subdued, at least for a while.

Printed in Great Britain
by Amazon

62676836R00127